the MATCH

SARAH ADAMS

Srishti
PUBLISHERS & DISTRIBUTORS

Srishti Publishers & Distributors
A unit of AJR Publishing LLP
212A, Peacock Lane
Shahpur Jat, New Delhi – 110 049

editorial@srishtipublishers.com

First published in India by
Srishti Publishers & Distributors in 2023

First Published by Sarah Adams

10 9 8 7 6 5 4

By arrangement with Sarah Adams, through BookEnds Literary Agency.

This edition is for sale in the Indian Subcontinent only

Printed and bound in India

This book is for all the four-legged superheroes of the world, saving lives, giving love and independence to those who need it!

CHAPTER ONE

EVIE

I wake up to the feel of Charlie's tongue grazing my cheek. I don't like being kissed like this first thing in the morning. Mainly because I don't like mornings, and I wish that he would get it through his thick head that I need every minute of sleep possible. But just like every morning, he's persistent. I am Sleeping Beauty, and he is the prince. Although, I'm pretty sure the prince didn't roll his tongue all over Sleeping Beauty's face like Charlie is doing now. What a different movie that would have turned out to be.

"Can you please just give me five more minutes?" I ask while shoving my head under the pillow in an attempt to block his advances.

But he doesn't like this game. Never has. It worries him to not be able to see my face. We've been together now for three years—and he's become the tiniest bit overprotective. But he's the best snuggler in the whole world, so I allow his slightly domineering attitude.

Plus, he really does know what's best for me. He's improved

my life in more ways than I can document. It's why I adore him. It's why I let him lick my face at 6:30 AM. It's why I sit up in bed and roll him over onto his back and rub his tummy until his leg starts shaking.

Oh, right. Charlie is my dog. Did I forget to mention that?

More specifically, he's my seizure-assist dog.

I was diagnosed with epilepsy when I was sixteen years old. It stole my adolescence. It stole my peace of mind. And more importantly—it stole my license. Turns out, the state doesn't like it too much if you randomly black out and convulse. Believe me, they will—under no circumstances—let you behind the wheel of a vehicle once they get wind of the E word.

No one sympathizes more with the poor girl in the Beach Boys song about her daddy taking her T-Bird away than me. Except mine was a 1980 slate-blue Land Cruiser with a cream-colored top. My daddy bought it for me a month before my sixteenth birthday. Not even a week after that sweet sixteen, I had my first seizure that changed my life forever.

Those next few years were hard, to say the least. I was scared of going anywhere or doing anything. One day I was a teenager, blissfully carefree about everything besides the chip in my hot-pink glitter nail polish. The next, I was painfully aware of how little a part I played in my existence on this earth.

Charlie didn't come into my life until I was twenty-three and still living with my mama and daddy because I was scared to live on my own. Actually, I thought I *couldn't* live on my own. But then I met a woman in a coffee shop who had an adorable white Labrador retriever at her side, a bright-blue vest strapped around its body with a patch sewed on the side that read *Working Dog, Do Not Pet.*

I'll be honest, the first thought that went through my mind was wondering if this dog could do my taxes. Turns out, they don't do that sort of work. The woman was kind enough to field all of my stupid questions, because in her exact words, "*No question is too stupid.*"

But I figured if she gave me enough of her time, I could manage to change her mind.

The rest was history. Joanna Halstead, the woman from the coffee shop—also known as my fairy godmother—quickly became one of my best friends. I learned that she owned a service-dog company called Southern Service Paws, and she trained and matched dogs with people living with all sorts of disabilities. Disabilities just like mine.

That's how Charlie came into my life. It's how I regained my independence and security. It's how I decided to live on my own. It's how my parents came to hate the company that I adore and am being groomed to take over when Joanna retires next year.

Well, *company* might be a bit of a stretch.

Company implies monetary value. And money is not something that Southern Service Paws has. It's more like Jo is grooming me to take over her heart. Something that has a whole lot more value than money, but a shockingly low credit score.

I am the only other employee that is paid a salary—the rest are volunteers. And, actually, *salary* is also another one of those deceiving words. When you hear it, you think benefits, 401ks, and down payments on pretty little houses. When I hear it, I just think of my apartment that is the size of my thumbnail and my kitchen pantry that is stocked with Ramen noodles and Froot Loops.

Luckily, I love Froot Loops.

I will eat nothing but sugary cereal for the rest of my days if it means I get to keep working for Jo and her company. Because I love what I do and the people I help. And as cramped as I am in this little place, I'm proud that it's mine—not my parents'.

In this new world I have carved out for myself over the past three years, I'm just Evie. Not Miss Evelyn Grace Jones, daughter to Harold and Melony Jones of the prestigious

Charlestonian family that resides SOB (South of Broad, aka Snootyville, and where I was raised). That name might not mean anything to you, but around here in Charleston, it's everything.

My family comes from what's known as "old southern money." You know the kind: big historical houses, prestigious country clubs that only accept members with names who have been on the list since it was founded, garden cocktail parties served by men in white jackets, and a unique southern drawl that says, *"I'm better than you."*

My daddy is an attorney and partner at Jones and Murray Law—the oldest and most elite law firm in all of South Carolina—and my mama is on the board of the Powder Society of Revolutionary Ladies. What is it they do? Mainly sit around in their finely tailored day dresses and drink martinis, planning more cocktail parties for their wealthy husbands to mingle and continue to pass their old southern money back and forth like playing cards.

Basically, I grew up exactly opposite of how I'm living now, and I couldn't be happier about it.

That thought reminds me of my schedule for the day, and I reach over Charlie, my 90 lb. golden retriever—who is more of a bed hog than any full-grown man—and pick up my phone. I do a double take of the time. That can't be right. It says it's 9:10 AM. How can that be when I set my alarm for 6:45 AM? Oh, wonderful. I forgot to set it. And now I'm going to be late for my client meeting.

"No, no, no," I say, throwing off my white comforter and jumping out of bed.

Charlie sits up, ears at attention and body poised for anything, watching me race across my studio apartment to the closet. I'm wearing a pair of cute new pink undies, and it occurs to me how sad it is that Charlie is the only male in my life to see them.

I trip over a shoe before I look in my empty closet and

remember that I put off going to the laundromat last night so I could finish binge-watching *The Bachelor*. Don't judge me. It's the only romance I have in my life right now.

Charlie walks up beside me and gives me a look that says, "I told you not to shirk your responsibilities." He's so much more adult than me.

I put my hands on my hips and frown down at him. "I have twenty minutes before I need to be at the coffee shop, and I have nothing to wear, so quit giving me that high-and-mighty look, or I'm going to shave your fur and wear it as a coat like Cruella de Vil."

He rolls his eyes at me. You might think it's impossible for a dog to roll his eyes. That's only because you haven't met Charlie. I smile and rub his adorable head because I can never be mad at him for more than two seconds.

Thankfully, I spot my turquoise summer dress I wore yesterday. It's laying crumpled on the couch in a tight little ball that would make my mama gasp with disbelief. Her maid would never allow one of her dresses to crease. *How atrocious.*

Crossing the room, I shake out my dress, give it one good sniff, and then decide that wearing it one more day won't hurt anyone. It smells a little too much like the burger I ate last night, so after pulling it on, I douse myself in vanilla body spray.

Now I'm a walking ad for Bath & Body Works, and I consider requesting some sort of royalty from them.

The clock continues to race, and I look like I'm in the middle of a challenge on a game show as I rush around my apartment trying to gather everything I need for the meeting, take my meds, and get Charlie fed. *I better win a million dollars when I beat this clock.*

"Charlie, find your vest," I tell him while hopping on one foot and pulling my white tennis shoe on the other.

Yes, I wear tennis shoes with sundresses. Mama swears that *this* is the reason I'm not married yet. I think it has more to do with the shockingly small pool of men that want a serious relationship with a woman that has to take a service dog with her everywhere and might drop down with a seizure in the middle of their dinner date.

And to be honest, I just haven't been looking for a man all that much. My days are full of work, and I don't have much time to devote to weeding out the guys who only want to sleep with me from the ones who I can count on to show up if I mark him down as my emergency contact.

I check the time on my phone and then give myself two minutes to brush my teeth and wipe the mascara out from underneath my eyes. I wish I had more time to spend on my face. I hate feeling rushed or unprofessional for a meeting, because it makes me wonder if Mama is right and I don't have my act together. But there's just no time to worry about that now.

In record time, I swipe on some pink lip balm and knot a loose braid over my shoulder all the way to where it stops right above my hip. I've been growing my blonde locks out for a few years now, and it's grown so long that I half-expect a prince to throw a rock at my window and tell me to let down my hair.

Do I have a fairytale princess obsession? I blame it on those Wednesday cotillion lessons I had to attend in high school.

Charlie pulls me out of my wandering thoughts and keeps me on track by dropping his blue vest at my feet. He's better at finding things than I am. After buckling it around him, I give him a quick kiss on his head.

Since the coffee shop where I'm supposed to meet my new client is right down the street, I plan on walking instead of calling a ride. Honestly, not being able to drive has been one of the hardest parts of living with a disability. There are so many nights where I wish I could hop in my car and run down to the drugstore to pick up a pint of ice cream. Or when I run out of tampons, it would be so nice to make a run myself, instead of having to call and wait for an Uber or order off of a one-hour grocery delivery service. Without fail, my delivery person ends up being a young guy. And every single time, he blushes when he makes the drop.

"Evening, ma'am. Here are your military-grade tampons and overnight pads. I hope you don't die of anemia tonight."

At 9:20, Charlie and I are on the sidewalk, jogging toward the coffee shop. Literally, jogging. My braid is bouncing around my face, and I realize that I probably should have worn bike shorts under my dress. Someone catcalls at me from somewhere across the street, and my suspicions are confirmed.

Somehow, I remembered to grab my binder full of information to share about our matching process as well as our training methods and fees before I darted from the apartment. I wish I could say that our dogs come free of charge to qualifying recipients, but we just aren't there yet. Right now, our dogs come with a hefty price tag, and there are many people who could really benefit from having a service dog but can't afford them due to the massive health bills that also come along with having a disability.

But, hopefully, after the big fundraiser Jo and I are putting on next month, that will all change.

For the past few months, we've been in contact with lots of major businesses and have coordinated a fancy silent auction of their goods and services that will raise money to help us be able to give away our dogs 100% free of charge to those who qualify. The recipients will have to prove that they are financially capable of providing food and necessary medications and vet visits for their dog, but that's it. If all goes as hoped, we will make this a yearly event.

I clutch my binder tightly under my arm as I race toward Hudson Roasters. When a bead of sweat runs down my face, I wonder if it would have been better to just reschedule.

I'm meeting a man named Jacob Broaden to discuss having his ten-year-old daughter matched with one of our dogs. Maybe I would have canceled if it wouldn't have been for her particular disability. Epilepsy. It's not as if we've never matched anyone who shares my same disability before, but for some reason, knowing how young she is makes me feel a kinship to this girl. I feel like I owe it to her to show up today.

The dad sounded nice enough over email—if not a little… eccentric. Although, I think he might have been in a hurry when he sent off the email, because he misspelled a few words. His choice of five exclamation marks at the end of every sentence was intriguing as well. Actually, now that I think of it, I'm just hoping he's not a psycho. I really don't want to get stuffed in someone's trunk today. That would really solidify my parents' point that the lower class can't be trusted. But he said he has a daughter. How creepy can someone with a daughter really be? Unless the daughter was just a cover…

Maybe I should have worn a longer dress. Suddenly, I'm very aware of how much of my legs are showing.

As we round the corner to the coffee shop, Charlie and I slow our pace. It's as hot as Hades today. I'm sweating like I've been sitting in a sauna with a fur coat, and my vanilla body spray is emitting from my skin in toxic quantities. Yeah, I'm fur-coat-sauna-sitting sweating.

Mama would be so proud. I'm really putting my best foot forward today.

Before I reach the door of the coffee shop, I come to a stop, closing my eyes and trying to catch my breath. I mentally remind myself of all the major points I need to cover today and hope I don't forget anything. It doesn't matter that I've been doing this for three years now; I never fail to grow excessively nervous before these first meetings. I think it's because I know firsthand how much having a service dog can change someone's life, and I don't want to do anything to deter them from taking that step.

I look down at Charlie, and he winks at me. I'm telling you, my dog is special.

I take one last glance down at my florally patterned summer dress and do a quick check that all my lady parts are where they should be and have not escaped from the scooped neckline during my jog. But *ha ha,* who am I kidding? None of my lady parts are big enough to move, let alone escape their confines. There are perks of being tall and lean—being a member of the itty-bitty-*you-know-what* committee is not one of them.

I open the door, and Charlie walks through with a loose leash like a perfect little gentleman. During the first year after I adopted Charlie, I felt like my eyes were constantly glued to him and his to me. I used my face and hands, asking him to stay, wait, go ahead, or lie down at my feet. Now, it feels as if Charlie knows what I'm thinking before I think it. He and I are so tuned to one another that I honestly forget he's there. He's a part of me. My second skin. *A very hairy second skin.*

It's an odd thing when there's no one in the world you trust more than your dog. But that first time I had a seizure alone in my apartment, and Charlie did exactly what we had trained him to do—push the medical alert button on the wall that calls Joanna and then my parents, and then turn me on my side and lick my face to help me regain consciousness sooner—it sealed my trust.

And today, I hope I can help a little girl and her daddy find that same trust.

After stepping inside the coffee shop and letting the cool air rush over the beads of sweat on my forehead, I scan the room, looking for a man and young girl. Mr. Broaden gave me a brief description of himself in his email, so I scan the room, looking for a tall man with "hunny"-colored hair. Though, I really hope that his fingers hit the keys wrong and he actually knows how to spell the word *honey.*

I'm scanning, I'm scanning, I'm scanning, and….bingo!

There's a tall man with dirty-blond hair, a to-go cup in each hand, walking toward a young girl sitting at a table. This has to be them. Charlie and I approach the two, and the girl notices us first. Her eyes light up when she sees Charlie, and I recognize the look. It's the same one everyone gives my dog. It's a look that says she's seconds from lunging at him, and I'm going to have to tenderly ask her not to pet Charlie while he has his vest on.

Mr. Broaden notices that something has caught his daughter's eye and he turns.

And then, *BAM*. The most spectacular pair of blue eyes hits me, and I almost feel like taking a step back. I'm staring into his eyes and dreaming of swimming in the shallow part of the ocean where you can still see your feet but the water is so blue that it looks like God dipped his brush in it after painting the sky. I immediately appreciate the way his eyes perfectly contrast the white cotton t-shirt that's straining over his chest and shoulders.

I mean, *wowza*. Is this the kind of dad hospitals are cranking out these days? Where do I sign up?

I'll take one dad with dirty-blond hair, tan skin, 6 ft tall, glittering blue eyes, and a chiseled body that makes my face turn into molten lava, please. Actually, better yet, I'll just take this one. Thanks.

It's impressive how quickly my mind absorbs the information that his ring finger is blissfully empty. Not a tan line in sight.

"Mr. Broaden?" I ask, sounding a little too excited for my taste. *Take it down a notch, Evie.*

"Yes?" he says tentatively, and I notice him briefly take me in. His eyes scan all the way down me until they land on Charlie and stop. He frowns and looks back up at me.

That's a little bit odd.

I move my binder under my arm and then extend my hand to him. "I'm Evie Jones. It's so nice to meet you in person!" My southern accent is friendly and inviting, and if we're being honest, a little bit adorable, but he's not taking my hand.

Why isn't he shaking my hand? He's staring at it like he's

just escaped from a deserted island that he's been stranded on for most of his life. Human contact is foreign to this man.

My smile falters, and an odd feeling settles in my stomach. Finally, he seems to remember some sort of manners and shakes my hand. The moment his skin settles against mine I feel my whole body break out in chill bumps. Until this moment, I've been completely unaware of how important it is to me to have a man with hands so large they completely engulf mine. My hand looks like a tiny baby hand inside his, and I love it.

Mr. Broaden pulls his hand back, and I'm pretty sure he takes a step away from me. The bad feeling returns.

"I'm sorry, but…do we know each other?" he asks, his voice deep with only the slightest touch of a southern accent.

I'm not exactly sure how to respond to his question since we technically have met, but only over email. But he should know that already. He looks blindsided. Like I'm an insane woman who has just approached his table and he's concerned I'm going to try to kidnap his daughter and run away.

It's at this point that I realize the little girl at the table is biting her lip and focusing intently on the paper cup in front of her. She looks just about the right age to spell honey with a *U* and two *Ns*.

CHAPTER TWO

JAKE

All of the alarms are sounding in my mind. Who is this woman? Why is she standing in front of me, looking at me as if I should know her? Is she a client of mine? No. I definitely don't know her. Believe me, I would remember.

She's exactly the sort of woman I would take one long look at and then mentally transcribe in my little black book of *DO NOT EVER CONTACT AGAIN.* I'm writing her name inside, shutting it, wrapping a chain around it, bolting it, and dropping it to the bottom of a lake.

This woman is trouble. Gorgeous, tempting trouble.

She's too beautiful. And that immediately turns me off to her, because I just got off the phone with *Too Beautiful.* Not even five minutes ago, *Too Beautiful* was calling from Hawaii to tell me that she wouldn't be able to visit Sam this weekend like we'd planned because her new boyfriend surprised her with a trip to some tropical resort. She said it as if I should be happy for her. I'm not happy for her. I kind of hope that the shark from *Jaws* comes and swallows Natalie up while she's floating on a yellow tube in the ocean.

In case you're currently worried about my mental health, you should know I haven't always been this vengeful. Not sure if that makes it better or worse. I didn't get to my current level of angst overnight. It took months of watching my daughter cry in her bedroom when her mom didn't show up like she said she would, didn't call like she said she would, wasn't there for Sam like she promised she always would be.

Yeah, I don't have any illusions anymore. *Too Beautiful* only sticks around until she gets bored.

I watch the woman carefully, not willing to let my guard down around this woman for one second. Her wide smile falters, and she looks at my daughter, Samantha, with a question in her eyes. This concerns me even more. It concerns me more than the fact that I've already memorized exactly what shade of green Evie Jones's eyes are.

Mrs. Jones—the woman I know I've never met before this moment—comes to some sort of conclusion, and she looks back up at me. She smiles again, and my stomach tightens. I consider finding the dang key to my black book and fishing it out of the lake.

"I'm guessing you're not the one who emailed me?" asks Mrs. Jones.

"Emailed you?" I ask, feeling like a patient learning he has amnesia. "No, definitely not."

She nods and chews her bottom lip briefly while casting her eyes down at her dog. *Her service dog.* There's a binder tucked under her arm with the words *Southern Service Paws* written across it.

Ahh—and now I have it.

Sam has been leaving their pamphlets around our house for weeks. She's been begging me endlessly to let her get a service dog ever since she saw an interview of a woman and her service dog on an episode of *Ellen*. But I've been firm in my answer of no, and that answer still stands.

I'm not entirely sure how to proceed here. I'm mad that my daughter has evidently gone behind my back and contacted whomever this woman is without my knowing. But I also know that she's had a hard year with her mom leaving and then being diagnosed with epilepsy, so I don't want to pile on by reprimanding her in front of this woman. At the same time, it's not okay for her to be pulling stunts like this. Ever since she was diagnosed, she's been acting out in strange ways, and I'm not always sure how to handle her.

When I told her that her mom couldn't (wouldn't) make it to her birthday party last month, Sam told me to cancel the whole thing. I wasn't going to, but she completely freaked out, crying and yelling that birthday parties were stupid anyway and she didn't even want one. She's quiet these days, too—holing up in her room more than I think is healthy.

I wish more than ever Natalie had stuck around. I'm in over my head here doing this parenting thing alone. Sam needs her mom, but she needs her mom like she used to be. Not this new woman who's obsessed with the size of her waist and how many likes she got on her Instagram bikini photo.

But this isn't the time to fume over Natalie.

I turn to Sam and raise an eyebrow. "Did you email Mrs. Jones?"

"Miss," says the woman quickly and then smiles. "It's just *Miss* Jones. Evie, actually."

I choose not to dissect exactly why she felt the need to clarify that and move on.

"Did you email her?"

Sam dodges my gaze and looks down at her hot chocolate. She bites her lips together and then crinkles her nose. That's really not fair. She knows that's her secret weapon to get out of trouble, and she's using it now.

"If I admit to it, am I going to be in trouble?" Sam was only born ten years ago, but I swear, she's sixteen.

I refuse to look at Evie. There's no need. I'll be done with her in five minutes, and she'll be on her way, and I'll never think of her and her cute accent again. "How about if you fess up to it now, I'll only take away your iPad for one week instead of two?"

Most kids pout right about now. Not Sam.

"Five days and you have a deal." Her brown eyes look up at me, and she's Natalie in the flesh. This girl is going to be trouble.

I can hear Miss Jones try to hide a chuckle from beside me, but I still refuse to look at her.

"One week. It was wrong of you to go behind my back, and you know it." I go easy on Sam because, honestly, she's a good kid, and I know that even though she looks tough, she'll cry in her pillow tonight if she knows she has disappointed me. And even though I'll never admit it to her, I'm impressed that she managed to hack into my email, impersonate me to set up this meeting, and then convince me to take her out for hot chocolate at the agreed meeting place.

I hope she channels this cleverness to cure cancer one day and not to rob a bank.

"Okay," says Sam, tucking a lock of her dark-brown hair behind her ear. "I'm sorry."

Sam and I smile at each other for a minute, and I think I've handled this situation well. I don't always come out on top of these parenting moments, but this one feels like a win.

Miss Jones clearing her throat beside me reminds me that I've still got a loose thread to tie up.

Or cut off.

I turn to the woman beside me and force my eyes to see her without really *seeing* her. "I'm sorry to have wasted your morning, Miss Jones. But as you can see, there was a little miscommunication between my daughter and me." I'm just about to turn my back to this woman and join Sam at the table when Miss Jones speaks up.

"The morning doesn't have to be a waste. I'm already here, and I have all my information with me. If you're interested, we could still—"

"I'm not interested," I say, cutting her off.

I can tell I've startled her, because her glittering green eyes are wide and her lips are separated. I don't want to be a jerk to this woman, but I'm also not in the mood to deal with her or her sunny smile. And definitely not her long legs that I'm refusing to notice. Is she wearing tennis shoes with a dress? Did she jog here? Never mind. I don't care. Miss Jones needs to go.

"It was nice to meet you, and again, I'm sorry for taking up your morning." There. I said it in a way that was final but still nice enough that people will want to cast me in a children's television show where I pull on a red sweater and pretend to like everyone.

I glance at Sam, and she looks so disappointed that it physically hurts me somewhere in my chest. I know she thinks having a service dog is going to solve all of her problems, but she's wrong. A dog can't keep her safe. But I can, and I will. I'm not about to just step back and let a dog do the responsibility that is mine. If I've learned anything this year, it's that I can't trust anyone else to love and care for my daughter the way I do. Definitely not a dog.

"Are you sure you don't want to hear just a little bit about the company or our process? I'll even go so far as to mention that no question is too silly." This woman is unbelievable. I've already sat down, and she's making me drag my gaze back up to her.

"In the email, it said that your daughter has epilepsy." Miss Jones's smile grows as if we are talking about a mutual favorite TV show rather than a life-altering disability. It grates on me. She looks down at her dog, and her smile grows more devastating. "This is Charlie. He's been trained as a seizure-assist dog, but he also alerts—"

I hold up my hand to stop her. I'm not proud of how condescending that made me look, but honestly, this woman is just not taking the hint, and I want her to go away. "I don't think you're understanding. We don't want to hear about your company or the dog."

"No, *you* don't want to hear about the dog," Sam says under her breath but at a volume definitely meant for me to hear it.

I look at Sam and prepare to tell her to watch it because she's already on thin ice when Miss Jones pipes in again. "If Sam is interested, I would really love to get to tell you about Charlie and how he's—"

Now, before you judge too harshly what I say next, you should know that I've had a bad week. Nothing has gone right. I've been looking into private schools for Sam to attend in the fall where they can give her more attention than she'd get in her public school, and she's hated every single one of them that we've toured. I've had to tell her that she can't go to Jenna Miller's eleventh birthday party sleepover three times, and I had to deal with Sam storming up the stairs all three of those times with the words *I hate you* lingering in the air between us.

On top of all this, she had a longer than usual seizure last week that scared the heck out of me, and I haven't slept in the past six months since she was diagnosed. I can't stand the thought of her having a seizure in the night and me not knowing about it, so I get out of bed at least fifteen times a night to check on her before I usually just give up and make a pallet on her floor.

Because of all these things, I stand up so fast that my chair scrapes, and everyone in the coffee shop turns to watch me be a complete jerk to this woman.

"Stop. I told you we don't want to hear about your company's dog. I don't know if you're hard up for the cash or what, but you should know that you're coming across as an annoying car salesman about to get fired if he doesn't meet his quota for the week."

I know... It was bad.

Miss Jones shifts on her white-sneaker-clad feet, and her dog's ears shoot up. I'm prepared for all sorts of replies from her, including her siccing her dog on me for being so rude. I'm not, however, prepared for her smirk. "So, I'm a man in this analogy?"

I'm honestly not sure how to respond to that, so I settle for a very mature shrug.

She scoffs and shakes her head at me. I see pity in her eyes, and I don't like it one bit. Mainly because I feel like I need it, and I despise feeling like I need anyone's help.

"Good luck to you, Mr. Broaden." She leans in close to me, speaking low in my ear and alerting my senses to the fact that she smells as good as she looks. "You're going to need it when you try to walk out of here with your head shoved so far up your butt."

I'm a statue as I watch Evie Jones and Charlie walk out of the coffee shop, her sundress swaying with her hips, and my daughter's angry gaze burning a hole in the side of my face.

CHAPTER THREE

JAKE

Sam doesn't speak to me all the way home. Doesn't even take the bait when I ask if she wants to stop by her favorite ice cream shop and get a double scoop. Shawn Mendes's falsetto is blaring over the speakers, and I honestly have no idea how else I can redeem myself in her eyes.

I'm practically screaming *LOVE ME* to my ten-year-old daughter, and she's plugging her tiny little pierced ears, holding all the power.

How did this happen? How did I get here? Shouldn't she be the one begging me for mercy after the stunt she just pulled?

Instead, I'm seconds away from offering to clean her room and do her homework for a month. I'm a total schmuck, but I don't care. Sam and I have always had a close relationship. Even before Natalie left, I was the one who Sam gravitated toward. I've always been able to see how brightly I shine in her eyes. But right now, they look dim, and she looks more disappointed in me than ever. I will do anything to see her smile right now.

"I've gotta stop off at the office real quick to pick up a few plans," I tell her as I pull up in front of Broaden Homes.

It's my residential architectural firm—as in, I built this little company from the ground up. It's not the biggest firm in town, but it's not the smallest either. Honestly, I'm doing pretty well for myself, and as I walk through the large, light-oak doors of the historic downtown building I renovated and turned into our offices, I feel a shot of pride. I also feel a little longing.

Ever since Natalie left and Sam was diagnosed with epilepsy, I haven't been able to devote as much time to the business as I would like. The two other architects I have employed here are working double-time to pick up the extra slack I keep dropping. But being a single parent in the summertime is hard enough. Add in a newly discovered disability and an endless string of sleepless nights, and you get *nearly impossible*.

"Jake, what are you doing in here today?" asks Hannah, one of my two head architects on staff, as she steps out of her office.

It's a smallish building with only three smaller offices for the architects and one large common space for meetings and assistants to work. But it's a beautiful space, even if I do say so myself. Floor to ceiling windows line the front of the building; the flooring is made of wide, natural plank wood; and a massive, 15-foot-long farmhouse table is in the center of the common space for meetings.

"I just wanted to stop in and grab those plans of the Halbert's build." *And feel like myself again for a minute.*

Hannah levels me with a look before putting her hands on her hips. "I thought you were giving that project over to Bryan?"

"I was. I did." I run my hand through my hair, wishing I didn't have to get through a customs checkpoint before making it into my own office. "Last night I thought of a few ideas for the mudroom problem we were having, and I thought I might take a look at the plans again. I think if I move it—"

"That sounds like something *Bryan*—the man you handed

the project over to because you were so exhausted you were falling asleep on your desk in the middle of the afternoon—should be worrying about."

I'm mad that she's right. I'm exhausted and stretched thin. It's why I decided to cut back my hours, delegate more projects to Bryan and Hannah, and devote more of my time to Sam this summer. But it's hard. I love my job, and I love giving my brain the ability to create. Forcing it to turn off like this feels like I'm cutting off my leg. I don't know how to walk anymore.

"Okay, you're right. Let me just look at those plans really fast, and then I'll be on my way."

Hannah gives me a flat smile that alerts me to what's coming. She steps toward me, puts her hands on my shoulders, and physically turns me toward the door. "Go home, Jake. This is your day off. Let us do our jobs."

I'm letting her push me through the door, but I'm not happy about it. "But you're not doing your job; you're doing *mine*. I don't like it, Hannah. I feel like I'm working you guys into the ground."

"Neither of us has kids or spouses, Jake. We like being worked into the ground by our taskmaster boss. It gives us something to gripe about when we go home to our families at Christmas," she says, pushing even harder now.

"I'm going, I'm going." There's a good chance Hannah will kick me if I don't leave now.

I get back in my truck and look to Sam, waiting for her to smile up at me like she usually does. She doesn't, and honestly, it's the most annoying thing in the world to have a ten year old give me the silent treatment. I let her, though, because I'm not entirely sure I don't deserve it.

Miss Jones's sweet southern drawl pulls at my memory. *You're going to need it when you try to walk out of here with your head shoved so far up your butt.*

Pulling into the driveway at our house, I click the button to open the garage and notice that my sister June is sitting on the front porch swing zeroed in on her phone. I arranged for her to come stay with Sam for a few hours so that I can go to the grocery store and shop in peace. And *wow* that statement makes me feel like the physical manifestation of my mom from twenty years ago.

Do I give my man card over to someone directly or mail it in somewhere?

But honestly, I don't know what I would have done without the help of my sister (and my other three sisters) this past year. At one point in my life, I lamented the fact that I had four of them—all younger than me. Growing up, it was like I was always sneaking into a sorority house, trying not to get noticed as I tiptoed past each of their rooms. Someone was always crying. Always heartbroken. Always threatening to run some dumb teenage guy over with her little Honda Civic.

Now that we are all grown adults, living our own lives, I wish they would move in with me and never leave.

June glances up when she sees us approach and smiles wide. It falters when she sees Sam open the truck door and dive out before I've even had a chance to put it in park. It's as if I've kidnapped her and she would rather open the door and hurl herself out onto the concrete while driving 70 MPH down the interstate than live the rest of her life with me.

Sam's flip-flops flap angrily, and her ponytail swings like a pendulum all the way into the house. She doesn't even look back at me—just slams the door shut behind her.

I wince a little and turn to my baby sister whose eyes are now as wide as saucers.

"What in the world was all that about?" she asks as I make my way up the front steps and join her on the porch swing.

"She's mad at me."

June laughs. "Yeah, I gathered that. But why? I've never seen her throw a fit like that. Usually, she just goes quietly and hides in her room." June is the only one of my sisters who isn't married yet, so she's been around this past year more than anyone else.

"Yeah, well. Unfortunately, those outbursts are becoming more normal by the minute. She even slammed her door in my face the other day. Nearly gave me a bloody nose."

"Yikes. So what are you doing wrong?" she asks with a playful grin.

I know she didn't mean it seriously, but the comment still stings me somewhere vulnerable. I feel so out of my element lately. I'm quickly approaching the years where Sam will enter puberty, and then I'll have a whole new pile of worries and insecurities on my plate. Right now, I'm just obsessed about making sure Sam doesn't have a seizure while she's in the shower where she would fall and hit her head. In a few years, I'll be worrying about seizures AND the boy who keeps her out past curfew.

My hands find my face, and I rub my palms across my eyes all the way up through my hair. "I wish I knew. I'm 99% sure I'm failing at this single-parenting thing."

June shifts beside me and puts her hand on my back. "Oh, come on now, it was only a joke. You're doing a great job with Sam." She rubs circles on my back like I've done for her a hundred times. My reply is a half-hearted grunt.

"I'm serious!" She leans in and lays her head against my shoulder. "You're the best dad I know, besides our own. Top-notch, really. I can't think of anyone else in the world who could handle all that you've gone through this year with so much ease."

With so much ease? Last night, after Sam went to bed, I was so angry with how my life has turned out this year that I tore a pillow in half. I'd never felt so powerful and masculine until feathers went flying everywhere, making it look more like a scene from a 1990's slumber party.

I shake my head and sit up straight, dragging a deep breath

into my lungs. "I feel like I'm losing her, June. She's only ten, and she's gone through so much heartache this year. It's like I can physically see her shutting down."

June wraps her arm around mine, and we start to swing. "You've both had a tough go of it. But I think it's just an adjustment period. As long as you keep showing up and proving that you love her enough to stick with her through her anger and outbursts, she'll pull through it all. And you'll both figure out how to live with her seizures. It'll just take some time."

I nod, wondering when my baby sister got smarter than me. Truthfully, though, I think it happened a long time ago.

"I wish there was something I could do to cheer her up."

"Well, maybe there is," says June, looking up at me as if I've never even considered exploring this idea before now.

"I asked if she wanted to go out for ice cream, but she didn't seem too thrilled by that idea." Apparently, when your dad shuts down your masterful plan to con him into getting you a service dog, and then when you have to watch him act like a jerk to a perfectly nice stranger, you don't have much of an appetite for bubblegum ice cream.

"Hmm. Maybe there's something I can do with her while you're at work. Is there a movie she's been wanting to see?"

"No."

"Does she need any new clothes? I could take her shopping."

"She hasn't been interested in clothes lately."

"Well…is there anything else you can think of? Anything she's mentioned lately that she really liked? Or wanted? Anything she's shown interest in that would get her excited about life again?"

I stop our swinging, and my gaze turns toward the house as if I've suddenly developed x-ray vision and can see right through the walls to the stack of pamphlets piled up on the kitchen counter.

My answer has been in front of me all along, and I dislike the idea just as much as I did yesterday. I am still holding tight to all of the reasons I think getting a service dog would be a bad idea, but I'm feeling just desperate enough to let myself see that maybe it's exactly what Sam needs to give her something to look forward to.

But more than anything, I really don't like that I'm about to have to eat a whole truckload of crow.

CHAPTER FOUR

EVIE

"I don't think it's supposed to look like this," I tell Joanna, stepping away from my easel to inspect it.

She leans around her own masterpiece (literally, it looks like it could hang in a museum somewhere) to look at my sorry painting. Honestly, it looks as if Charlie painted that bowl of fruit. *Not true*—Charlie would have painted a better version. His attention to detail is impeccable.

Six weeks ago, when Joanna announced to me that she was going to be heading into retirement at the start of the new year, she decided that she needed to seek out a new hobby that could help occupy her time when she was a lady of leisure. Not sure why she felt the need to drag me along on her hobby-seeking adventure since I'll be the one to absorb all of the work she'll be giving up, but I've been along for the ride ever since.

So far, we've taken up power yoga (and then set it right back down), built a raised vegetable garden and planted ten different types of green plants before Jo decided that she didn't like being in the sun so much and wanted an indoor hobby, and took two improv classes until the guy who never stepped out of his pirate character told me my hair was beautiful and that he'd like to see what it looked like on one of his dolls at home.

Yeah.

So, when Jo suggested we take up painting in the comfort of her kitchen while we sip white wine and listen to music, I was all for it.

Joanna scrunches her nose and shakes her head. "I don't know how it's possible, but I think you might be gettin' worse." I love her accent. It's thicker than mine because she's from the deep south of backwoods Alabama.

I give a short laugh. "No, don't sugarcoat it for me. Be honest and tell me how you really feel, why don't you?"

Jo flashes me a sassy grin. "Honey, you know I love you more than a stick of butter. I don't need to lie to you about your artistic abilities to prove it."

And I do know that she loves me, which is why her honesty never hurts. It's why I'm laughing at her comment instead of silently brooding over it like I would if my mama would have made it. Because if Melony Jones would have said something like that, it would have been so I could see exactly where I fell short. Exactly why I needed to either hire the best private tutor and spend countless hours a week perfecting my technique so she could hang the finished product above her mantel for her supper club to *ooh* and *ahh* over, or hide it away forever, and for heaven's sake, never let anyone know I have flaws.

By contrast, Jo stands up and fluffs her messy top knot —*seriously, can I please have long, gorgeous, white hair like her when I grow up?!*—and tops off my glass of wine before telling me to paint a line down the center of my orange.

"Then it'll look like a big round butt," she says with a satisfied smirk. "And that, darlin', will make you laugh every single time you look at it."

I nearly spit my wine back into my cup. Drinks are never

safe with Jo. You never know when she's going to say something that makes you shoot it out your nose.

"Where's Gary tonight?" I ask later after she and I packed up our canvases and moved to the couch. Her painting looks like a masterpiece of bright, delectable fruit. Mine, a plump booty covered in an orange spray tan. "And why doesn't he ever get dragged along on these hobby adventures?"

Gary is Joanna's husband—and is just as likable as she is. He's a sixty-six-year-old journalist who can work from anywhere and loves his job more today than he did the day he started thirty years ago. Joanna and Gary Halstead are just the sort of people to make my mama and daddy turn up their noses. *Gracious me, do you mean he had to work for his money???*

The Halsteads moved into the Charleston area about five years ago simply because they'd always wanted to live here. That was when Joanna founded Southern Service Paws. These people are as down to earth as the dirt itself.

I aspire to have what Jo and Gary have—the kind of love where a man will still walk into a room and pinch my butt after forty years of marriage. And I know this from witnessing it a few too many times for my liking.

A mischievous glint enters Jo's eyes, and she wags her eyebrows playfully. "Gary's not invited because I don't like to mix my hobbies. And he already participates in a very favorite pastime of mine."

"Ew," I say, shoving my face into one of her oversized throw pillows dramatically.

Suddenly, I'm thirteen, and she's my mama telling me about the birds and the bees. Except the irony is that Mama never actually told me about the birds and the bees. She gave me a book and walked away, because Melony Jones doesn't have personal conversations.

I remove my face from the pillow and toss it at Jo instead.

"Gross. I don't want to know about your nighttime hobbies with Gary!"

She catches the pillow, laughing. I know she takes great amusement in the fact that I turn red easier than if I were on the beach with no sunscreen, because she always, always, *always* takes her inappropriate jokes a step further.

"I never said they are *nighttime* hobbies. Honestly, Evie, where's your creativity? Thinking like that is going to give you the most boring marriage on the planet one day."

La, la, la, not listening.

Don't get me wrong. I love a good inappropriate joke. But from the first day I met Joanna and Gary, they became the parents I never had—meaning, the parents I wish my current parents were. Because of this, I absolutely do not want to hear about my surrogate parents' bedroom endeavors.

I curl up in a ball in the corner of Jo's massive couch and shut my eyes. This day felt way too long, and now it's catching up to me. "I don't think you're going to have to worry about the creativity in my marriage, because it's starting to look like I'm going to die a lonely old maid. Just me and Charlie forever."

I gaze longingly at Charlie curled up at my feet. There's so much comfort in him resting. If he is resting peacefully, it means I'm safe too—no danger of a seizure.

"He won't live as long as you."

My eyes fly up to Jo, and I take in her smiling face. If I had another pillow, I'd throw it at her too.

She laughs. "I'm sorry! I was just tryin' to lighten your heavy mood."

"By telling me my dog is going to die?!"

She shrugs. "My humor is dark."

I shake my head in a mock reprimand and sink back into my corner. I wish my couch was this big and comfy, but that tiny loveseat was hard enough to fit in my apartment.

"Joking aside, I have no idea how you're still single, Evie. You're gorgeous. Funny. Driven. Leggy."

Epileptic.

"As it turns out, men don't really like to approach a woman with a dog wearing a bright-blue vest and a patch sewn on that says, "*Hi, I'm single, and occasionally I lose consciousness and convulse on the ground.*"

I can see in Jo's eyes that she wants to make a sarcastic joke about the patch reference, but she refrains and instead says, "I wish there was something I could say to make it better. But I know there isn't."

Reason #12,345 why I love Jo. She understands people because she's a good listener. She's been listening to people with every disability under the sun for the past five years of working for Southern Service Paws. She understands that sometimes people just need to talk and be heard—not fixed.

"Can we change the subject?" I ask, feeling a little too spent from this day to go down a deep, heartfelt tunnel.

"Sure." She pulls her legs up onto the couch to mirror my position. I swear she looks closer to thirty than seventy. And yet, she's sixty-five years old. "Tell me how your meeting went today."

I groan. Maybe I should just go home. Apparently, there is no acceptable topic for me and my *I-hate-everything* mood tonight. "I wished him good luck trying to walk with his head up his butt."

Jo's mouth falls open just as I suspected it would. "Gracious, girl! Why'd you say that?"

I skew my face up and then shove it into the collar of my t-shirt to hide. What I said to Mr. Broaden was so unprofessional and a drastic overreaction to what he said. Sure, he was a class-A jerk to me, but I shouldn't have responded the way I did. I should have smiled politely, thanked him for his time, and then went home and stuck a hundred pins in the voodoo doll I made of him. Instead, I cast a bad light on our company.

"Well, in my defense, he was rude to me first. But still, I shouldn't have said what I did. And definitely not in front of his ten-year-old daughter."

"All right, here's what's going to happen. I'm going to pop some popcorn, and then you're going to start from the beginning."

And that's what I do. I tell her everything. Well, almost everything. I leave out the part about him being ridiculously hot and me replaying the scene in my head a hundred times, except changing the course our conversation took and ending it with us making out in the corner. She doesn't need to know any of that.

When my monologue is finished, Jo laughs and tells me she would have done the same thing. But I don't believe her, because she treats the company like it's her baby. She's helped train over sixty dogs that have literally changed people's lives—giving them freedom in ways that medicine never could. She would never have let one stinging comment from an attractive guy undo her like it did me.

Jacob Broaden struck a nerve inside me. It still hurts.

Before I leave, Joanna and I discuss the plans I made that day for the fundraiser, and then I spend the rest of the night continuing to obsess over that five-minute conversation in the coffee shop. I teeter between embarrassed of my actions and spitting angry that he would say something like that to me, because:

1) YES, I am hard up for money, and how dare he point that out.

2) Everyone knows that car salesmen are probably the most annoying humans ever, so I take great offense to that comparison.

3) He was right.

I was pushy and obnoxious. I was acting like I would be fired if I didn't meet my quota, because something in me actually does feel that way—not that Jo would actually fire me, but like I constantly need to prove my worth by helping every single person struggling with a disability. Every time I match someone with one of our dogs, I feel like I'm earning my keep in this world. Like maybe, one of these days, my parents will see the grand total of people I've helped and finally say, "*You know, Evie, I'm glad you took your own path in life. I'm proud of you!*"

I pop that dream bubble and move on.

Later that night, after Charlie and I are back in our own little corner of the world, we spend our time curled up on my tiny loveseat, watching *Friends* reruns while I eat sherbet ice cream out of a mug. I think Charlie has a crush on Rachel, because any time she comes on the screen, his ears perk up. *Your ears never perk up for me like that anymore, buddy.*

And then I realize that I'm jealous of the attention my dog is paying a fictional TV character, and I decide I really need to get a life. As if my mama could somehow sense that I am at an all-time low and could possibly be swayed into becoming her mini-me like she's always dreamed, my phone pings.

MOM: Tyler told your daddy that he asked you out again for this weekend and you turned him down. When are you going to start taking your life seriously and claim the future you're destined for?

EVIE: What a little tattletale.

Remember the name of my daddy's law firm: Jones and Murray Law? Well, Tyler owns the Murray part of that title. He is two years older than me and the son of my daddy's best friend (who used to own the company before he had a heart attack two months ago and handed the company down to Tyler.) The law firm has been in the hands of our families for the past three generations. This match between Tyler and me has been in the making since our great-grandfathers shook hands on opening day of the firm.

Only families as delusional as Tyler's and mine would expect their children to marry in order to ensure that a business and all of its money stays in the proper hands. I think the plan is for me and Tyler to marry and for me to immediately birth a son who they will both leave the entirety of the company to since my daddy was never given a son. Because let's face it, folks, this is the wealthy South, where a woman's only job is to look pretty, birth babies to take over her husband's empire, and help him close business deals by fluttering her lashes and making the best old-fashioned for his colleagues.

The sad part is, I almost agreed to this life that I never fit in, because I felt like I didn't have any other options. I was scared to live alone with epilepsy, and since I didn't have any men busting down my door to marry me, my only option was to powder my nose, hike up my pantyhose, and agree to my parents' plan for my future.

That is, until I met Joanna and she gave me Charlie. Suddenly, a bright new future rolled out in front of me. One all sparkly and new, where I could live independently and work for my own living doing something I actually enjoyed. And most importantly, one where I didn't have to marry Tyler Murray and his lying playboy butt that shouldn't be trusted farther than you could throw it.

I left home three years ago and moved into my Thumbelina apartment because it was all I could afford. My parents immediately cut me off, in hopes that I'd starve and come running back to them wearing the patent-leather heels Mama has been polishing for me since I was in her womb.

I would rather eat dirt.

To make sure I didn't have to do either of those things, I took odd jobs babysitting at night; and during the day, I worked side by side with Jo, molding adorable little puppies into dogs that save lives. It felt monumental the day she told me I could move from volunteer into a paid employee position in the company.

. . .

MAMA: Evelyn Grace, why do you insist on acting so childish? You are twenty-five years old. It's time you started acting your age and thinking about your future.

I'm twenty-six, but whatever.

EVIE: I happen to like Froot Loops far better than the high-fiber cereals, so I think I'll just keep on the way I'm going. Thanks, though. Say hi to Tattletale Tyler for me.

I know she won't like that. Mama hates when I make jokes, especially during a conversation that she thinks should be life-changing for me.

Several minutes go by, and I turn off the TV and brush my teeth before climbing into my full-sized bed. My phone pings again. I groan and roll over to grab it off of my bedside table, pulling Charlie in a little closer to give me the moral support I need before reading whatever biting thing my mama has texted me.

But when I unlock the screen, I'm confused to see a number I don't recognize.

Unknown Number: Hi, Miss Jones. This is Jacob Broaden. I have no doubt that I am the last person in the world you want to be hearing from right now, but I was hoping we could talk.

I squeal and drop my phone like it's suddenly morphed into a hot coal. *Jacob Broaden is texting me??* Do I want him to be texting me?

Yes. No. Yes. No.

See…I told you I'd been teetering all night. What could he possibly want to talk about? After our encounter this morning, I doubt he's wanting to shoot the breeze.

. . .

EVIE: Why? Are you in the market for a used car?

UNKNOWN NUMBER: I see what you did there. I deserve it. That's actually why I was hoping to talk. What do you say? Will you meet me at Hudson Roasters tomorrow at 9AM and help me pull my head out of my butt?

UNKNOWN NUMBER: Was that gross?

EVIE: Very.

UNKNOWN NUMBER: I regretted it instantly. Will you meet me?

I'm biting my lip and smiling down at my phone like a fool. Charlie looks at me and rolls his eyes at me again.

One minute ago, I hated Jacob Broaden and was contemplating adding a pin to a very special spot on his voodoo doll. Now, I'm daydreaming of that corner in the coffee shop. Which is exactly why I should decline his offer and suggest he meet with Joanna instead of me if he is considering going with our company for a service dog.

It makes sense. I mean, my body is breaking out in a flush just thinking of his steely blue eyes. But then again, I have first-hand experience with the same disability as his daughter. Who better to advise him than little ol' me?

For no reason other than that I'm a saint and only have the child's heart in mind, I pick up my phone and text him back.

EVIE: Fine. Try not to bite my head off this time, all right?

UNKNOWN NUMBER: Where would the fun be in promising that?

CHAPTER FIVE

JAKE

Walking into Hudson Roasters, I have a distinct feeling that I'm walking right to my death. I don't know exactly why I feel this way. It's not rational. It's not as if I suspect that Miss Jones is going to pull out a knife and stab me. But it's more that I've been putting up walls around myself since the day Natalie left—big, ugly forcefields of solitude that keep beautiful women far away—and I'm a little afraid that the woman I spent most of the night dreaming about might have a really tall ladder.

I woke up in a cold sweat the moment her pink lips collided with mine. It was ridiculous, and I blame it on my late-night texting with her. I didn't mean to flirt. I had only intended to apologize and request a very professional meeting between the two of us to discuss the potential of purchasing one of her company's dogs. All business. Very buttoned up.

But the moment I pictured her green woodland eyes, the flirtatious replies rolled off my fingers like it was a newfound superpower. I wanted to make her laugh. Why?

Because I'm stupid, that's why.

But not today. Today, I plan on being the epitome of professional. I am a neurosurgeon walking into the operating room. I've scrubbed up, gloves are on, scalpel is in hand, and I'm ready to extract only the information I need.

I open the door to the coffee shop, and the smell of roasted coffee beans hits my senses. I've already had two cups of coffee today because I woke up at 4:30 AM and couldn't go back to sleep after my dream about Ev—Miss Jones.

No one likes that guy who shows up to a coffee meeting and then says he already had his coffee that day, so I fall into line behind a man in a nicely tailored suit and wonder if I should have dressed up too. Maybe it would have aided my efforts of being professional with Evie—DANG IT—Miss Jones!

I'm looking down at my jeans and gray Henley tee when I feel a warm hand on my forearm. I turn around, and my eyes collide with a woodland forest. And just like that, I'm dead. She brought a freaking ladder. It's all over for me.

"Mr. Broaden, good morning." Miss Jones is all business too. This is good. I'm definitely not wondering if her lips would feel as warm and soft as they did in my dream.

"Miss Jones, thanks for meeting me. Can I get you a coffee?" I notice that she has the same binder from yesterday tucked under her arm. The dog is here again too. I wonder if she's brought him to give me a demonstration of his skills.

Something different, my eyes note without my approval, is that she's wearing a pair of tight jeans with a rip on the thigh.

It's fine. I'm fine. Moving on.

"I was actually going to ask you the same thing." I frown at her, and so she adds, "I buy all of my potential recipients a coffee during these meetings."

"But do all your potential recipients insult you at your first meetings?"

She smiles and tucks her blonde hair behind her ear. "Oh,

yes. You'd be surprised the number of times I've been likened to a man."

I cringe, thinking back to that comment. The reminder that I was horrible to this woman hits me in the chest. "Right. In that case, can I get you a muffin as well?" I aim a smile at her, and then when I realize it probably looks flirtatious, I wipe it away.

"Chocolate chip, please."

Honestly, I'm a little struck that she agreed to the muffin so easily. Usually, women would never admit to wanting a pastry full of calories and sugar. I expected her to reject it or suggest a veggie omelet bite instead. I like this better, though.

Once we both have our coffees and pastries in hand, we make our way to a table by the window. We sit down, and I note that her dog, Charlie, lays down at her feet without her even having to ask him.

I honestly had no idea dogs could be that well behaved. He's huge. If he wanted to, he could be knocking over tables and swiping all the muffins off of the barista's counter, but instead, he's nearly invisible. It's impressive the way he tucked himself at her feet, half-in/half-out of the table. I wonder if Miss Jones was the one to train him.

She must see me staring at him, because she smiles and looks down at him. "This is Charlie. He's four years old and a major bed hog."

I'm choosing to pass right over the thought of Miss Jones in a bed.

"Is he a potential dog you would match with my daughter?"

"Only if the good Lord calls me home today." Her comment is so shocking that my eyebrows shoot up. She laughs and picks at her muffin, taking one small bite—a chocolate-chip-only bite. "Charlie belongs to me, not the company. He's been my personal seizure-assist dog for the last three years." Did she say seizure-assist dog? Charlie is *her* service dog? She sees the shock on my face and continues,

"That's partly why I was determined to speak with you yesterday. I know exactly what it's like to be in your daughter's shoes."

Oh, well, great. Now I'm sure I could win an award for being so rude to her yesterday. Any day now, I'll be receiving a pin that I'll be forced to wear on my shirt that says, *I'm the biggest jerk in the world! Ask me how I accomplished it!*

"I had no idea," I say, still trying to absorb the information.

She laughs, and the sound trickles down my back. "Of course you didn't. How could you have when you wouldn't let me say more than three words at a time yesterday?" Her smile turns mischievous, and my stomach tightens.

I like that she's not letting me off the hook easily. "Yeah. About that. I'm really sorry for the way I treated you. It really wasn't like me, and you kind of caught me on a bad day."

"Said every jerk since the beginning of time," she says with a smirk as she pinches off another chocolate chip.

"You're going to make me grovel, aren't you?" I think I might be flirting again, but honestly, it's not my fault. She's giving me these eyes that say she's taken off her suit jacket and rolled up her sleeves. Business is forgotten.

"Possibly. I'm hoping I can squeeze at least one more muffin out of it."

I contemplate buying her the whole display case. There's not one part of me that likes where my head is at. Miss Jones is capturing my attention like no woman has before. It doesn't feel safe. This must be how a bug feels right before it gets zapped.

I clear my throat after a sip of coffee burns my mouth and nod toward her binder. "I feel like I should be honest with you. I'm not completely sold on the idea of a service dog for Sam yet."

"Okay." She draws out the word like she can sense there's more and doesn't know how to respond yet.

"I just don't want you to get your hopes up on my purchasing a dog since there's only a small chance that I will. Today, I'm just hoping to get more information."

She's smiling at me curiously. "Mr. Broaden, this is twice now that you've made a comment implying that I am desperate for you to buy one of my dogs. Why is that?"

I tell myself to not say what I'm thinking, but it doesn't work. "Well, to be honest, I've seen the average price of one of your dogs. They cost a fortune. I can only imagine that the commission is enough incentive for you to pressure me into buying one." *Wow*. I had no idea I could be any more rude to this woman than I already have been. Turns out, I had more left in the tank than I suspected.

Miss Jones breaks out in a mirthless laugh. She's looking at me like I just ate cat food, thinking it was caviar. She pulls her feet up in her seat and sits cross-legged, and leans forward, resting her elbows on the table like she's about to tell me a juicy secret.

"Jacob, may I call you Jacob?" I consider telling her to call me Jake but decide against it. "To continue your metaphor, these dogs are not used cars I'm trying to move off of a lot. They are highly trained animals that enhance the quality of—and often save—the lives of those living with disabilities. They do cost a lot of money to purchase, but that's only because it costs an enormous amount to care for a service dog. Not only do we have to pay a breeder, but the extra health tests that a service dog has to undergo are not cheap."

I open my mouth to say something—anything—but she's apparently revoked my talking privileges, because she plows on. "And then there is food, grooming, training equipment, and the teeny-tiny salary that my colleague and I make in order to eat. And if you still don't believe me that I'm not making commissions off of our dogs, I will be happy to show you my checking account, and you'll be impressed to see that the total is exactly the same as my age."

At this point, I'm wishing I could crawl under the table and disappear.

She still doesn't give me a chance to talk. "I'm not in this for the money. I train and match dogs with recipients because Charlie gave me an independence and security that I thought I would have to sacrifice when I first started having seizures. I want others to have a chance at that same security."

I know she's telling the truth. I can see it in her eyes. They are like perfect open windows to her soul. Her passion is contagious, and I wish I hadn't made that stupid comment about the price of the dogs. I knew she wasn't making money off of them. I think I'm self-sabotaging because I'm scared of how impressed I am by her.

I drag in a deep breath. "I think I should just wear a sign around my neck that says *I'm sorry* any time you're around. I honestly didn't mean anything I said a minute ago. I'm just… looking for reasons to not get a dog for my daughter."

"Can I ask why you're here then? What made you text me and schedule another meeting?"

There are two answers to that question. I'll only give her one of them.

"Ever since Samantha was diagnosed with epilepsy, six months ago, she's changed. She used to be such a vibrant little girl, and now she's closed off. She doesn't smile as much, and she's acting out in ways that seem too grown-up for a ten year old."

Miss Jones smiles. "Like breaking into your email and impersonating you to get a meeting with a service dog company?"

I smile back and nod. "Like that. And yesterday, when I turned you down for the meeting, Sam wouldn't speak to me all the way home and then slammed the door on me after we got there." I can't believe I'm telling her all of this. And the way she never looks away from me is making me want to squirm. "Anyway…this has been the only thing she's shown any excitement or interest in since learning of her condition, so I thought maybe I should at least hear you out."

Miss Jones holds my gaze. Her eyes narrow slightly, and I wonder what she's seeing. Her head tilts, and some of her hair spills over her shoulder. It's curled in long, loose waves today, and before I can tell my brain to stop it, I wonder if she's curled it for me.

"You're not sleeping, are you?" she asks.

Her question is so out of left field that my head kicks back. How does she know that? Why is she asking? I'm curious where she's going with this, so I answer honestly. "No. I wake up every hour to go check on her. I wanted her to sleep in my room with me, but she refused. She thinks my room is too boyish."

I recall how I went to the home improvement store and almost bought three cans of bubble-gum-colored paint for my room before I chickened out.

"Does she spend most of her time in her room by herself?" she asks, and I nod. "And I'm guessing you've probably stopped letting her go to her friends' houses?"

How could she possibly know that? Suddenly, I'm in an interrogation room, and she's just grabbed the light and shined it in my face. It feels blinding.

"But I still let her invite them over," I say, and there's definitely a defensive edge to my tone.

"But you're a single dad, so I'm guessing that the other moms haven't been too excited about that prospect."

Okay, who is this woman? Does she have a crystal ball shoved in her purse somewhere?

I lean forward. "Do you think that's why none of her friends have come over?" I don't like how insecure my voice sounds right now.

Miss Jones smiles, but I don't feel patronized by it. More like, I feel as if she sees me and understands something. Something that I don't even know yet. She leans forward again, and I resist the urge to lean closer too.

Nope. I'm gluing my butt to this seat.

"You're not doing anything wrong, and everything about your daughter's actions is normal." Her words help me breathe for the first time in six months. "Samantha has just had life as she knew it ripped out from under her. Her freedom is gone. Her friendships are gone. The small amount of independence she had probably gained from growing older is gone."

Her mom is gone.

"But it doesn't have to be that way," she continues. "I am a perfect example. Charlie has given me the ability to live alone with confidence that if I have a seizure, I'm going to be taken care of. And I know that thought sounds daunting to you right now, and you'd probably like to shrink your daughter and put her in your pocket so you can always watch over her, but believe me, you won't be doing her any favors. She needs freedom. She's not broken, and she can live a full, independent life just like her peers with the help of a dog just like Charlie. Help give your daughter her independence back, and I guarantee you will see your old Samantha again."

Shoot. Just like that, Miss Jones moves to *Evie* in my mind.

CHAPTER SIX

EVIE

I've only seen Jacob and Samantha twice since the day, three weeks ago, that he filled out an application to purchase one of our service dogs. And both times were to introduce Samantha to one of our dogs and see if they were a good fit.

The first dog, Max, I could tell straight away was not right for Sam. He's an amazing dog and very gentle, but he was more interested in watching me than Sam. She was excited and engaging with Max, but he looked as if he had a show recording on his DVR that he couldn't wait to get home to.

I think Sam and Jacob both started to get a little nervous at that point that a service dog wouldn't work out for her like they had hoped. But I assured them it was normal to not match with a dog right away and that choosing the right service dog is a lot like choosing your soulmate. You don't always find Mr. Forever on the first date.

Or in my case, the second, third, or eighteenth. But I'm getting off topic.

The next option was Daisy. She's basically Charlie's twin,

just a little smaller. When I brought her to visit Sam, it was an instant connection. I let Daisy off the leash, and she went straight to Sam and laid her head in her lap. It was that magical moment when I saw both human and animal sigh with relief that they had found each other.

It's hard for people who don't need the hope that a service dog can provide for them to understand the bond that forms between a dog and a person. But as someone who knows first-hand what that sigh of relief feels like, it brings tears to my eyes every time.

Today is the official start of what we call "training camp." It's a week-long program where I help Sam and Daisy bond and show Sam exactly how to work with and utilize her dog.

I've instructed at least twenty of these training camps over the past three years, but never have I been as nervous as I am now, standing outside of Jacob Broaden's front door.

He and I have not interacted at all outside of updates concerning Sam's application and scheduling days to meet the dogs. No texts. No phone calls. And he's been all business when we correspond through email.

I thought that he had been flirting with me that night he texted (and a few times over our coffee meeting), but I guess I was wrong about whatever I thought I was picking up on. My antenna must be busted. And now, I'm staring down the black front door of his gorgeous house, and I can see just how wrong I was.

I knew from Jacob asking me to meet him and Sam at his office for the last two visits that he is an architect. But this home is the physical representation of just how out of my league this man is. Like, he's playing for the major leagues, and I'm not even on the farm team. I'm eating a box of candy that I snuck into the game up in the very last row of the nosebleeds, just happy to have scored a free ticket from one of my friends.

I may come from a prestigious family with a fortune that

could solve the nation's debt deficiency, but I'm always acutely aware that it is not *my* money or the future I want to have. I'm just Evie. A girl floating from cereal box to cereal box, trying to figure out exactly what it is I want out of life (and also trying to collect all of the prizes in those cereal boxes to get that free MP3 download).

I wipe my sweaty palms on the side of my dress and then ring the doorbell. I'm armed with a service dog on either side of me (Charlie and Daisy), and I'm eager to get going on this day of training. I'm also interested to see if Jacob purchased any pastries for our day of training. My stomach rumbled loudly on the way over, making my Uber driver look even more uncomfortable than he did when I first got in his car with not one, but *two* service dogs.

Why does this woman need two of them?! Is she going to drop dead in my car or something???

While I wait, I assess the large modern swing on the front porch. My mind takes a speedy nosedive, and suddenly, I'm making out with Jacob on that swing as the sun is setting behind us.

The door opens, and I jump as if Jacob might have just caught me kissing him in my imagination.

Dang it. He looks good. Too good. He's wearing a black t-shirt (it fits him so well I'm skeptical that he didn't pay $50 to have a $10 shirt tailored), brown chinos, and a leather watch around his wrist. How does this man manage to make wrists look sexy? It's not fair, and I'm worried that I might be drooling.

Nothing about Jacob Broaden screams money. At least not in the way Tyler's ridiculous suits do. But he has this air of confidence that says he should be taken seriously, and it leaves me feeling a little shaky legged.

"Morning, Evie. Come on in."

Now that is one thing that *has* changed. After our heart-to-heart at the coffee shop, Jacob has stopped calling me by the formal *Miss Jones* that makes me feel way too much like my mama. Don't get me wrong, he's still polished and business-like, but I like to imagine that maybe he sees me as a friend now. Not sure why that gives me hope, because remember, I'm up in the nosebleeds just lucky if my binoculars reach as far as the field.

"Good mornin'!" I step inside the house, and a choir of angels starts singing around me.

This place is…glorious. That's the only word I could possibly use to describe it. It's a big, open floor plan with high, vaulted ceilings lined with dark wood beams, and from where I stand at the doorway, I can see everything from the living room, to the dining room, to the cabana outside. I can see it through the floor-to-ceiling windows that make up the wall of the living room. Oh, and there's a pool out there too.

I grew up in a mansion with a maid staff, and yet it never gave me the urge to dive onto the plush living room rug and make snow angels the way this house is.

Everything is white and light-colored wood with contrasting black-steel trimming on the massive windows. It's sophisticated yet homey, and it smells like vanilla and teakwood and something else that I'm realizing is Jacob Broaden's natural man musk.

I'm really trying to control myself to not go run and dive onto that big gray couch. I had no idea that architects make this kind of money.

And, *oops,* I apparently said that out loud, because Jacob replies with a shy grin, "Not all of us do. But I own my own firm, so I make a little more than the average."

I like that he's not the kind of guy to be in your face about how much money he has in his bank account.

There's a small awkward pause while I continue running my eyes over every inch of the house that I can see.

"I designed the house. Do you like it?"

Do I like it? I have to scoop my jaw up off of the floor just to respond. “I love it. I think I could fit twenty of my apartment inside it.” I probably didn’t need to say that. In fact, I wish I hadn’t. It’s only going to prove to him what a small fry I am compared to him.

I’m resisting the urge to open my arms wide and turn a full circle in slow motion. That’s what living in a 500 sq ft apartment will do to a person. I’m a madwoman, escaped from my cell, and there’s no telling what I’ll do next.

I turn just in time to catch Jacob’s eyes dart up to mine as if he had just been checking out my legs.

That gives me a nice little boost of confidence until he says, “Your shoes…”

I look down at my scuffed up, white tennis shoes, and now I’m a ripe strawberry. “Oh. I’m sorry. Are you a shoes-off house?”

I’m frantically trying to toe out of my sneakers when Jacob’s calloused hand lands on my forearm, but then he pulls it away quickly like I burned him. “No, I wasn’t insinuating you had to take them off. I was just wondering if you always wear tennis shoes with your dresses. I remember you were wearing them that first day at the coffee shop too.”

He remembered that? I force my skin to cool and meet his gaze. “Not just with dresses. I wear them all the time. Because of my seizures, I’m not able to drive. I live close to downtown, so I usually walk most places. Helps to wear tennis shoes.” I lift my foot and wiggle my shoe back and forth like a dumbo.

He looks thoughtful after my comment. My wiggling foot isn’t making him smile. He runs a heavy hand through his perfectly mussed hair and puffs out a heavy breath. “That’s something I hadn’t even thought of yet. Driving. Sam won’t be able to drive, will she?”

I shrug, ignoring my urge to wrap my arms around his middle and tell him everything is going to be okay. It will be okay. They will find a new normal, and life will go on—just in a new direction.

But for now, it's important for me to be honest. "Depends. If her medication helps and she makes it the state's specified number of months without a seizure, she'll be able to. But if she's like me…then no."

I can see his mind processing that information, and it immediately triggers my memories of being sixteen and angry at my life too. But you know what? I got through it, and I learned to love my new life. Hopefully, Sam and her daddy will too.

I turn around and face the main living area of the house again. Everything looks so clean. Surely, a single dad doesn't have time to keep a house this clean all the time. *Unless he isn't single.* There is absolutely no reason why that thought should crush me as much as it does, but I feel as if I've been stuffed inside a trash compactor and it's turning me into a tight little square.

Wanting to escape my feelings of dejection, I invite myself and the dogs farther into the immaculate house.

Seriously?! Where's he hiding the little knick-knacks and doo-dads that prove they really live here?

I briefly consider lifting up the couch cushions to see if I find any crumbs or loose change living underneath. Would he think it's weird if I open that hall closet and have a little look around? I wonder if his room is on this floor or up the stairs? Does he sleep on a king bed? I think he would have to, otherwise those long legs of his would dangle off the end.

"Evie!" Sam's voice breaks from the top of the stairs, and she comes barreling down, all teeth and sparkling brown eyes. She really is adorable. Her face looks open and excited today. I remember that feeling well.

"Hey there, darlin'!"

For a brief moment, I think Sam is going to run right up and hug me, but in the end, she doesn't. She looks like she lost the courage to do it.

I glance back at Jacob, and he looks puzzled—as if he were wondering the same thing. His hands are shoved in his pockets, and he looks more than uncomfortable—like he has no intention of ungluing himself from the front door. He's re-enacting an 1800's BBC movie where the gentleman is afraid of being caught alone in the room with the lady.

Don't worry, Jacob. You won't be forced to marry me.

Sam looks up at me. "Can—can I pet her?" She glances down at Daisy—whose tail is wagging and looks as if the only thing she wants out of life is for Sam to wrap her up in a hug—and then back up at me.

I know why she's nervous. Everyone is at first. They see the big, scary *Do Not Pet* patch on the bright-blue vest and worry that they are going to be doing something wrong.

"Of course you can. Daisy is your dog. I want you to pet, snuggle, and play with her as much as you can."

"Really? That's not against the rules?"

I shake my head, trying not to smile too big and make her feel silly for asking. "No. Not against the rules at all. The more you and Daisy bond, the better care she will take of you."

"Okay, cool."

Sam drops down to her knees in front of Daisy and reaches out to pet her. She's cautious at first, running her hand over Daisy's head and neck, and then something snaps in Sam, and her restraint flies out the window. She wraps her tiny little girl arms around Daisy's neck and shuts her eyes with a peaceful smile. The sight tugs somewhere deep inside me.

I know this feeling.

Suddenly, my back feels hot, and I'm aware of a new presence. Jacob has peeled himself away from the door, and he is now standing right behind me, looking over my shoulder at his daughter. I don't want to look at him. Honestly, I'm too attracted to him. I'm afraid that if I look into his eyes at this close proximity, I might burst into flames.

Out of my league.

"She looks happy," he whispers close to my ear, doing nothing to help my buzzing nerves.

I turn my head ever so slightly and see that he is looking down at Sam, and to be honest, he looks like he could cry. Training camp weeks are always emotional for everyone involved—including me—but this…this feels different. I feel what he's feeling, and I want to cry too.

I now understand what it's like to be those weird blue people in *Avatar* that touch tails. I so misjudged them.

"Can my daddy pet her too?" Sam's voice feels like a bucket of water.

I shake myself from my emotional connection with Jacob and focus on the real reason I'm here. "Yep. He sure can. Seizure-assist dogs have to be working 24/7, and because of that, we want Daisy to be able to be a dog sometimes too. It's best to not let other people pet her while you're in public because we want her to stay focused on taking care of you. But when you're home, she can definitely enjoy some TLC from your daddy and friends."

We spend the next few minutes going over what we will work on that day, and Sam looks like she could combust from excitement. Before we move into the living room, Jacob speaks and makes me fall in love with him in a single statement.

"Oh, by the way, there are chocolate-chip muffins in the kitchen."

CHAPTER SEVEN

EVIE

I'm running behind. *Great.* Mama's going to love when I show up to this swanky restaurant in my tennis shoes and a whole (*gasp*) five minutes late.

I can picture her now, sitting at the table, tapping her French-manicured nails on the table, apologizing to the waiter for her inconsiderate daughter causing such an inconvenience to him and his fine establishment. As if he really cares that I've delayed their ordering by five minutes. She's also probably given him at least one other instance in which I've let her down during my lifetime.

As Charlie and I spring from the Uber and dash into the restaurant, I'm almost willing to bet all twenty-six dollars in my bank account that our waiter knows I turned down THE Tyler Murray's hand in marriage.

I approach the table just in time to see my mama finishing up a monologue. The waiter looks at me with pity swimming in his eyes. I smile at the poor man who will have to wait on us this evening, because I know that no amount of money will be enough to erase the backhanded compliments my mama will offer our lowly servant tonight.

"Well?" I ask him. "Do you think I should have accepted his proposal or not?"

He presses his lips together in an apologetic smile. *Listen, lady, I just want a good tip tonight.*

"Oh, for heaven's sake, Evelyn Grace, don't be so dramatic."

I turn my eyes to the woman I'm forced to call mother and suppress my overwhelming desire to laugh. I'm dramatic? The very lady who has probably alerted the whole serving staff of this restaurant to the fact that I'm five minutes late is calling me dramatic?

"Hi, Mama. Daddy." I pull out my chair and sit down, and Charlie takes his rightful place at my feet.

Daddy gives me a half-hearted smile that doesn't reach his eyes and grunts, going right back to perusing the menu he has held in front of his face like it's Captain America's shield. He's been to enough of these "family" dinners. He knows how it's going to go down, and he is not excited about it. *That makes two of us, buddy.* I wish I could check out like he has since I was sixteen years old.

Charlie senses my tension. He lays over my feet and keeps glancing up at me.

"I assume you have a good reason for being late to our dinner?" says Mama, not even waiting for my butt to warm in the seat before she begins her berating.

"Yep. I sure do." I lift my menu and begin reading. Goodness, I hope they are paying for dinner tonight; otherwise, I'll have to ask for a nice crisp water and a side of free cherries from the bar.

"Do you care to explain what that reason might be?" She's blinking at me so rapidly I consider suggesting some eye drops.

Setting down my menu, I say, "Honestly, Mama, I don't think any reason I give you will be good enough in your eyes for my disgraceful tardiness. So, let's just pretend that I had to save a child from a burning building and leave it at that."

That does NOT make Melony happy. Her bright-pink lips are pressing into a line. "Must you always act as if I'm the devil? Is it really so horrible of me to wish for my daughter to be punctual to an event one of these days?" Got it. We've started the manipulative portion of the evening. That was quick.

I look to my daddy, waiting to see if he's going to perform a miracle and intervene. His menu seems to have only become more engrossing. Stephen King has nothing on this restaurant's list of dinner options.

I sigh, mentally deciding to just say what needs to be said to get through this dinner as fast as possible. "I'm sorry I was late. I was across town training a little girl and the new service dog we just matched her with today. Training went a little later than I had anticipated, and I had to return the dog to her volunteers for the night."

This is the part where a mother should say, "*Oh, I'm so proud of you and the amazing work you do, darlin'!*"

Not my mama. She looks bored to tears. "You wouldn't have to be doing all this silly work if you would just take Tyler up on his offer."

Silly work? I dig my fingernails into my palms to keep from crying at the table. "I can't believe we are still having this conversation. I'm not going to marry Tyler, Mama. You'll just have to find some other way to secure the family business, because I don't care to sacrifice my happiness for it."

"Again. So dramatic. Tyler would make you plenty happy."

"How? By parading me around on his arm at cocktail party after cocktail party for the rest of my life?"

She's giving me a look that says she sees no issues with that scenario. Of course she doesn't. We couldn't be less alike if I were an alien freshly beamed down from space.

"Your daddy parades me around on his arm, and I happen to love it."

"Well, I'm glad for you, Mama. But I'm not the same woman as you."

She rolls her eyes. "Of course you are. You're a Jones just like the rest of us. Sooner or later, you'll get bored with this feminism kick you're on and come to your senses. I just hope that Tyler still wants you when you finally wise up."

I want to scream. I want to stand up and scream. Maybe then she would finally hear my voice over the crazy ones talking in her head. "This is not a kick, Mama. This is my life, and you need to get used to it. I don't want your money. Or Tyler's money. And I sure as heck don't want to spend the rest of my life having to turn a blind eye when he grabs a cocktail waitress' rear end."

"Evelyn Grace, what a terrible thing to say about a man. Now, stop talking about Tyler like that before he overhears you."

I frown. "What do you mean *'before he hears me'?*"

I look around, afraid that I'll find Tyler standing right behind me. Not because I'm afraid of him overhearing me say I think he would be a no-good, cheating husband (I'll say that to his face), but because I don't want to have to spend any amount of time with him. Ever.

"Quit craning your neck like that. It makes you look like a giraffe hunting for leaves. Tyler is running late too, but you want to look your best when he arrives."

"What?! You invited him tonight?!"

"Shhh. Lower your voice, young lady. We thought it would be a nice reunion for you two since you won't spend any time with him. I can't believe you haven't even seen him since he moved back to town. Really, Evie, we raised you to have better manners than that."

I am so angry I feel like my head might pop off my body. I push my chair back and shoot to my feet. Charlie does the same.

He gives me the look that says, "*Let's do this, girl. I've got your back.*"

He was at my feet during my weekly hour with my therapist; he knows I have her approval to leave when Mama starts putting me down. "I cannot believe you went behind my back and invited him here. Actually, no. I can believe it." I shake my head. "I'm leaving. And until you can start learning to respect my wishes concerning me and Tyler, our family get-togethers are over."

This is the scene in every movie where my mama realizes the errors of her ways. Her mouth should fall open, and she should reach out to grab my hand to keep me at the table. She should apologize and tell me all she wants is for us to have a good relationship.

Nope. Maybe when hell freezes over.

Mama just sits back in her chair and lifts her brows in a taunting expression. "You're being childish again." That line should sting. It doesn't. She's used it too many times to count, so it just rolls right off my back. Or maybe it rolls right off my long giraffe neck.

I gather my purse and push my chair in to the table, not even bothering to reply to her. I think I would have more luck convincing the brick wall outside to be proud of who I am than my own mother.

"Evelyn." I pause and turn back around to the table. A false hope blooms in my chest that maybe she wants to make amends. How stupid. "And just what am I supposed to tell Tyler when he gets here to see you?" I stare at her, my mouth falling open a little. This woman is delusional.

"Tell him if he had been on time, he would have been able to watch my butt walk away himself." I shouldn't be the only one to be scolded for being late. But I know he'll get off scot-free because he's precious Tyler Murray. If we were to marry one day and he cheated on me, Mama would say it was because I wasn't giving him enough of what he needed.

Daddy lowers his menu slightly to peek at me over the top. "That was a little too crude for my taste, Evie."

Okay. Where is that nice waiter? I need to find him and ask him to hold me back before I jump over this table and fistfight my parents. I've never been one to resort to violence to solve a problem, but it's never too late to start.

I turn around and raise a lackluster hand over my shoulder. "Have a lovely evening," I say, in a bland tone that conveys that I mean absolutely none of it.

On my way out, I notice our trusty waiter headed toward my parents' table with two drinks—the only two drinks my parents have ever ordered in the history of their lives: a glass of champagne and an old-fashioned.

I step into the waiter's path, looking like I'm a gunslinger from the wild west. I wish I were wearing cowboy boots with spurs on the back so they could clink as I move. "Whoa, there. Are these going to the table I was just sitting at?"

I must have crazy eyes, because the waiter nods skeptically. He *should* be skeptical.

I give him my best John Wayne smile before I take my mama's champagne off the tray and shotgun it like I'm a college frat boy with major insecurity issues and something to prove.

After the bubbles have sufficiently burned my throat and threatened to come out my nose, I wipe my mouth with the back of my hand and charge out of the restaurant just hoping to high heaven that I don't bump into Tyler.

Here's the problem with not having a car or a license. When you pull an epic move like storming out of a restaurant and downing your mama's champagne on your way out the door, you're then forced to sit on the sidewalk with your service dog and find a ride home before you have to encounter the man you're avoiding. Not to mention the major buzz that's setting in because I forgot I hadn't eaten since the muffins at the Broadens' house that morning.

I'm quickly scrolling through my phone, hoping to find that an Uber is only one street over and can pick me up, like, two minutes ago, but instead, I'm met with a disappointing twenty-minute wait. That won't do.

I feel pathetic, small, and broken—basically, what I like to call the Melony Jones special—and I want more than anything to get in a car of my own and peel out of that restaurant parking lot, leaving glorious black tire streaks in my wake.

I dial the next best thing: Joanna. She'll probably peel out just to make me smile.

She answers my call with, "It's going that well, huh?" She knew that I was having dinner with my parents tonight.

"Can you come get me?" Suddenly, I'm twelve years old at summer camp, and I want to go home because the popular girls are picking on me.

I hear some shuffling on the other end of the line followed by the sound of keys jingling. "On my way; just drop me a pin with your location."

I don't mean to cry. I really don't. But the fact that Jo knows nothing about the situation and is likely in the middle of dinner with Gary, and she stops everything to come to my rescue, does me in. She acts like my best friend, my sister, my mama, and my grandmama all rolled up in one. Although, I would never liken her to my grandmama to her face because, *hello,* I don't have a death wish.

I hear the sound of a garage door opening, followed by the closing of her car door, just before I notice a truck pull up in front of the restaurant and stop. The restaurant is on the main street, and the only cars that stop out front are either cars dropping someone off or picking someone up. Just then, the truck's reverse lights come on, and I realize it's backing up to stop right in front of me.

I might have been concerned that someone is clearly going out of their way to kidnap and murder me, but I think I'm a little too dizzy and buzzed to care. Instead, I openly inspect the lifted, dark-gray truck and blacked out wheels. The windows are so tinted that I can't see inside. It's not a bad truck to have to be abducted in.

Charlie's ears perk up when the window starts to slowly roll down.

"Evie?" says Joanna. "Where should I head to?"

"Hang on," I whisper, wishing that window would roll a little faster. "I think I'm being kidnapped."

"What?!"

"Shhh."

The window finishes its descent, and I peer inside the dark interior, not yet certain who my captor will be. A male voice calls out. "Evie?"

Imagine my surprise when the driver leans toward the passenger window, and I'm finally able to see the face of Jacob Broaden and his bright-blue eyes staring back at me. "Are you waiting for a ride?"

Of course he would drive a truck that only makes him look hotter. Of course he would. I wish he drove a minivan with an ugly stick-figure bumper sticker of him and his daughter wearing mouse-ear hats.

"Who is that?" Jo practically yells in my ear.

I pull my phone away with a wince, almost certain I will never fully regain my hearing from that, and ignore her. "I—well, sort of. I was just in the middle of finding one."

"Lie!" Joanna shouts again. "You already found a ride, remember? Why are you lying to this man?"

"Shhh," I hiss at Joanna.

She makes a valid point, though. Why am I acting like I don't already have a ride?

"Hop in. Sam and I were just headed to dinner, but I can drop you off wherever you need to go first."

Hop in? Well, that's an idea. One that I should firmly decline. It wouldn't be good for me to get in that man's truck. I already have the teeniest bit of a crush on him (read: massive crush), and I know that nothing good can come of taking a ride with him.

All morning, I caught myself glancing at him when I should have been paying attention to Sam and Daisy. It didn't matter, though. He didn't catch my glances, because he seemed to barely realize I existed. He hovered on the outskirts of the room, only participating when instructed. But even then, he barely spared me a single look. His attention was zeroed in on his daughter and Daisy, which, honestly, only made my attraction to him deepen.

He might have been flirting with me over those first few texts, but now he has made it perfectly clear that he is not interested in me. That's fine. I'm not interested in him either. And I almost mean that.

"Oh, that's okay! I'm good to catch a ride with my friend across town. You guys go on to dinner." My smile is all stars and butterflies, but inside, I feel a little tremble. Why? Do I hope he fights for me? Or do I hope he drives off?

I am a human see-saw. Up and down I go. *Take me with you. Leave me be.*

"Who is this guy?" Joanna reminds me that she's still glued to my ear. "He sounds sexy." *You have no idea.*

"Come with us, Evie!" I hear Sam bellow from the backseat.

I want to step closer so I can see her, but I know that's a bad idea too. I need to keep my butt over here, far away from this family that I can very well see myself growing attached to. I'm already going to be spending every day this week with them; I don't need to heap more coals onto the already blazing fire.

"Yeah, come on," Jacob says with a cool-guy wave. His other hand is draped over the steering wheel, and he looks so effortlessly sexy. "Don't make your friend come all this way."

His persistence is throwing me off. Just when I think I understand what's happening with him, he turns the tables. Earlier today, he was Mr. I-Don't-Care-About-You, and now I could almost swear I see a hopefulness in his eyes.

"Well…" I glance around and remember that Tyler will show up at any moment. I really don't want to be here when that happens.

"For Pete's sake, go with the hot man!" Joanna says, and I hear her garage closing again. What a traitor. "I'm officially retracting my offer to come pick you up."

I turn my back briefly to Jacob and Sam and cup my hand around the mouth of the phone like I've seen people do in the movies. Apparently, this keeps anyone else from hearing what I'm saying. "Are you sure? I'm not sure it's such a good idea." I haven't told Jo yet about my teeny-tiny, almost non-existent attraction to Jacob.

"If he's half as cute as he sounds, I'd say it's a fantastic idea. And besides, you need more friends under the age of sixty. Honey, it's about time I kick you out of the nest. Fly, little Evie birdie, fly!"

I roll my eyes as she ends the call. I never get to end it first. One of these days, I'm going to end it mid-conversation just to throw her.

I turn around with a tense smile. "Well, my ride just bailed on me, so I think I have to take you up on your offer."

CHAPTER EIGHT

JAKE

How am I doing in my attempt to keep Evie Jones at bay? Not great, considering she's sitting in my passenger seat right now. I nearly ramped the curb when I saw her standing there with Charlie. She looked sad and concerned with her phone pressed to her ear. I threw the truck in park and almost sprang from my seat before I mentally grabbed myself by the collar and shook some sense into my sorry self.

"How are you?" I ask after Evie puts Charlie in the backseat with Sam and she buckles herself into the passenger seat.

This is ridiculous. I'm ridiculous. I saw this woman not even four hours ago, and I'm already feeling needy to know how she is? What she's been doing since she left our house? Why she looks so sad?

"Fine." She gives me the universal female answer for *everything is horrible,* but I resist asking any further questions, because I'm not her boyfriend. Never going to be.

Next time I date, it will be someone of average beauty and definitely not seven years younger than me.

"Thanks for giving me a ride," says Evie.

"Happy to." And I am. Actually, I'm way too happy to have her seated beside me. "Where am I headed?"

"Oh, here, I can type my address into your phone." Her emerald eyes, along with her soft vanilla scent, hit me for the first time since she got in the truck. She's saying normal words, and her tone is completely casual. And yet, my heart is racing as if she just whispered something dirty in my ear.

I hand my phone over to her, and once she's done typing in her address, we set out toward her apartment. Because I have no idea how to talk to this woman without accidentally flirting, I do the same thing I've been practicing all day in her company: keep my mouth shut. I also squeeze the steering wheel, because out of the corner of my eye, I can see an impressive amount of her tan legs, and I swear to myself that I will not give in and look at them.

I WILL NOT.

After a minute of silence, Evie adjusts in her seat to turn around and look at Sam. I'm not sure why this takes me by surprise. "What do you think about your first day of training with Daisy?"

Man, I like her southern accent. I grew up here. I'm used to women all around me having accents. Hers is different, though. It's sweeter, somehow.

"It was great. I wish she could have stayed with me tonight," says Sam.

"I know. It's sad to have to say goodbye to them at night, isn't it? But until you've learned everything you need to know about how to interact with her, it's better to let her sleep at her volunteer's house. But you did so great today. I was really impressed with how quickly you caught on to all of the techniques."

I catch Sam's eye in the rearview mirror and see the moment Evie's praise hits her bloodstream. She wants to smile. She wants to soak every ounce of that compliment up, wring it out, and then soak it up again. Other than my sisters, she hasn't had a woman offer her praise like that since Natalie left. I feel as if I can see the void inside her and watch Evie's words fill a small part of it.

"Thanks." Sam pushes her unruly hair that I have a hard time brushing behind her ear and looks out the window. Only when her head is fully turned do I see the slight grin touch the corner of her mouth.

I'm torn. On the one hand, I want Sam to receive the praise she needs. But on the other hand, I'm scared to death of Evie. After this week, she'll be gone, and it'll just be me and Sam again.

Evie turns back to the front, and I hear her take in a deep breath through her nose. She lets it out like it's the first one she's taken all day.

"How was your dinner?" I ask, proud that it sounded innocuous enough. Polite. Business talk between two colleagues.

"Dinner?" she asks with a furrowed brow.

"Yeah, weren't you just leaving that restaurant? I assumed you were eating there."

"Oh." She looks down at her lap. "I was supposed to, but… my company wasn't so great, so I left before eating."

My eyes slice to her, and my mouth goes rogue. "Was the guy a jerk to you?" I have no idea why I said that. I don't even know if she was there with a guy.

One minute, I'm driving Miss Daisy, and the next, I'm a psycho-jealous boyfriend, fighting some random jerk wad in a bar because he looked at my girl wrong. I've never been that guy before. Not even with Natalie, and part of me wonders if we really ever loved each other.

I think Evie finds my comment amusing. She relaxes into her seat, and I can tell she's fighting a grin by the way she's biting her lips together. "Uh, no. I was actually having dinner with my parents. But someone was…never mind."

My grip on the wheel relaxes. I see Evie's fingers (and bright-yellow nails) creep toward the release button for the center console. For a second, I think she is going to open it and look inside, but she catches me looking at her hand and pulls it away. All day, I caught her peeking around corners of the house when she thought I wasn't looking. I think I even heard her open a cupboard in the guest bathroom at one point. She wouldn't have found anything fun in there. I keep all my personal items in my bathroom.

Maybe I should find it creepy that she was searching my house. I don't. Actually, it makes me smile, because I know she's as curious about me as I am about her—even though I really shouldn't be. I wish I could put her out of my head.

Speaking of curiosity, I want to ask her more about her parents and this mysterious *someone* she stopped talking about, but Sam chimes in from the backseat before I get the chance.

"If you haven't eaten, you could come with Daddy and me to dinner."

I try to flash Sam a look in the rearview mirror that says *no she absolutely cannot!*

Evie is not coming with us to dinner. I can't handle any more hours with this beautiful woman than I already am. After spending the first half of the day together, I feel like I've been staring at the sun. I shut my eyes, and the image of her face is burned there. I might never see properly again.

Also, she made Sam laugh ten times today. Ten. I kept a tally.

Yeah, Evie's not the only one being creepy.

I realize belatedly that Evie saw me give Sam that look. I try to play it off and smile at Evie, but she just chuckles a laugh that sounds like she's giving me the middle finger in her head. She thinks I don't like her all that much, and although it's kind of torturing me, I'm also okay with her thinking that, because I've been working hard to give her that impression all day.

"Thanks for the offer, Sam, but I'm actually pretty tired, and I think I heard Charlie's stomach growl earlier. I should get home and feed him."

"You sure? You're welcome to join us." I'm all politeness now that I know I'm in no danger of her accepting.

She makes a guttural noise that says she knows what I'm doing. I glance up at her in time to see her lips mouth *liar liar, pants on fire.* She smirks and turns her face to look out the side window. I like that she never lets me get away with my rudeness.

Five minutes later, we are pulling up outside of a classic Charleston-style, tall and skinny house in the center of town. It's not bad. A little old and outdated, but it looks like a pretty nice place, all in all. I wonder what it looks like inside. Does she have feminine throw pillows sprinkled around the living room? Is she tidy or messy? Somehow, I instinctively know that she's messy. Evie just seems like the sort of woman to kick off her shoes haphazardly as she walks into her apartment and drop her purse somewhere random that she'll forget by the morning. I definitely have her pegged as an "unfasten her bra, pull it out her sleeve, and toss it over the back of a couch before she's even made it fully into the house" kind of woman.

I really want to walk her to her door and find out if I'm right.

Seeing me inspect her house, she says, "This isn't my house. I rent out their detached studio apartment around back."

Oh. Now I'm even more curious.

She gathers her purse and slings it over her shoulder. I notice that her hair gets caught under the strap, and I'm reaching up to pull it free when I notice Evie's eyes widen.

Bad hand!

I drop it and quickly turn to open my door. I'm getting out now. Why am I getting out? What am I supposed to do once Evie comes around to this side of the truck? Do we hug? *Definitely not*. Do we shake hands? *That would be strange.* Suddenly, I'm thirteen, I've just discovered that girls exist, and I have no idea how to act around them.

I hear Sam call out a goodbye from the backseat and watch Evie wave toward Sam when she and Charlie round the truck. If I'm not mistaken, she gives one appreciative glance to my truck before meeting my eyes. *What would I do if she gave me that same look?* I'm losing it.

"Well,"—she adjusts her hair out from under her purse strap —"thanks for the ride. Should I Venmo you some money for gas?" Wow. She really thinks I'm an A-hole.

I shake my head and stuff my hands in my pockets. "Not necessary. Glad to help out."

She's fidgeting, awkward, and won't make eye contact with me. Oh, right. She thinks I don't like her. Is she waiting for me to apologize for the look in the car? I should…but I don't because I'm afraid it would undo all the work I've done to keep her at bay.

"Okay. Well, I'll see you two tomorrow, then." Her tone is clipped, and I'm 99.9% sure she wishes I was dead.

"Right. Yeah. Sounds good."

I wish she would smile at me. I just want one for the road. She looks over my shoulder toward Sam's window, and then her face lights up with a smile that melts my insides. She looks back to me, and her smile drops. *No smiles for you, big jerk.* And then she and Charlie disappear around the house.

When I'm back in the truck and buckling up, Sam says, "She saw you make that face, you know."

I sigh. "I know."

"Why didn't you want her to come to dinner?"

At least a hundred answers fly through my mind, but I can't tell my ten-year-old daughter any of them. "Because…I didn't want her to feel uncomfortable having to eat with us."

"I think she would have liked to come."

I flip my turn signal and move into traffic, pretending not to be overly curious about Sam's statement. "Oh yeah? Why do you think that?"

"Because she peeks at you as much as you peek at her."

Never mind the fact that statement makes me sound like a massive creeper…

I look at Sam in the rearview mirror and see her satisfied smirk. "We're just friends, kiddo. There's nothing else between Evie and me."

"Well then, you should have made her come with us. Friends eat dinner together."

The problem is, I don't want to be friends with Evie. I want to take her on a date, and run my hands through her long hair, and find out if her lips feel as soft as they look.

CHAPTER NINE

EVIE

I'm sitting at the venue Jo and I booked for the fundraiser benefit, waiting for the caterer to meet me so we can go over the menu, when my phone buzzes.

JO: You need to go shopping.

EVIE: Because you hate my clothes?

JO: Because you need a new dress for the benefit. Something short and black.

EVIE: I was thinking I would wear my silver one again.

JO: Exactly. That dress has seen better days. You need to go shopping. Let's go Friday.

Ugh. I hate that Jo is right. That silver dress is the last connection I've had with my old life. I'm pretty sure when Mama bought me that dress, it cost more than all of my current wardrobe piled together. But just because it was expensive back then, doesn't mean it still looks expensive now—unless peplum dresses that have shrunk a few too many sizes in the dryer have suddenly come back in style.

EVIE: Fine. You win. I'll buy a new dress. But it has to be from somewhere that I can use a 20% off coupon.

JO: No way, missy. You haven't let me buy you anything all year. This is my treat.

That's true, too. Jo is always trying to buy me things, but I don't let her. I can't exactly be a pioneer, forging my own path in life, if I'm constantly letting someone go in front of me and whack down all the weeds. I have to do it. I have to get my hands dirty.

But since this night is really important for our company, and I have invited quite an impressive list of people that I'm hoping will give us loads of money, I decide to give in this once and let her spoil me.

EVIE: If I let you buy me a dress, does that mean I have to let you pick it too? Because anytime you dress me up, I end up looking less like a lady and more like a lady of the night.

JO: **Pretty Woman* gif*

EVIE: Does that mean yes?

JO: *Another *Pretty Woman* gif*

EVIE: You're hopeless.

JO: And you're more prudish than my Grandma Sue.

EVIE: I love you.

JO: I love you too.

I hear the door to the venue open, and I look up with a smile on my face. My smile immediately falls at the sight of my caterer walking beside my mama, as *buddy-buddy* as I've ever seen two people. They are laughing about something, and Mama gives the caterer a playful smack across the arm. "Monica, you're so bad. I had no idea that you were capable of being so conniving."

The woman beams at Mama. "That's only because you've never harassed my servers and then tried to get out of paying me for my services."

What in the name of Sam Hill is my mama doing here with my caterer?

I stand up with an angry scowl on my face. “Mama, what are you doing here?”

“Now, is that any way to greet your mother?” She’s smiling like she does when she’s trying to fool everyone around us into thinking we’re a happy, do-anything-for-each-other family. We’re not. And honestly, I’m so done pretending.

I cross my arms. “How do you two know each other?”

Poor Monica sees my face and starts looking worried. She takes a small step back to let my mother take the lead. “Did you not know? I’ve been using Monica’s catering company for years. She provides the most delicious food for all of the Powder Society’s functions.”

I want to groan. Of course I picked the one caterer in town that was tied to Melony Jones.

“I think it’s safe to say that I did *not* know that.” *Or else I would not have used her.* “But how did you know we were meeting today?”

Mama smiles a syrupy sweet smile to Monica over her shoulder. “Will you give us a minute, Mon?” Mon! Bleh. Excuse me while I go fire my caterer immediately.

Monica leaves my mama and me alone together. I spot the fire alarm only a few feet away, and I consider pulling it.

“Now, Evelyn Grace, can you please try, for one moment, to not treat me like some sort of almighty tormenter in front of my caterer?”

“*My* caterer! She’s my caterer today! I’m just trying to figure out what the heck you’re doing here.” I’m as close as cat's breath to purposely spilling my coffee all over my mama’s pink linen dress.

She sticks her nose in the air a little higher. “If you must know, Monica and I were together yesterday, discussing the menu for an upcoming Powder Society meeting, and she mentioned that she was meeting with a client today by the name of Jones and wondered if I was related to an Evie." Oh, yeah…Monica's got to go. "I told her you were my daughter, and she mentioned your fundraiser. Imagine my embarrassment when I had to pretend like I knew what she was talking about! My own daughter not inviting me to a fundraiser she is hosting!" She's shaking her head, and honestly, that pity card she's trying to fly in front of my face is looking pretty flimsy these days.

"Mama, you have made it perfectly clear that you do not support my decision to work for Southern Service Paws. So, excuse me if I didn't think it would interest you to be invited."

"We are the Joneses, Evelyn Grace! We go to every fundraiser in town. Imagine how it would look if word got out that I wasn't even invited to my own daughter's event?"

And this, ladies and gentlemen, is the mother that raised me. She is putting up a big fight, not because she's hurt that I didn't want her at the fundraiser, but because she's afraid of what people would think. This is so classic Melony Jones. It's how she's acted every single day of my life.

Maybe I should move to a new town. Somewhere far away where the Jones name means nothing.

But I relent because I don't have the time to go eighteen rounds with her. "Fine, Mama. Consider this your and Daddy's official invitation. It's Satur—"

Mama holds up her hand and then starts rifling through her purse. "Don't bother. I already have all the details on this *laser-printed* invitation I took off of Deborah's fridge." She levels me with a frosty scowl. "Because *Deborah* and her family received one."

I knew she would mention something about the printing. Mama is the queen of event planning. She would rather saw off her arm to pay for the finest engraved linen invitations than have to settle for mere laser printing.

I gesture toward the invite. "So, apparently you didn't have to do too much acting when Monica told you about the event since you had already stolen that invitation from one of your friends. Remind me, do they teach theft in cotillion? It's been so long I don't remember."

Mama's eyes narrow dangerously. "Now that's enough sass from you, young lady. Like it or not, your daddy and I will be at the benefit." She tucks her stolen invite back into her Coach purse.

She turns away and starts swinging her hips as she walks toward the door, and without looking back, she gets one final punch in. "By the way, I already talked with Monica, and the drumsticks you originally ordered will never work for a black-tie event. I had her change the menu to salmon and chicken cutlets. If you want people to give like millionaires, don't expect them to eat with their fingers like cavemen."

I'm looking around for something I can throw at this woman, but whether because of the good Lord's mercy or my own bad luck, there's nothing nearby.

She pauses with her hand on the door. "Oh, and I expect you to send a proper invitation to Tyler and his parents."

"Sure. I'll get right on that as soon as pigs fly."

Mama swivels her lazy frown back at me. "I raised you to have more class than that. This is proof you've been spending too much time with that Joanna woman. Act like a southern lady, dear. Not a backwoods bumpkin."

I watch her disappear through the door and hear her chuckle with Monica on the other side of it. I wonder if this is how the rest of my life is going to be. Will I ever be outside of my mama's reach in this town? Is there anyone who works within the state of South Carolina who hasn't worked for Melony Jones in some fashion?

Southern Service Paws is usually my safe haven, but now it feels like Mama has wiggled her way in the back door somehow.

I despise the idea of accepting my parents' money or using

their name in any way, but I do know that if word spreads around town that they are attending the benefit, all the other elitists will come too. No one wants to be the couple that didn't attend the same event as Melony and Harold Jones. And likely, if they see my mama offering up a check, the money will pour in like manna from heaven. Now that I think about it, it was selfish of me not to invite them in the first place.

For the sake of the company, I can lay down my pride long enough to add my parents' names to the guest list. But under no circumstances will I be adding Tyler Murray's name. I'm not that selfless.

I pick up my phone and see that Joanna has texted me again. Just seeing her name on the screen helps my shoulders relax and my breathing to normalize. She has given me a place in this world that I never expected to have; the least I can do is help the company she loves thrive.

JO: After we find you a dress, we need to find you a date.

EVIE: I have one. I need to buy Charlie a tux, though.

JO: I was thinking more along the lines of that sexy dad that gave you a ride home last night.

EVIE: You've never even seen him.

JO: I don't have to. When a man has a timber to his voice like that man's, he has no choice but to be sexy. Bring him!

EVIE: No. He doesn't like me. Besides, shouldn't you be discouraging any fraternization between me and our clients?

JO: We're not a PR team for a presidential candidate. Fraternize all night if you want :)

Dang it. I was really hoping she would ban any thoughts of making out with Jacob Broaden. It would be easier to swallow his rejection if I knew I couldn't have him even if he *did* like me.

CHAPTER TEN

EVIE

I sling my purse over my shoulder and gather Charlie's leash. It's been a long day of training at Sam's house, and she's honestly done amazing. She's picked up the techniques so quickly that I'm considering asking her to drop out of elementary school and come to work for me as a trainer.

Sam approaches me slowly as I gather my things, her bare toes scuffing the plush rug. She's after something. She glances toward the kitchen where Jacob disappeared a moment ago and then back to me.

"Spill it," I tell her when she works up the nerve to meet my eyes.

She smiles—something she's started doing more and more over the past two days—and asks, "Do you think…well…there's this birthday slumber party at one of my friend's house coming up…"

"Mmhmm," I say, setting my purse down and giving Sam my full attention. "Go on."

"Do you think Daisy will be ready by then to go with me… you know…if I can convince my daddy?"

"I don't see why not. I think you and Daisy are bonding quickly." And that's the truth. I've been impressed with how attentive Daisy has been to Sam. Anytime Sam simulates a seizure, Daisy has snapped into action immediately, rolling Sam onto her side and going to alert Jacob before returning to Sam's side and licking her face until the "seizure" subsides.

"Oh, great." Sam doesn't look relieved, though. This conversation wasn't really about asking if Daisy will be ready or not.

"Are you sure that's all you wanted to talk about?"

"No." Sam gives me a crooked grin that has seriously started to melt my heart.

I learned this morning when I asked if Sam's mama could come around sometime during the next week to get acclimated with Daisy that the woman left a year ago and there is no chance of her coming back into their life. Jacob is single—a fact that doesn't affect me whatsoever—and Sam is essentially motherless. I don't know where this incredibly stupid woman has gone, or why she left, but I know that she left this fragile family devastated.

"Actually, I was kind of hoping that maybe you could talk to my dad about the slumber party for me. He doesn't think it would be safe for me to go, but since you have epilepsy and live on your own with Charlie, you could convince him that I would be fine, and he would listen to you."

Ha! Listen to me? I think I'm the last person in the world that Jacob Broaden wants to listen to. It's clear as day that the man is only tolerating my presence because of Daisy. He doesn't meet my eye when he's in the same room as me. He goes through ridiculous feats to stand as far away from me as possible and only responds to me in one-word answers.

I have no idea what I did to make this man not like me so quickly, but I wish I knew, because then I could bottle it up and spray it all over myself before I go to the grocery store. Maybe then it would keep all of those weirdos from hitting on me. Why can't the normal ones ever hit on me? You better believe that if a man is talking to me in a grocery store, he smells like body odor and Funyuns and is advising me on which foods to buy that will "enhance my hourglass figure." True story.

"I don't know, Sam." I look down at Charlie, and his eyes say it all. *Bad idea. Do not engage. Set down gently and walk away.* He's so smart.

Sam, however, does the dirtiest, meanest trick in the book. She reaches out and grabs my hand with big ol' Bambi eyes. *The little terrorist.* "Please, Evie. You're my only hope. I've tried, but he won't listen to me. I really want to go to this party. Everyone is going to be there, and I really miss my friends."

So, this is what it feels like to have your heartstrings tugged like a puppet?

Charlie whispers for me to stand firm. I tell him I never stood a chance. "All right," I say with a sigh. "I'll see what I can do."

"Really? Great!" Her eyes light up, and you'd think I just told her she could eat ice cream every single meal for the rest of her life. But then I realize how badly I've been played when she starts pushing me toward the kitchen where Jacob has been banging pots and pans around for the past ten minutes.

"Sam, no, not right now!" I say, digging my feet into the rug, but this little girl must be freaking Superwoman, because I'm no match for her. Suddenly, I'm being tossed into the kitchen, and I stumble forward as if I've just been shoved into battle.

Even better, Jacob saw the whole thing. The whole entire thing. My cheeks turn red under his blue gaze, and I consider doing a spin move around Sam and dashing out of the house. Screw the Bambi eyes; I'm not falling for her rotten tricks again.

But like every masterful con artist, she continues to hold the upper hand. "Hey, Daddy! Evie wants to ask you something!"

I thought we were friends, Sam!

His brows sink low, and he crosses his arms. I know, without a doubt, that if I were to ask him if Sam can go to a slumber party right now, he would take me by the shoulders and shove me right out of his lovely house. I'm pretty sure that he'd also tell me just where I can stick my advice.

I can't do that to Sam. I can't just sabotage her chances like that. So instead, I'm Katniss Everdeen. *I volunteer as tribute.*

"Yeahhh. Actually, I was hoping that maybe I could invite myself to stay for dinner." And also hoping that a sinkhole could magically appear and swallow me up. "I'm...running low on food"*—oh gosh, make it stop*—"and since training went a little late today, I'll miss dinner if I have to go all the way to the store."

The only way I can describe the way Jacob looks right now is thunderous. Thor has nothing on him. "Mmhmm," he grunts through pursed lips, and honestly, I want to grab the frying pan off the stove and bang it against his head until he learns to be nice. How dare he make me feel terrible for inviting myself! *Have you no Southern manners?!*

I back-pedal as fast as I can. "Nevermind!" I laugh, and it sounds shrill. "I just remembered I have a can of soup." Lie. I have a half-eaten pouch of Sour Patch Kids and an expired jug of milk in the fridge. "You guys have a good night! See you tomorrow!"

I whirl around and make a beeline for the door, grabbing Charlie's and Daisy's leashes in the process. Only problem is, I went the long way—out of the kitchen and through the living room toward the front door—and just as I'm about to make it to the entryway, I run smack into a hard wall. Not actually a wall.

A Jacob wall.

He took the shorter way, apparently, and cut me off.

"Oof," I grunt when my head comes in contact with his right pectoral muscle, and let me tell you, that man must work out every day, because I'm fairly certain I have a concussion now.

He grabs my shoulders to steady me, and when our eyes meet, he takes a wide step back. *Do not touch the leper.*

"Evie, stay for dinner," says Jacob, but his tone reads: stay at your own risk.

"No, thanks. By your reaction back there, it's apparent that my company would be nothing short of torture. So, I'll just be on my way." I try to go past him, but his hand catches my bicep before I can pass. His touch makes my stomach drop and my nerves sizzle like a drop of water on a frying pan.

His hold was tight at first, but when I freeze and look down at his hand wrapped completely around my arm, he loosens his grip.

Jacob lets out a long breath from his nose. "Please stay. I want you to stay." This man is nothing short of a mystery.

I'm plucking petals off of a daisy. *He loves me, he hates me, he loves me, he hates me.*

Which petal will we end on?

I look up to Jacob and force a smile that I don't at all feel. I'm ready to give him a very polite "over my dead body" when I see the smoldering look in his eyes. He's serious. I don't know how I know that, but somehow, I know that this man really does want me to stay for dinner.

Because I'm not generally a masochist, my feet should be carrying me as far away from this fickle mister as fast as humanly possible. But instead, my arm is burning where he's holding it, and I begin dreaming of that porch swing again. "Okay, I'll stay."

He smiles. Actually smiles. There are crinkles beside his eyes, people! "Okay, good."

We stand like that for a minute, and I'm not entirely sure what's happening or how to breathe anymore. Charlie must sense my heightened heart rate and think that Jacob is upsetting me, because he suddenly angles his furry golden body between us and looks up at Jacob with the most human look I've ever seen him give. *Hands off my lady.*

Jacob and I both chuckle at my little chaperone, and he releases me. I miss his touch right away.

Jacob turns on his heel and disappears back into the kitchen, and I'm left wondering what in the heck just happened.

I turn around and bend down to unlatch Charlie's and Daisy's leashes when I catch Sam's face across the room. She's leaning her hip against the side of an armchair, and her arms are folded, a smug grin on her face. I furrow my brows in question, and as a response, she waggles hers.

Oh no. What have I done?

CHAPTER ELEVEN

JAKE

I'm standing across the kitchen, watching as Evie finishes painting the last fingernail on Sam's hand. Sam is smiling from ear to ear, and she keeps looking up at Evie with a studying look as if she's memorizing every tiny thing Evie does so that she can perfectly replicate her actions later. Sam adores Evie, that much is apparent. And honestly, I understand the sentiment.

The woman is gorgeous. Funny. Strong. Kind-hearted. She has overcome a difficult disability and not let it dictate her life. And she has the most beautiful, full pink lips I've ever seen. Okay, I doubt that Sam has noticed that last part, but believe me, I have.

Did I mention that Evie is painting a rainbow pattern on Sam's nails? That probably doesn't seem like a big thing, but for my little girl that has resisted everything happy and cheerful over the past six months, it's huge.

I was quiet during dinner, partly because I have no idea how to interact with Evie, but also because I was enjoying hearing my daughter talk. I didn't realize how starved I was for the sound of her voice. It didn't sound heavy like it has been lately. She didn't give short, clipped answers. She told Evie things that I had no idea about (Jenna Miller already got her first kiss?! Where have I been? And isn't eleven years old a little young for that??)

Evie should have felt bored by a young girl's monologue on preteen romance, but she wasn't. She was enthralled, sitting on the edge of her seat, one leg propped under her (I'm realizing Evie will never sit normal in a chair) and those emerald eyes wide with interest. I was floored when she asked Sam if there were any boys she was interested in. Even more floored when Sam said yes.

Note to self: hunt down Tate Bradley and explain to him in perfect detail what will happen to him if his lips get anywhere near my little girl.

After dinner, Evie helped me clear the dishes. When she came to stand next to me at the sink, every muscle in my body tightened with awareness of her. She feels like a magnet. I'm being pulled to this woman, and I'm helpless to stop it.

I want to stop it. I need to stop it. She's too young for me. Too pretty. I bet she has drooling men trailing after her everywhere she goes. I don't want to compete for a woman's attention again. I don't want to constantly worry if she's cheating on me with a guy from the gym, or if she's going to up and leave in a month when she has a doctor offer her a ticket to Hawaii.

But at the same time, I see what a good impact she's having on Sam. She has connected with my daughter in a way that even my sisters haven't been able to since Natalie left. I can't overlook that. Does this mean that I'm coming around to the idea of dating again?

"Daddy, can Evie tuck me in tonight? I want to show her my room."

I sigh and rub the back of my neck. What's the protocol for this? Do I let Sam get attached? Do I protect her already-broken heart? I don't know what the right answer is here.

"It's fine with me if Evie wants to. But I don't want to hold her up if she doesn't have time for it." I give Evie a questioning look. I'm putting the ball in her court because I don't know what else to do.

She smiles down at Sam. "Plenty of time. Show me that room, darlin'."

I hug and kiss Sam goodnight and watch as the two disappear up the stairs, Charlie and Daisy following close behind.

All while I'm washing the dishes and loading them in the dishwasher, I'm aware that I should feel nervous by the amount of time they are spending together upstairs. I don't. It feels right. Like this friendship between them was always meant to be.

As I'm loading the last bowl in the dishwasher, Evie's white tennis shoes enter my sights. I know for a fact I've never been so attracted to a woman in tennis shoes before now.

"You've got a great kid up there," she says, and that answers the question that's been flying around my brain for the last half-hour.

I don't want to push Evie away anymore. If she's up for a friendship, so am I. But ONLY a friendship. I need to dip my toes in and see if the water's warm before I'm ready to take a dive.

"I wish I could say I had something to do with it. But it's all Sam. She came out that great all on her own."

Evie smiles, and I want to let my eyes trace the outline of her mouth, but I don't because yeah...*friends*. "Somehow I doubt that's completely true. I've seen how you are with her." We stare at each other for a moment, and then Evie shuffles her eyes around the room. "Well. Thanks again for dinner. Have you seen my phone? I need to call an Uber."

She starts looking around the kitchen, and I wait until her back is turned to me to say, "It's a nice evening. Do you want to go sit on the porch until your ride gets here?"

Evie's body stops. Apparently, I've shocked her. "Do you

mean you want me to wait for my Uber outside and not in your house?"

"What?" Oh, great. She thinks I'm being a jerk again. "No. I meant…do you want to sit on the porch *with me*? You know, talk together. With words."

I'm ten years old, and she's the cutest girl in class. I'm begging her to accept my Valentine heart, and she's staring at it like it's poison.

A grin finally cracks on her mouth, and she tucks her hair behind her ear. "Words? I wasn't sure you knew how to use those. At least, not outside of insinuating I look like a man or accusing me of extortion."

I smile and shrug. "Occasionally, I can find a few nice ones."

"And are you going to use those nice ones if I sit on the porch with you?" I hate that she's skeptical. I hate that she has a right to be. But I love the southern lilt to her voice.

I cross my heart. "The nicest."

Evie brushes past me with narrowed eyes and a wary smile as if I'm some feral predator lying casually in the tall grass. She's a doe, prancing by but cautious that I might pounce at any moment.

She doesn't know just how much I want to, but not in the way she thinks.

When we make it out onto the porch, I gesture for her to sit down on the swing first. I think I spot the apples of her cheeks turn pink, but I can't be entirely sure. She sits down, and now I'm certain I see a secret smile on her mouth. I briefly glance at my pants, wondering if my fly is down or something.

Still zipped.

I take care to sit as far away from her on the swing as possible, but my body still hums with awareness of her. We start swinging, and the dogs settle down on the porch by the front door. It's a deep swing, but I'm tall enough that my feet are fully planted on the ground. Evie's toes are barely touching, and for some reason, that makes me smile.

Seconds pass, or minutes, or hours, I don't know. All I know is that we are both quiet and sitting stiff as boards, and I've never felt more awkward. I steal a glance at her and find her stealing one too. I'm not alone in this awkwardness.

"Okay. What are we doing here, Jacob?" she finally asks.

"Call me Jake. Everyone else does."

She laughs a little laugh that sounds borderline annoyed and pulls her legs up under her to face me. She's wearing a long burgundy skirt today that's kind of flowy and has a slit up to her tan knee. It's paired with a fitted white tee, but about an hour ago, she got cold and pulled a gray crewneck sweatshirt from her bag and put it on. Her hair is down and wavy like she's been swimming in the ocean today and then let it dry in the sun. She looks effortlessly beautiful, and YES, I realize I shouldn't be noticing any of this, but I freaking am because I have no self-control.

"Alrighty then, *Jake.*" She says my name almost like she's giving me a friendly shove to the chest. "Now I really want to know what we're doing out here. What's happening right now?"

I like that she's direct. I don't think that's a normal quality in women. I wouldn't actually know because it's been a minute since I've played the field (evidence being the fact that I just used the phrase, *playing the field.)*

"Well, Evie, this here"—I put on the same playful, sarcastic tone she's wearing and gesture between us—"is called friendship. It's a concept where two people—"

This time she really does shove me in the arm, and I break off with a chuckle. "I know what friendship is! I just want to know why you are suddenly feeling *buddy-buddy* with me when it's been clear up until this point that you don't want me around."

It's time for me to be direct too. I purposely meet her gaze. "I've wanted you around."

That statement cracks through the air like a bullet from a gun.

She wants to smile; I know it because there's tension at the corners of her mouth, but she doesn't. "You have a funny way of showing that."

I sigh and face forward. "You're right. I've not been the friendliest. And the truth is, it's because ever since my wife left, I feel a little hesitant around beautiful women."

Oh, awesome, Jake! How about you just go ahead and tell her all your deepest pain, why don't you?! Maybe she'd like to hear about how you were pantsed in the hallway in the ninth grade and it's scarred you ever since???

"You think I'm beautiful?"

I laugh and meet her sparkling eyes, glad to know she's not making a run for it. "Oh, come on. I know you own a mirror. You don't have to play coy."

"But if I play coy, I might get more compliments from you."

My heart flips over. She wants more compliments from me? Wants me to flirt with her? I think she realizes how that sounded, because she starts squirming in her seat. She shifts forward and then bunches her long hair up on her head and wraps a hair tie around it until it's an oversized bun that somehow makes her look even cuter. "Okay, then, *friend*. Tell me something about yourself I don't know." She's deflecting, but I can still tell that her face is flushed.

"I started my architecture firm five years ago."

She scrunches her nose, and shakes her head, and then turns to fully face me on the swing. As she pulls both of her legs up under her, one of her legs brushes against mine. Her back is leaning against the armrest, and I couldn't get away from her gaze even if I wanted to.

"I don't want to talk work. Tell me something interesting about you. Like…what color Skittle is your favorite?"

"I don't like Skittles."

Her mouth falls open. I am a serial killer in her eyes now. "You don't like Skittles?!" She shakes her head. "What's wrong with you?"

I laugh. "Many things."

"Wait. Do you not like *all* candy? Are you one of those guys who only eats lean proteins and greens? I mean, it would make sense based on the way you look, but..."

My smile is wide and cocky. "The way I look?"

"Now who's being coy?"

I laugh fully and realize I could sit here and talk to her all night. That thought scares me as much as it excites me. "I like brownies—extra fudgy and with chocolate chips, slightly underbaked."

Her blonde brow raises. "Really? Okay, I can respect that. I love chocolate."

Are we really having this conversation? It's so casual and sweet and unimportant and...exactly what I've been missing in my life lately.

"What's your favorite color Skittle?" I ask.

She lays her head on the back of the swing and pulls the sleeves of her sweatshirt down over her fists. "Red. Do you have any siblings?"

"Four sisters."

"Four! Goodness gracious! Are you close with them?"

"Very. I couldn't have gotten through this year without them." I can feel the conversation drifting toward the therapist's couch again, so I steer it away. "How about you?" Somehow, I can picture her fitting in with four sisters.

She shakes her head. "It's just me and my parents. And before you ask me that question, no, we do *not* get along."

"Really? Why not?"

She chuckles a little, but it doesn't sound like the happy kind. "They want me to be someone I'm not. They have very clear expectations for me and who I should be. From the day I flung my toddler beauty pageant crown in my mama's face, I've been letting them down."

"I'm sorry. That's gotta be hard." I can't imagine anyone ever being disappointed with this woman. I mean, she trains service dogs for a living, for crying out loud.

She smiles softly, and her green eyes pin me in my seat. We are locked in a stare as the porch swing continues to sway us back and forth, and I never want this game to end. Except, it does when Evie's eyes fall to my lips. Did she look there intentionally? My stomach swoops, and I'm wondering how friendly it would be to tug her over to me and find out if her lips taste like strawberries. I've been dwelling on that important question since I saw her apply a pink lip balm earlier.

"Can I ask you something that's a little out of line for the business friendship we have?" she asks, her voice breathy and nervous.

"Sure. I'm all ears."

She smiles tentatively, and I wonder if she's going to ask me out. Is that something women do these days? It's pathetic how old that thought makes me feel.

"Will you consider letting Sam go to the slumber party with her friends?"

And just like that, I'm a popped balloon—air rushing out of me as I fall and land deflated on the ground.

In the tiny span of time between her potential and actual question, my mind took a hundred different turns, none of which I can voice out loud because I'm too much of a gentleman—or at least I pretend I am.

"The slumber party?" Now I'm just stalling, feeling like I need a minute to reel my thoughts back in.

"Yeah. Sam told me about the slumber party at her friend Jenna's house. She really wants to go, and I think that it would be good for her." She bites the bottom corner of her lip, and I realize that she's nervous. She's afraid I'm going to resort back to my caveman ways and beat the ground, telling her to get out of my house.

I've got news for her: I'm not going to be that guy again. I'm done being the jerk around her, so I smile and purposefully relax more into the swing. "She gave you her doe eyes, didn't she?"

Evie's face lights up. "The biggest eyes I've ever seen! I think she even managed to let a single tear pool in them. How does she do that?"

I laugh. "She's an impressive human being. But honestly, Evie…I don't know about the party. I don't think I'm ready for her to do something like that."

"But Sam is." Her words feel like a hammer to my chest. "She and Daisy are doing great together. Trust Daisy to do her job. She's going to take care of Sam if she has a seizure, and she'll alert Jenna's parents, and they can call you." I don't respond right away, so Evie reaches out and lays her hand across my forearm that has been draped over the back of the swing. "You can't keep her in your pocket forever, Jake. Just because your daughter has epilepsy, it doesn't mean that she has to be treated like a toddler for the rest of her life. She's going to need to grow up and learn to live with her disability. Trust me."

I do trust her. Or at least…I'm starting to.

I puff out a breath, trying for once not to overthink anything. "All right. I'll let her go."

Evie smiles wide and squeezes my arm. I swear I'm going to lean across the swing and kiss her. I have to. Every inch of me is aching for it.

Honk. Honk.

Evie and I both jump, and she pulls away, springing to her feet and grabbing the dogs' leashes like we were just caught after curfew doing something we shouldn't. I wonder if she could read my thoughts a moment ago, because she seems suddenly reluctant to meet my eyes. Would she hate a kiss from me?

GET IT TOGETHER, JAKE. You can't kiss her! You're not ready for this, remember?

"I think you're making the right decision about the party," Evie says as she's running down the porch stairs in a full gallop. "I'll see ya tomorrow!"

I'm watching her leave my house, and honestly, I hate it. I want her to stay. It's stupid. I'm being stupid. But just before she gets in the Uber, a thought hits me, and I call out to her. "Evie, wait."

Charlie and Daisy jump in the backseat, and Evie pauses before getting in to look at me. "That's what Sam was trying to get you to ask me earlier, wasn't it? When she pushed you into the kitchen? She wanted you to ask me about the slumber party, but you knew I'd say no, so you covered by inviting yourself for dinner." I state this like I'm at a murder-mystery dinner and I've just solved the case.

A smile grows on her lips, confirming that she threw herself under a bus to protect my daughter's chances of happiness. "Night, Jake."

"Goodnight, Evie."

Tomorrow can't come fast enough.

CHAPTER TWELVE

Training Camp Day 3:

JAKE: Thanks for braiding Sam's hair tonight before you left. I can never get it right.

EVIE: Not a problem. I like braiding hair. Maybe I'll quit the service-dog business and go to hair school.

JAKE: Can you wait to do that until after you've finished working with Sam and Daisy?

EVIE: Bossy much? But okay. We only have two days left anyway.

JAKE: Yeah…two days.

Training Camp Day 4:

EVIE: Dinner was great. Thanks again for inviting me to stay. I swear I really do have food at my apartment.

JAKE: It was nothing. Made sense for you to stay since training went late.

EVIE: Which makes it even nicer of you to offer.

JAKE: Stop it. You're making me blush.

EVIE: I don't believe it. I need photographic evidence.

JAKE: Are you trying to get me to send nudes?

EVIE: What? NO. Now I'm blushing.

JAKE: I need photographic evidence.

EVIE: …

Training Camp Day 5:

JAKE: Last day of training today.

EVIE: Yep.

JAKE: Sam's going to miss you.

EVIE: Sam can come see me anytime she wants.

JAKE: Good to know. Come hungry today. I'm going to feed you pancakes before you guys start your session.

EVIE: Do you talk this dirty to all your female friends?

JAKE: Just you.

CHAPTER THIRTEEN

EVIE

My intentions were noble when I set out for the bathroom. I swear it. Put a Bible under my hand and I will—okay, well, that's taking it too far because clearly my intentions were as noble as sin.

I'm standing in the middle of Jake's bedroom, looking around with hungry eyes. I'm a jewel thief inside of Tiffany's, and I don't know where to start.

Jake was on a work call when I left him, and Sam was in the living room. I walked toward the downstairs bathroom, innocent as the day I was born, until I was out of Jake's eye line. Then, I shut the bathroom door from the outside—I obviously missed my calling as a spy of some sort—and then hurried down the hall where I suspected Jake's room to be.

I don't know why I feel the overwhelming need to be in here. I think it's because Jake still feels like a mystery to me, and I'm hoping that if I have this inside look at his personal life, I'll stumble across the secret to who he is. During our last five days of training camp, Jake has been kind and friendly. But that's it.

Nothing more. Nada. His attention is zeroed in on Sam or work or Daisy. He smiles at me. He asks if I want anything to drink. But that's it.

I wouldn't think anything strange about it if it weren't for the texts I get like clockwork every night. I've never been so glued to my phone before. It always starts with something innocuous and then quickly dips into flirtatious. It's like he has another Jacob Broaden stuffed in a closet somewhere and only lets him out after 8 PM.

I open his closet, and unfortunately, no one jumps out.

Now, I realize that I am a borderline stalker woman right now. It's creepy that I'm tiptoeing around his room, running my fingers across his rumpled gray bedspread, and smiling that he doesn't bother to make it before he leaves in the morning. I really want to pick up his shirt laying across his bed and smell it…but I said that I was only BORDERLINE creepy, and I stand by that, therefore I refrain.

The ugly truth is, I saw the signs saying *Beware: Crush Ahead,* but I blew right past them. Jake has stolen all of my brain space.

He is all I think about, and it's really making me nervous. I don't want to fall for him. I still feel like he's too far out of my league. So, I guess, by me tiptoeing around his room like this, I'm sort of just torturing myself with what I'll never have.

My eyes narrow on a book beside his bed, and my greedy little fingers snatch it up. What does a man like Jake read before he goes to bed?

TWILIGHT?! No. You've got to be kidding me. This one life choice of his has me rethinking everything. There's no other explanation for a thirty-three-year-old man reading a book about teenage vampire love: he's a psychopath.

Yes, I realize that's rich coming from a woman snooping around a man's bedroom.

"Find anything interesting?" Jake's voice sounds behind me,

and I snap the book shut and spin around to face him, holding the book behind my back.

I'm caught red-handed. The jewels are behind my back, and it's incriminating enough to send me to prison for the rest of my life. I don't dare speak. *I have the right to remain silent.* I've seen enough cop shows to know that anything I say will be held against me in a court of law.

"Whatcha got there?" He's smiling, and I'm turning into a tomato.

"I was looking for the bathroom."

"In my bedside table?"

He's stalking toward me, and I'm quaking in my tennis shoes. Where's Charlie when I need him? *Attack, boy!*

Jake stops just in front of me, so close that I can feel the heat rushing off of him in waves, and I have to tip my head up to look at him. It's doing nothing to help my flaming cheeks. I don't think he's ever stood this close to me before, and I'm wondering if maybe this is 8-PM Jacob Broaden, freshly escaped from whatever cell he's normally kept in.

He reaches around me, his arm brushing against my shoulder, and I think I accidentally shudder. No, I know I do because he notices and smirks. *Hello, 8-PM Jake.*

After retrieving the evidence from behind my back, he chuckles. I can't look away and neither can he. He's holding the book between us now but doesn't bother to look down at it. "Were you about to call Child Protection Services to have Sam removed from my guardianship after seeing this?"

"The number is halfway typed in my phone." I don't like how wobbly my voice sounds. But how else am I supposed to sound when I'm face to chest with a superhero that just finished fighting crime? Because that's clearly what Jake is. It's the only logical explanation for all the muscles.

He smiles. "Sam said she wanted to read it, so I thought I would read it first to see if it's appropriate for her."

"A likely story." I can't let him know that I think he's probably the best dad I've ever seen before. The way he loves and cares for Sam only adds to my attraction for him.

"It's not at all an appropriate book for her." His eyes drop to my mouth. "Too much longing and wanting."

Between Edward and Bella, right? Because my mind is screaming that he's talking about us, and I have no idea what to do with that information. I want Jake to like me; I want him to *want* me. But I also don't dare believe that he really does. I don't have anything to offer him.

"By the way, your boss is here," he mentions casually as if that isn't the most startling information I've heard all day. It has the same effect on me as a hypnotist snapping his fingers.

My head rears back. "Joanna?!"

He nods, but his eyes are still trying to tell me something. "That's why I came to get you. But I figured I should let you have a few minutes to creep around my room first."

My cheeks heat again. "You knew I was in here the whole time?"

His smile grows. "I don't mind. Snoop anytime you want."

"Why would you be okay with that?" It's a dare as much as it is a truth.

He's quiet for a minute, and then he looks over my shoulder as if he can't look me in the eye when he answers. "I guess I… want you to get to know me."

"Oh."

His eyes hook mine again. "So we can be real friends. Not just work friends."

Oh.

Again with this friend crap?! I try not to let my dejection write itself across my face, but it's probably no use. I've never been good at hiding my feelings. He's probably reading a Post-it on my forehead at this very moment that reads, *Hi, I'm Evie. I want you to like me romantically, but you don't, so I'll probably cry on my car ride home.*

"Do you know why Joanna is here?" I'm ripping the Post-it off and changing the subject. "She never comes to my training days anymore."

He shrugs his big shoulders, and I'm mesmerized by how the fabric of his shirt pulls tight. "I guess you're in trouble."

Not likely. If I had to guess, I would say that Joanna is going to be the one in trouble at the end of this day.

I try to step around Jake, but he cuts me off. Maybe Jake isn't the only superhuman, because I halt my body so fast that I almost knock myself backward. Thanks to my reaction time, neither of us are touching, but that doesn't help all the chills racing across my body.

"Wait. I want to know what you think of my room." His voice is playful, and this is seriously throwing me off.

He's like a bully that pulls my hat down over my eyes in the hallway and then keeps spinning me in reverse circles so I'm never able to catch my bearing. *Business. Flirting. Stoic. Friends. Flirting. Quiet.*

But he's very clearly not going to let me leave this room without an answer, so I sigh and take a long, exaggerated look around the room (as if I didn't already do a thorough investigation a few minutes ago).

"It's nice," I say and then get ready to leave.

"No, no, no. Tell me what's going on in your head. What do you think? What stuck out to you?"

"Why do you want to know?"

He smiles. "Because…I don't know. I just do."

"Okkayyy. I like the vaulted ceilings." Ceilings are neutral, right?

"What else?" His smirk says this is some sort of game to him, but I haven't figured out the rules yet. Or the objective.

"You're being weird."

"Says the uninvited woman standing in my bedroom."

"Right. Well…I guess I like that you don't make your bed."

He chuckles, deep and full, and I'm pretty sure that if my hand was on his chest, I would feel the force of it. "I knew that's what you'd like most. I wanted to see if I was right. And I was."

I narrow my eyes. "No you did not! How could you possibly have known that?"

He shrugs again. "I guess because I picture your place being messy." He's pictured my place?

"Should I take offense to that?"

"Not at all. I just mean that you…you're not uptight. Life moves too fast for you to take time to put your things away. It's refreshing."

Oh good. The claw of heat is creeping up my neck again, and I'm about to be full-on strawberry. "I haven't confirmed that my place is messy."

He looks down at me and lifts a brow. "Is it?"

My shoulders slump. "Yes."

He smiles, and those shoulders of mine are perking right back up. I need to get out of here. He's being strange, and I like it way too much. It makes me wonder if maybe his house is so clean because he needs someone else to help him and Sam live in it a little more. Someone like me.

"I need to see what Joanna is doing here." I push past him, and this time he lets me go.

CHAPTER FOURTEEN

JAKE

I let Evie leave my room and have a few minutes alone with her boss before I join them. Okay, fine, it was me who needed a few minutes alone to process. Evie was in my bedroom. And she looked perfect there. Too perfect. This room had never felt so bright before.

I watched her in the doorway for a minute before she noticed me, and I felt desperate to know what was going through her head. Did she like this space I've set up for myself? Or did she think it was dull?

She touched my bedspread. What does that mean? I'm pretty sure it can only mean one thing. I mean, it's been a while since I've been around a woman who wasn't my wife, but I'm thinking that snooping through a man's room and casting longing looks at his bedspread can only mean one thing: she's attracted to me.

What the heck am I supposed to do with that thought?

Friendship was fine when there was only a small probability that a woman like her could be attracted to me—a single dad with so much baggage that I have to rent a U-Haul to hitch to the back of my truck—but after seeing her smile when her fingers landed on my bed, that complicated things.

I don't know what else to do, so after peeking down the hallway to make sure no one is around, I shut my bedroom door and pull out my phone to dial the one person I know can tell me what to do. "June! Thank God you answered," I say when my baby sister picks up.

"What's wrong? You sound crazy."

"I am crazy," I say, scraping my hand through my hair. "I think she likes me."

"No way! Did she steal your baseball cap at recess?"

"Shut up. I'm serious. And I'm freaking out."

June chuckles a minute, and then I hear her shuffling some baking pans around. "Okay, hang on. Let me go outside so I can talk to you and not have Stacy listening in. YES, I see you tilting your ear toward me, Stacy! Mind your own biscuits." June and her best friend, Stacy, own a trendy donut shop they opened a year ago called Darlin' Donuts. I'm proud of June. Everyone in Charleston loves their donut shop. The storefront itself looks like something right off a Pinterest page. Everything is white with pops of bright color, and each of their original-flavored donuts have names like "Just Peachy" for their peach-flavored donut, and "Slow as Molasses" for their cinnamon-molasses donuts, and then my personal favorite "Kiss my Grits" for their newest savory-grits-inspired donut.

"Okay, I'm ready. Spill."

I sigh and go into my bathroom and shut the door just in case anyone is in the hallway and can hear me. "Do you remember the woman, Evie Jones, I was telling you about the other day?"

"The hot toddy that works for the service dog company?"

"I never once called her a *hot toddy*."

"You should. I bet she'd love it. Ladies love a sexy nickname." Oh my gosh. Why did I call her again?

I sigh loudly into the phone so she knows I'm done with her game. "Anyways, I just found her in my room."

"NAKED?!" I cringe hearing that word come off of my sister's tongue.

"No, you perv. Fully clothed. I just mean that she was in my room, looking around because…I think that she likes me. Likes me-likes me." Wow, yeah. I hear how immature that makes me sound, but whatever.

June chuckles. "Okay, what's the problem? That seems like good news to me. Worthy of celebrating."

"It's not."

This time she sighs. "You're going to self-sabotage this, aren't you?"

"Most likely. Which is why I'm calling. I need you to tell me what to do so I don't jump out my bedroom window just to keep from having to face her again."

"Do you like her?"

I pause for a moment. "Yeah. A lot."

"Okay, good! Then just freakin' chill. No one is asking you to propose. Do you know how many guys' rooms I've snooped through when they weren't looking? It's how we make sure you're not a creeper with lots of—"

"Don't finish that sentence."

"Stuffed animals," she says, and I can hear her smile.

"That's not what you were going to say."

"Nope. It wasn't. But seriously, just chill about it all, okay? Don't push her away, but you don't have to decide anything yet either. I assume you guys are already something of friends if she felt intrigued enough to play spy in your room. So maybe just keep being her friend until you're sure you want to take that next step into Relationship Land. And if the situation arises for you to play tonsil hockey—"

"UGH. Goodbye, June."

"Byyyeee."

I end the call and plant my hands on my bathroom counter to stare at myself in the mirror for a minute. It's literally been over eleven years since I've kissed anyone other than Natalie. This past year has been so insane with the divorce and Sam's diagnosis that I haven't even had a minute to think about being a normal male.

I'm thinking about it now, though.

June's right. There's no need to rush it. It's better for everyone if Evie and I just stay friends for a while. I can't do the dating thing the way a normal man my age would, anyway. I have to be cautious because of Sam. Evie would be dating both of us, and since she's not even thirty yet, I don't know if that's something she would even want. I need to inch toward the line. Feel her out.

I can hear June's voice in my head, saying, *I think you mean UP.* No, June, I don't mean up.

I'm going to take things slow with Evie. Christmas slow. Painfully slow. No-one-can-even-see-me-moving *slow.* And if she sticks around—if she can handle the lack of speed—I'll consider Relationship Land.

I walk into the living room just in time to see Evie physically pushing her boss toward the door. "Thanks for stopping by! You can be on your way now."

"But I only just got here!" She's digging in her heels and smiling ear to ear. I don't even know this woman, and I can tell she's messing with Evie.

"And you didn't need to come in the first place, so go before he comes back!"

"Too late," I say with a smile. "He's back."

Evie turns around with wide eyes—she might as well have a canary sticking out of her mouth. Sam snickers from her perch on the couch's armrest, and Evie narrows her eyes at her, which makes Sam burst into laughter and fall back onto the couch. What am I missing here? Why does Evie not want me around her boss?

Joanna gives Evie a smug look before crossing in front of her to get to me. She holds out her hand and smiles wide. "I know we met briefly a few minutes ago, but let me formally introduce myself. Joanna Halstead. I'm the founder of Southern Service Paws, and I'm pleased as punch that you chose us to provide a dog for your precious daughter."

Joanna is polite and engaging, and I still can't figure out why Evie looks like she's standing on pins and needles over by the door. Her hand is on the knob as if she's ready to thrust it open and shove her boss out at any moment.

"I'm the one who's grateful. Evie had every right to ignore my call and refuse my application after the way I treated her that first day."

Joanna waves away my comment with a good-natured smile. "Water under the bridge. Believe it or not, you're not the first parent to not want a service dog for their child. It's a little scary deciding to allow your baby's safety to be put in the hands of a dog—or paws, I should say. But believe me, those paws are more than capable."

"I see that now, and I'm excited to see what Sam's new future will look like with Daisy. And honestly, it's all thanks to Evie. She's put in so much time here with my daughter, and I'm really grateful for all of her help."

Joanna beams at me like I couldn't have given a more perfect answer. She tosses a glance over her shoulder to Evie who opens the door and gestures for Joanna to walk out. Joanna just turns back to me, a new devious smile in place of the previous businessy one. "Evie really is the best. Never have I seen a heart bigger than hers."

"Yep, I have a big ol' heart! Well, thanks for coming to check on everything, Jo! Tell Gary I said hi!" Evie's tone is shrill and panicked.

Joanna pays zero attention to her. Her eyes narrow on me, and I have a feeling I'm about to find out why Evie has been so adamant to get Joanna out of my house. "Mr. Broaden, has Evie told you about the benefit she's been planning? We're hoping to raise enough money to be able to give the dogs we are currently training to future recipients, free of charge. It was all Evie's idea."

"JO, YOUR CAR IS ON FIRE!" Evie yells.

Joanna just bats her hand behind her and waits for my answer.

"No, she didn't. That is really incredible, though. When is it?" Why didn't Evie tell me about it? Suddenly, I remember our first conversation where I accused her of trying to make a big commission off the dogs, and I feel even worse about my prior behavior. Is that why she didn't want to tell me? Because she didn't want me to see it as her being defensive?

"It's next Sunday night. Going to be quite the shindig—a black-tie affair and all the bigwigs in town were invited."

I nod, still wondering where this is going and how I play a part in it. "Sounds really nice."

"Oh, it will be! But you know what's not so nice?" She puts on a dramatic pout. "Evie can't seem to find a date! What a pity it would be for a pretty thing like her to have to get all dressed up and show up to the event all by her lonesome. Oh, wait! You wouldn't be interested in being her plus-one, would you?"

Ahhh, and there it is. Everything makes sense now.

Evie lets out a long, defeated sigh and shuts the door. Her cheeks are the color of a candy apple, and I'm suddenly enjoying Joanna's company more than I've enjoyed anything before. "Don't answer that, Jake. Joanna is a scheming old hen who needs to stick her nose back in her own business."

"Don't call me an old hen or I'll fire you, little missy."

"Don't call me *little missy* or I won't come to painting night Wednesday." I can't decide if these two women act more like sisters, friends, or mother and daughter. I like them, though. And I really like knowing that Evie needs a date. Also, HOW does she not already have one? That question perplexes me. Evie should have a line of men wrapped around the block, begging her to date them.

"It's black-tie, you said?" I ask, my voice making both of their heads turn and acknowledge me for the first time.

Evie's brows pull together. "Yesss. Why?"

"Because it would be embarrassing to show up in jeans to a black-tie event."

Joanna's face grows into a smile, but Evie still looks skeptical. Honestly, I'm going out on a limb here by inviting myself as her date. I'm really banking on the fact that she and Joanna seem close and Evie would have told her if she already had one. But I'm painfully aware that this could all blow up in my face.

"You really don't have to come with me. I'm sure I can find someone to go if you're busy. Joanna never should have put you on the spot—" I cut her off because she sounds nervous but not entirely like she doesn't want me there.

"I want to go with you."

I am Ryan Gosling now. No one can touch my smoldering confidence. It's all fake, of course, but she doesn't need to know that.

"Really?" The hopefulness in her voice only boosts my confidence more.

I shrug my shoulders. *Yeah, no big deal. I go to fancy benefits all the time and definitely won't have to go out to buy a new suit.* "I do. I think it would be fun—if you're up for taking me."

She's trying to hide a smile as she tucks her hair behind her ear. "Yeah, okay, I guess that will work then."

CHAPTER FIFTEEN

EVIE

"So, she's really mine now?" asks Sam.

"She's really yours."

"Like she gets to sleep with me from now on?"

"Yep."

Sam smiles and lets her toes skim across the pool water again. She's only dipping her toes in because she's wearing little-girl skinny jeans and could only roll them up to the ankles. I'm wearing my favorite yellow cotton dress, so I'm able to dip my legs in from the knee down.

The water feels like a bath, and the setting sun is warm on my skin. Charlie is lying down on the side of the pool to my left, and Daisy is lying down on Sam's right. Other than our different hair colors, we look like a mirrored reflection of each other.

I feel a tether to Sam that I can't explain, and I wonder if it's because I see her as a younger version of myself. We sit quietly together by the pool while Jake is inside putting out a few fires with a contractor over the phone. I glance over my shoulder and catch a glimpse of him standing at the window, phone pressed to his ear, but his eyes glued to me and Sam. His brows are pulled together, but he doesn't look angry—just thoughtful. My skin grows hot knowing Jake is watching me.

All I want to do is obsessively think about what took place this morning in his living room with Jo. Does he really want to go as my date to the benefit? Was it a pity offer? I want to murder Jo for asking him like she did—or kiss her, I can't decide. But when I get home and give my brain the free rein it wants to turn that conversation over and over and dissect it like a mad scientist, I'll know for sure.

"Soooo, my dad says I can go to the slumber party."

"I know! That's so great. Are you excited?"

Sam kicks some water. "Kind of."

I look down at her. "Just kind of? I thought you'd be super happy he gave you permission."

"I am." Except, she's not.

I bump her little shoulder with mine. "Tell me what's up."

She breathes in and out for a minute and then finally lets the truth out. "I'm kinda scared. I know I put up a big fight about wanting to go…but now that I can…I'm scared I'll have a seizure while I'm there."

I understand that, and unfortunately, the chances are pretty high that she will. Stress and sleep deprivation are triggers for a lot of people. "You might. But if you do, Daisy will be there to take care of you."

And I have no doubt that Daisy will. I've been working with them all week, and what I've seen leaves me with nothing but confidence.

Sam turns her face away from me to pet Daisy. "It's not that I'm afraid of the seizure. I'm…I'm afraid of what the other girls will think of me if they see me have one."

Unfortunately, this is the one thing regarding disabilities that service dogs cannot protect us from—other humans. People can be cruel, especially kids, so I understand Sam's worry.

"I wish I could tell you that everyone will always understand your seizures—but they won't. You can't control other people, but you can control who you surround yourself with. So, if you think that these girls will be mean to you if you have a seizure, don't go—they're not worth your friendship."

"Have you ever had anyone be mean to you after seeing one of your episodes?"

I don't like this question. It fills my mind with uncomfortable memories that I would rather never think of again. Ones I've buried six feet under the ground and promised never to revisit. Looks like I'm grabbing a shovel.

"Unfortunately…yes." I had a seizure during English class my junior year of high school. I am one of the lucky few who convulse during an episode (did you catch my sarcasm there?). Let me tell you, the jocks of the school loooovvedd that. They spent the rest of the school year reenacting my seizures every time they passed me in the hallway, but they must have been very into drama since they made sure to take their reenactments way over the top. I'm just lucky to have been in high school before the time of social media. I can only imagine how scary high school would be for someone with a disability in the age of smartphones.

And you know what? As it turns out, I don't think Sam needs to hear this whole story. It probably wouldn't make her feel much better. So I keep the full story to myself but decide that, one day, if I feel she needs to hear it, I'll tell her.

Wait a second.

Why in the world am I picturing myself in Sam's life as she's growing up?

"I had some not-so-nice people say some not-so-nice things about me when I was young. But you know what…" I look down at Sam and brush her hair behind her ear. "I survived. It hurt at the time, but now I'm a strong woman who lives with a very scary medical condition, and I have every right to feel proud of myself for that. And you do, too. Don't ever let anyone make you feel bad about who you are or scared to live your life. You're more than your seizures. And I'll be happy to remind you of that anytime you doubt it."

Sam smiles and then surprises me by leaning into me and wrapping me up in her darling little arms. "Thanks, Evie. I'm glad I emailed you that day…even if I did lose my iPad for a week."

I laugh. "Me too, darlin'."

A few minutes later, I hear the sliding door open, and Jake steps out wearing a pair of aviators in a way that would make Tom Cruise envious. "What are you two ladies doing out here?"

"Just enjoying your incredible pool," I say, holding my hand above my eyes to shade them from the sun. I should have put them in front of my eyes to shade them from Jake. I can't handle how good he looks drenched in the orange sunset. He's already tan, but the warm glow only adds to it, licking at his muscular forearms and making the man look downright illegal.

"I'm glad someone's enjoying it," he says, coming to sit down on the other side of Charlie.

"Yeah, we never use it," says Sam, a sad tone touching her voice.

"Never?" I'm shocked. What kind of crazy person would have a pool this glorious and never use it?

"Between work, and school, and doctor's appointments, we just don't have the time."

"Then make time!" He should be put in jail for owning a pool that could be featured on a design show and not finding time to use it.

He chuckles and shakes his head a little. "It's not that easy."

"It really is, though."

He's trying to sell me *adulting,* and I'm not buying it. The real problem has been hovering in Jake's and Sam's eyes all week. They haven't picked up the pieces of their life yet. They got hit with some tough stuff and haven't decided to move forward. I'm about to slingshot their butts into *moving on*.

"Life isn't worth it if you can't play a little. You've gotta steal fun when you can," I say while standing up.

Jake looks up at me with a crooked smile. "Like when? What do you suggest when every day is booked solid and I can barely find time to tie my shoes?"

"Get some slip-ons." I flash him a haughty grin. "And allow me to point out that you're not busy right this minute."

His smile falters ever so slightly. "I don't have my swim trunks on."

Oh, silly little practical Jake. As you're about to find out, I don't give one hill of beans if your trunks are on or not.

I smile wickedly, and then, before he has time to process the evil about to befall him, I give him a shove from behind and dump his practical butt in the pool.

He comes up out of the water like a cologne ad that never made it to live television because it was too sensual. His navy shirt is clinging to his chiseled body, and his hair is dripping wet before he dashes his hand through it, sending glistening water droplets through the air—and basically, I've never been prouder of a decision in my entire life.

Sam has dissolved into a fit of laughter beside me, and I'm pretty sure that Charlie just called Jake a moron under his breath. (Obviously, he likes Jake, but I think he's a tad bit jealous of our new friendship. He can go cry to Rachel Green.)

"Laugh it up, chuckles," Jake says with a heart-melting smile. "You're next."

I see what he's doing. He's inching toward the edge of the pool with a smirk that says *I'm coming for you*. Jake is so certain that I'm going to scream and run away like the girl who just got her hair done and would rather die than ruin her blowout. He doesn't know me very well yet, and my hair appointment is so overdue I think my hairstylist has given up on me completely.

Ladies, if you don't take any other advice from me, listen to these words, because they are the most important you will ever hear: if a sexy man is in a pool and smiling at you like Jake is smiling at me, don't waste a single moment standing on the side.

Before he has a chance to make it to the stairs, I take off running and cannonball in right beside him.

CHAPTER SIXTEEN

EVIE

I'm wringing out my hair from my shower and listening to Leon Bridges croon over the speakers. I have a sweet, warm, scented candle lit on my coffee table, and everything is right with the world. It's been a good week. A good day, especially.

I can't put my finger on it, but something about me feels different. I'm still working my same job; I still have my same thimble-sized apartment; there is still the same chance I'll have a seizure today as there was yesterday, but something feels different. It's like I had a pile of books stacked on my desk, and although I can't be certain, I think someone came in at some point and rearranged them. I'm rearranged.

Laughing in the pool tonight with Jake and Sam made me feel a sense of belonging. It scares me as much as it excites me, but I don't want to give into the fear. I still feel like I'm sitting up in the nosebleeds, but maybe I'm ready to walk down a few flights of stairs to get closer to the field.

I think Jake feels this way too. I could try to talk myself out of it—run a fake play on my own heart and choose to believe that he's not interested in me. But here's the thing: I catch him looking at me a lot. And it's not a normal look. It's a smoldering, knock-your-socks-off-kissing-until-midnight kind of look. He's at least attracted to me—I know that much.

So, what kind of dance are we doing here?

I just finish squeezing the water out of my hair and neatly hang up my towel on the drying rack (ha ha, just kidding! It's laying in a bundle on the floor where it will probably live for the rest of the week), when I hear a knock at my door.

"Did you order cookies again?" I ask the lazy dog lying on my bed.

He gives me a look that says *stop blaming your poor eating habits on me* and then lays his head back down. It's a good thing he's so cute.

I open the door and then realize I should have looked through the peephole first. I could have just opened the door to a murderer, or a rapist, or—*gasp*—my mama. But thanks to my incredible luck in life lately, I open the door to none other than Jacob Broaden.

"Jake!" I say, and *whoa* I need to simmer down because I sound WAY too excited to see him. Play it cool. I'm supposed to be walking down the stairs toward the field, not full-on sprinting and skipping steps.

He likes it, though, because he smiles when he says, "Hey, Evie."

Then his gaze drops and takes in what I'm wearing.

And this is the moment that I remember what a lovely ensemble I am wearing. I have on an XL shirt that says "Dolly is my spirit animal" which lands just above my knees, tall socks, and NO BRA. To make it worse, I am wearing flannel PJ shorts under my shirt, but there's no way you can see those, so basically, I look like the world's biggest hussy right now. But it isn't my fault! I obviously wouldn't have worn this if I knew Jake was coming by.

Although, I have to admit that I am enjoying the appreciative look in his eye.

No. Bad, Evie.

I fold my arms across my chest (but let's face it, my boobs are so small that this part is only for show) and feel the need to blurt, "I'm wearing shorts!" And if that wasn't stupid enough, I uncross one arm to lift up my shirt just enough to show him my green-and-red-checkered flannel bottoms.

He's so smug now. I swear he looks like a man that's just been told he won GQ magazine's Sexiest Man of the Year award. I'm squirming under his gaze, and he's loving the effect he has on me. "I like the Christmas trees on them," he says, and YES, I do wear Christmas PJs in July.

"It feels wrong to leave something in my drawer all year just because it's 80 degrees out. Do you want to come in?"

He nods and my heart races. Jacob Broaden is going to come into my apartment. My tiny, minuscule mouse hole that really should be called a playhouse rather than an apartment because it looks like dolls could fit in here easier than humans. He ducks his head as he steps through the door, and *oh my gosh,* I just remembered that I'm a slob.

I quickly survey what I like to think of as my *boho* apartment through the eyes of Jake and see what he's seeing.

Unfortunately, since my whole apartment is only one room, he gets to see it all. Unmade bed. Cereal bowls stacked up on my itty-bitty kitchen counter (but the butcher-block top still looks adorable). Half-empty cups of old coffee sitting on my end table. Clothing dotting the hardwood floor. And is that…? Yep! My bright-pink bra is defiritely draped over the back of my couch from where I took it off as soon as I got home earlier.

I make a lunge to grab it before Jake sees it, but it's too late. He's looking at it now and smiling. I grab for it anyways and tuck it behind my back, aiming a tight smile at him. "Clearly, I wasn't expecting company."

"I'm glad. I like seeing how you live." He looks right at me, and I think I might fall over. This apartment is too small, and he's too big for it. If he moves, I'll bump into him.

I don't think I've ever been so nervous having someone in my space before. Jake is so grown and adult and hot. And I'm… well, I'm grown too, but I definitely don't feel adult. Never have. Probably never will. I've given up any aspirations of becoming the woman who rinses out her mug and puts it right into the dishwasher when I'm done with it. I don't need that kind of pressure in my life.

My nerves are sizzling like bacon in a frying pan, and I feel the urge to bounce. Why is he here? I only left his house about two hours ago. His presence in my apartment doesn't make sense.

"Did I forget something at your place?" I ask after a minute more of his quiet surveying. I want to blindfold him.

DON'T LOOK AT MY CRAZY.

"Nope."

Oh, great. Now he's walking fully into my apartment and sitting down on the couch. I want to laugh—no, I do laugh—because he makes my loveseat look more like an armchair.

"Okaayyy. Well, don't take this the wrong way, but what are you doing here?"

He grins, his dimples come out to play, and now I'm way too aware that it's after 8 PM. He's not texting me. He's in my living room, breathing my air, and adding at least ten degrees of heat to the room.

"Do I make you nervous being in here?"

"No." I shift my weight to my other foot, shove my pink bra under the blankets of my bed, push my hair behind my ear—*don't like that*—untuck my hair. "Okay, maybe a little. Is this payback for me snooping around your room?"

He chuckles and moves his big arms to spread out over the

back of my loveseat. He looks mighty comfy there. Like a man that's in no hurry to leave. What the heck is happening?!

"Actually, I came by to bring you an invitation." He eyes me, and his brows pull together. "Are you going to stay over there all night?"

If this were a movie, this is the part where the camera would pan to me and I'd be gone. It would have to tilt up to find me plastered in the farthest upper corner of my apartment, like Spiderman.

Why am I being so weird? I'm twenty-six years old and acting like I've never been alone with a man before. So what if Jake is here at my apartment? No big deal. Friends visit other friends' apartments all the time. I just wish this friend was wearing a bra.

"An invitation?" I ask, moving closer to Jake. He scoots toward one end of the "couch" and makes room for me.

Okay. I guess I'm sitting there. With Jake. That's fine.

I sit down, and we are so close now that I feel like I might as well be sitting on his lap. I adjust so that my legs are up in the seat with me and I'm somewhat facing Jake. Because having my feet touch his leg is way better than the whole right side of my body. Well, not better. Just friendlier and less steamy.

He reaches in his pocket and pulls out a folded piece of paper and hands it to me. There is a very childish drawing of a girl jumping into a pool drawn on the front. "I had no idea you were such an artist," I say with a grin.

"I could say the same about you." He nods his head toward my fruit masterpiece leaning up against the wall. "Gotta say, I didn't take you for a butt girl."

My face flames and I laugh. "It was supposed to be an orange."

"Mmhmm. Sure it was."

"Oh, go home and finish *Twilight*," I say while shoving his shoulder.

He laughs, and honestly, I love the sound. It echoes off the walls, and somehow my apartment suddenly feels safer and homier.

"So, what's this?" I'm opening the invitation and reading the few scribbled lines stating a date and time. *SATURDAY, 12:00.*

"Sam and I decided you were right, and we should make more time for fun. So, this is your official invitation to our pool party this weekend."

I look up from the invitation, and I feel my smile growing too big. My smile is more appropriate for winning a new car off of *The Price Is Right* than accepting a pool-party invitation. "I love this idea. Count me in."

"Before you agree, you should know that my entire family will be there."

Okay, okay, okay. Just chill the freak out, Evie.

I want to dissect every part of what he just said and look for all the hidden meanings. Meet his family? This has to mean something, right?! But instead, I answer, "How entire are we talking? Like distant-crazy-Uncle-Fred-who-drinks-too-much-and-might-try-to-cop-a-feel *entire*?"

He laughs and rubs his hands over his legs and dark denim jeans. "Just my parents, sisters, and their families."

"That doesn't sound too bad. In fact, it sounds like fun." Someone sign me up for a movie deal, because I'm such a good actor right now that no one would suspect I'm completely freaking out. Jake wants me to meet his family. Wants me to spend the day with his family. Which reminds me of something.

"Wait, where's Sam right now?"

"My sister is at home with her. I had to run into the office for a little bit."

Right. The office. HIS office. The one he owns. I have to stop thinking of these things, because all they do is remind me that there is no way this guy should be interested in me. I'm the furthest from successful anyone could be. Just ask my mama. She'll tell you.

"So, work usually keeps you pretty busy?"

He sighs one of those heavy man sighs that sounds like he's literally holding the world on his shoulders. "Yeah. But I've delegated a lot of my work to the two other architects in the firm, though."

"You don't sound as relieved as a person normally does after a statement like that."

"I guess it's because I'm not really all that relieved. This is going to make me sound like the world's worst dad, but…I love my job. It's been hard for me to give up most of my work to be home with Sam."

I shake my head. "That doesn't make you sound like a bad parent. I think, if anything, it shows how amazing you are. You're giving up something you love to be there for your kid." I wish I wasn't having to say all this out loud. It's forcing me to think of all of the incredible qualities of Jake that I've been trying to ignore.

"Thanks. It was easier to balance it all when…" His words trail off, and I know what he's not saying.

"When you were married and had a second parent at home with Sam?"

His blue eyes lock with mine, and he nods. "Sorry. I don't mean to keep dropping that in every conversation."

"It's okay. Really. It's a part of your life, so why wouldn't I want to talk with you about it?" And then, suddenly, I realize I'm not such a good actor after all because I'm letting my interest in him show way too much. I clear my throat and look down at my knees. "How were Sam and Daisy getting on after I left?"

"Great. Sam is like a new kid with Daisy. She seems so much lighter and more excited about life." He chuckles. "She even put a fake spider in my sock drawer earlier today. You have no idea how good it is to have her interacting with me like that again."

I smile. "That's wonderful, Jake. I'm so happy for you guys. I know what it's like to find that security, and honestly, there's nothing quite like it."

"Is that how you felt when you first got Charlie?"

I smile at the memory of those first few weeks of finding my new independence. My parents hated it, but I thrived in it. "Yep. It was pretty wonderful. I didn't move out of my parents' house until I was twenty-three because I was so scared of what life with epilepsy would look like living on my own. But Charlie and I clicked right away. My parents didn't support my decision at all to leave their house because...well, I think they liked being able to keep me under their thumb. So when I moved out, Joanna became more of a mama to me than my own mother ever was. She helped me set up a landline here that attaches to a special button Charlie can push when I have a seizure."

I pause and point to the round yellow button on the wall by my bed. "It speed-dials Joanna's number. She usually waits about ten minutes for my seizure to pass and me to regain consciousness and then calls me to make sure I'm okay."

"Wow," Jake says, looking stunned.

"I know. Charlie's pretty incredible. And even though we can't technically train a service dog to alert before a seizure, he has. Charlie alerts me about thirty minutes before almost all of my seizures, and that gives me a chance to go lie down in a safe place."

"That's...I don't even feel like the word amazing is good enough. Do you think Daisy will do that with Sam?"

"Hopefully. But only time will tell. Just keep an eye out for Daisy doing anything out of the ordinary. It could be her trying to signal you."

Jake nods thoughtfully for a moment, and I think he's about to say something profound. "And to think we would never have found any of this new independence for Sam if it weren't for you telling me to get my head out of my butt."

He and I both laugh at the memory. I still can't believe I said that to him, but I don't regret it anymore. Not if it got us to this place.

Jake's eyes land on mine again, and his playful smile dies away. Something is changing in the air, and my body is fully aware of it. He shifts his arm and gently grasps a lock of my damp hair between his fingers. "I'm serious, though, Evie. Thank you. I owe you." His low voice is rolling over me, and I'm a little worried his finger is going to brush against my neck and feel my hammering pulse.

"You're welcome."

His eyes narrow ever so slightly, like he's contemplating something. He looks down at his fingers that are caressing that one lock of my hair and then back up to my eyes. I'm holding my breath, and I don't dare move. This moment can go from nothing to something in a split second, and I'm just waiting to see what it will be.

And now he's leaning forward…oh my gosh, he's leaning forward, and he's going to kiss me. "Evie," he whispers, and I can feel his minty breath on my lips. He said my name as both a statement and a question. What he means is, *Evie, can I kiss you?*

To which I'm responding with a YES by leaning forward too. His hand leaves my hair and moves to cup my neck, and now I'm certain he can feel my racing pulse. He's moving so slowly toward my mouth, and I'm dying. It's been so long since I've been kissed—and NEVER have I been kissed by a man like Jake. I want to fist the front of his shirt and drag his mouth to mine as quick as possible, but I'm being a lady about it and letting him come to me. No one wants to look desperate.

And then, I close my eyes and *finally* feel his warm lips press against mine in the lightest, most feather-soft motion. I inhale deeply and skim my hands up his shoulders to tentatively rest them on the back of his neck. I want to sink in and live inside this kiss for the rest of my life, but I can't because suddenly there's a KNOCK KNOCK at my door, and I swear I'm going to murder whoever is on the other side.

Jake and I both forget we are grown adults and catapult apart on my loveseat so fast you would think we just got caught making out in a closet during a Sunday school class.

CHAPTER SEVENTEEN

JAKE

While Evie is walking to answer the door, I lean over to rest my elbows on my knees and scrape my hands through my hair. What the heck was I thinking kissing her tonight? I know it looks bad, but that's definitely not why I came over here. I was really only intending to give her the invitation and run. *Just your friendly neighborhood postman.*

But no. I saw her, and my body suddenly had other plans. Plans to kiss her, apparently.

What now? I wanted to move slowly. S-L-O-W. This little action just changed things. Now I have a conversation on the horizon that I'm not at all prepared for.

Well, I'm a little prepared for it. The more time I spend with Evie, the more I can't imagine not dating her. But I don't know if I can trust myself. I've made a poor decision concerning a woman before and look how that turned out. Although, I know I don't want to spend the rest of my life alone…so I'll have to face my fears at some point. Looks like that point is now.

I hear Evie open the door, and then she gasps. Her gasp has

me looking toward the door just in time to hear her say, "Mama. Daddy. What are you doing here?"

Oh, super.

I shoot up from the couch, and in a split second—because Evie's apartment is made for ants—I'm standing beside her at the door. Her mom's eyes are wide as they look from me to Evie and then slowly down Evie's body in the same way one might look at a prostitute they've just encountered on the sidewalk.

I don't know why I suddenly have the urge to defend myself. SHE'S WEARING SHORTS! I'm a grown man. Evie's a grown woman. But Evie's mom has the look of a woman about to rail on her daughter. Instinctively, I move to shield Evie. "Hi," I say, sticking my hand out toward her dad first. "I'm Jacob Broaden."

He shakes my hand with the same gusto of a dead fish and cocks one eyebrow. "Harold Jones."

Wait a second. I pause mid-handshake. Harold Jones? As in, *the* Harold Jones from the long line of Joneses that have made up the majority of our city's wealth for generations? I knew Evie's last name was Jones, but I guess I never thought to ask her if there was any connection because she just seems so…normal.

I slide my wide eyes to Mrs. Jones, and she rolls her eyes at Evie.

"I can see you haven't told him who your relatives are." The woman sounds like she's never been more bored in her life. She looks at me again but doesn't even offer me her hand. "Melony Jones."

Oh yeah. I know who she is. Everyone in Charleston knows who this woman is. And she's just as off-putting as I had imagined.

Suddenly, I feel like laughing. Here I was, thinking that Evie would be impressed with my little architectural firm and my 2,000-square-foot house, when she grew up with the leading socialites of Charleston in a 12.5 million dollar home. I know this because I read the magazine article about it last month. I feel a little stupid.

She gave all of that up to live in this shoebox? What am I missing here? I have a whole new appreciation for Evie. Not because she came from money, but because she turned out like *this* despite her entitled upbringing.

Mrs. Jones turns her sharp eyes to Evie, and apparently, she's done with me. I'm just a small fly; I've been swatted away. "Evelyn Grace, are you going to make us stand out here all night?"

"I'm entertaining right now," Evie says through her teeth. I'm impressed by her backbone. She's not cowering under this woman's haughty glare—and believe me, it's more than a little intimidating.

"Clearly," Mrs. Jones says with another accusatory glance at Evie's bare legs.

I take one more look too because I'm a man and *goodness* she has good-looking legs.

"But you've been taught better than to leave your parents standing out in the heat like this." Mrs. Jones pushes past both of us and steps into Evie's house uninvited. It's shocking. I don't think I've ever seen anyone do that before.

Mr. Jones pulls out his phone and frowns down at it. He answers it, turns around, and walks back out without even so much as a glance to the rest of us. These people are something.

"I can't do this right now, Mama. I don't want to inflict our crazy on an innocent bystander." Evie gestures toward me.

I have no idea what to do right now. Do I come to her aid? Do I turn into a bouncer and throw these people out? I'm not prepared for this, but I want to help somehow.

Mrs. Jones acts as if she doesn't hear Evie's comment. "We won't be long." She runs her finger across the small entry table and then examines it for dust. "Honestly, Evelyn, what has happened to you? This place looks like a pigsty."

I expect Evie to take offense to this, but instead, when I look at her, I notice that she's looking at me—and she looks amused. No, not amused. She looks like she's about to crack up laughing. And then I realize she's looking at my hair.

I glance in the mirror on the wall and find that my hair is sticking up in all directions from where I ran my hands through it while Evie was getting the door. But this, coupled with Evie's little outfit, looks more than incriminating. I quickly smooth it down.

"If you're just here to comment on my cleanliness, Mama, you can just walk right back out. I'm happy with the way I live."

"That's not why I'm here. Although, I do feel compelled to mention that if you would stop being foolish and accept Tyler, you would be able to move out of this cardboard box."

Wait a minute. Who's Tyler?

"I don't live in the 1800s, Mama. I'm not going to accept a man's proposal just because he has a big estate. Am I the only one who thinks this idea is ludicrous?"

Proposal?! Apparently, Evie's not as unattached as I thought…

Mrs. Jones's eyes suddenly shift to me, and I can see her sizing me up. "Is *he* the reason you're not accepting Tyler?" She's looking at me, but it's clear that she's not talking to me.

"Okay, this conversation is over," says Evie. *Hmm.* Not going to lie, I kinda wish she would have answered that question. Evie walks back to her door and opens it. "Time to go, Mama."

Mrs. Jones turns a smirk to me. "If my daughter won't answer me, I'll ask you. Exactly who are you to Evelyn?"

"He's a friend," says Evie before I have a chance to open my mouth.

Mrs. Jones makes a guttural noise and then starts to stroll toward the door at a leisurely pace. "I only came by to inform you that your cell phone bill was overdue. If I don't see your payment in our account by the end of the week, I'll be forced to have your phone turned off."

Turned off? Is this woman insane? She sounds more like a villain in a movie, threatening to bash Evie's kneecaps in if that AT&T money doesn't show up soon.

This reminds me of something Evie said the first time we had coffee about her bank account matching her age. At the time, I thought she was kidding. But now, I'm genuinely concerned.

"Of course," her mother continues, "if you decide to have a relationship with Tyler, all of those ugly bills will go away. And you are welcome to come live in the guest house for free until you and Tyler marry."

"Great, not going to happen," Evie bites out. "Message received. You can leave now. Tell Daddy I said thanks for stopping by to check on me." Her sarcasm is thick, and although I've never seen her like this, I understand it. Admire it, even.

I feel a protective energy coursing through me, and I'm powerless to stop it. If this villain in the baby-blue pant suit doesn't leave in the next minute, I'm going to end up throwing her out myself.

Mrs. Jones shakes her head at Evie. "You're making a mistake, dear. I just want the best for you and your future." That almost sounded nice. And maybe it would have been a kind parting had she stopped talking there. Mrs. Jones casts a disgusted glance over Evie's appearance one last time. "And for heaven's sake, Evelyn Grace, you shouldn't be so easy. It's unbecoming of the Jones name."

Okay, that's it. I'm following hot on Mrs. Jones's heels, but Evie reaches out and catches my chest before I can follow the monster out. She shuts the door quickly and puts her back to it like she doesn't trust me to not wrench it open and go after Melony Jones. Probably for the best. Not sure I trust myself right now.

I stare at Evie for a minute, waiting for the floodgates to

open or her fury to burn hot. Instead, her dimples pop, and she smiles. "Can I bring anything to the pool party on Saturday?"

My mouth falls open. "How are you so calm?!" I feel like the Hulk, ready to rip my shirt off and burst through the ceiling, and she is just standing there, looking like a springtime fairy. "How are you not spitting angry right now?"

She shrugs and steps away from the door. "I stopped letting that woman steal my joy about fifteen counseling sessions ago."

I don't know what else to do, so I walk to Evie and wrap my arms around her. I want to hold her close because, somehow, I get the feeling she and Sam share more than just the same disability. I think Evie is tough as nails, but she'll still cry into her pillow the second I leave.

For a moment, she seems shocked. She doesn't move. Her arms are limp noodles beside her body. But then they finally lift up and wrap around my waist, and she squeezes me back as tightly as I'm squeezing her. It's all I can offer her.

"They suck," I mumble into her hair, and she laughs.

"Yeah. They're not the best parents."

"Why didn't you tell me what family you were from? I had no idea."

She pulls away from me and starts busying herself by tidying things around her apartment. "Because number one, how weird would it have been if the second I met you, I said, 'Hi! I'm Evie Jones. You know? Of the famous Joneses who practically own this city?' And number two, I'm trying to make my own way in life without riding their coattails."

I watch her fold up a fluffy blue blanket. "I understand that." We are both quiet for a moment, and then, when I can't take it any longer, I finally ask what's been eating at me. "So who's this Tyler guy your mom was talking about?"

Evie grins like she can tell I'm jealous and likes it. "Have you heard of my daddy's law firm? Jones and Murray? Well, Tyler is Tyler Murray. He just inherited his daddy's half of the firm. Our parents have been planning on our marriage since we were kids so that they could always keep the company in trustworthy hands. Only problem is, I'm the only one who doesn't want the marriage."

Only one?

"So that means Tyler *does* want the marriage?"

Evie shrugs like it's not a big deal. Like this relationship I was beginning to picture between us didn't just grow fuzzier and more unclear. Is there even a chance for us now? If Tyler is one of the Murrays, I've no doubt he's a millionaire. By society's standards, he would be a catch. Do I even stand a chance?

Then again…Evie is standing here with me in her little apartment that she chose to live in because she didn't want the same life as her parents. So that's something. Isn't it?

"Tyler wants a pretty wife on his arm that will help him climb the social and economic ladder. Marrying a Jones is exactly what he needs to ensure that happens. He doesn't want me. He wants what we would represent together. If a Jones and Murray finally tied the knot and joined our companies together, investors would pour their money into their companies. It would be a boost unlike any other."

"And you don't want that?"

Evie laughs, and the sound makes my heart lighter. "I sent that idea down the stinker a long time ago. Honestly, Tyler and I dated for a while in high school, and that was enough to make me never want to be attached to that man again. And he's only gotten worse since we broke up."

I don't say anything for a minute. I'm not sure what to say. Evie accurately interprets my silence and goes on. "Jake. I don't…I don't know if it's necessary for me to say this to you or not, but there really is no chance of me ever wanting to marry Tyler Murray—or any man like him, for that matter."

I really want to let those words soothe my fears, but it just isn't helping me feel better about wanting to date her. If anything, it adds to my terror about a million percent. What if we get serious and then she decides to finally take Tyler up on his offer? I don't know. I can't think about that right now. I need to change the subject before I self-sabotage. "Did they say you're still on their phone plan?"

She gives me a look that says, *don't you dare make fun of me.* "It's cheaper that way. I hate being beholden to them, but I can't afford it without the family-plan discount." Right. This reminds me of something.

I walk into her "kitchen"—meaning I take two big steps to the right. I'm not sure you can actually call this a kitchen. It's really just a fridge and sink and a 12x12 slab of butcher block that, if you squint, might be able to pass as a counter. I open the top cupboard, and it's just as I suspected.

"What are you doing?" she asks, sounding a little panicked.

I reach inside and push aside the box of colorful cereal and an open pack of sour candy. When I spot a tumbleweed blow across the back, I move on to the fridge. I pull it open and find a carton of milk with a questionable date and a Tupperware container that's half-filled with what looks like egg salad, but I don't dare open it and find out.

She runs up and shuts the fridge door like I was peeking in her lingerie drawer instead of her fridge. Her cheeks are burning red, and suddenly, she looks like she might bite my head off. "If you're hungry, we can go down the street to a diner that stays open late."

"Evie, do you have money to get groceries?"

Her cheeks burn deeper. I could fry up a pancake on them. "Yes! Of course I do."

"Do you have money to buy more than a box of cereal?"

"I'll have you know that a serving of that cereal has HALF of the recommended dose of fiber for the day."

She's trying to play, but I'm not having it. I'm bad cop now.

Stop fooling around, things just got serious. “Come on. Get your shoes.”

I grab her hand and start dragging her toward the door. Charlie darts off his perch on the bed and grabs his vest. For once, he gives me a look that says he is on my side. Evie deserves to have someone on her side, and I’ve just decided that that someone is going to be me.

She hits the brakes and digs her heels in the ground. “STOP. Where are we going?”

I swear, I will pick her up and carry her over my shoulder if I have to. “The grocery store.” She’s fighting, but I’m a big bully, and she doesn’t stand a chance against my size. “I’m buying you some food to go in that fridge.”

“No! Jake. I’m fine, I swear. UGH. Let me go. Charlie, attack!!”

Charlie trots beside me. I pause at the front door long enough to scoop up her tennis shoes. At this point, I’m afraid I’m going to leave a bruise on her arm, so I let go and turn to face her. “Evie. You can’t live on cereal. And I will never be able to sleep at night, knowing that the woman who helped change my daughter’s and my life for the better is at home with no food. Now, either you can hop in my truck on your own, or I will pick you up and put you in myself, but either way, you’re going to the grocery store with me.”

I can’t tell if she wants to smack me or smile. I think there’s a hint of both in her face. “Can I at least put on a bra first?”

I smile. “I guess.”

She stares me down, and her eyes narrow in contemplation. “I don’t need a sugar daddy, Jake.”

“Good, because that term has always creeped me out, and I really don’t want to be associated with it.”

“I’m serious. I’m not helpless. I’m just a little broke until I get paid again, because my insurance went up again this month, making things a little tighter.”

"When is payday?"

"...Two weeks."

"Yeah. Come on." She looks so torn. If I don't want to throw her over my shoulder, I'm going to have to reason with her. "Please, Evie. Let me help. I promise this won't make you beholden to me. I can just help you with this one little thing to get you on your feet, and then I swear I'll never force my money on you again."

She grins a little. "All right, fine." She's crossing in front of me, headed for my truck. Bra forgotten. "But we're also buying the ingredients for your favorite brownies so I can make them as a thank you." She pauses at the right bumper and looks over her shoulder. Her damp hair is flowing in the wind, and she looks way too cute in that oversized shirt. "Except, I'm going to have to make it at your place because I don't have an oven."

CHAPTER EIGHTEEN

EVIE: I opened my pantry this morning and felt overwhelmed. I've never had so many breakfast choices before.

JAKE: Mix them all together.

EVIE: EW! Are you one of those people who stacks all of your food on top of each other at Thanksgiving?

JAKE: It all goes to the same place.

EVIE: *GIF of a woman yelling "murderer!"*

JAKE: So you're a gif girl, huh?

EVIE: I prefer them over words.

JAKE: *Gif of a person walking across the street*

EVIE: What in the world was that????

JAKE: I thought you preferred them over words. That was me saying I'm leaving to come get you soon.

EVIE: Wait, why?! I can call an Uber.

JAKE: I know. But I want to come get you.

EVIE: Stop being so nice to me all the time.

JAKE: But then someone might take my *nice guy* trophy away.

I'm sitting in Jake's truck, feeling baseball-sized butterflies fill my stomach. It's the day of the pool party, and in approximately ten minutes, I will meet every member of Jake's family. This still perplexes me. I honestly don't know what I'm doing here. I do know that I'm holding a tin of extra-fudgy brownies in my lap… but only because I spent the evening at his house last night making them. Sam helped while Jake hovered and kept trying to stick his finger in the batter. I swatted him no less than three times, and the whole thing felt oddly domestic.

I want to love it. I want to let myself be ridiculously happy with what seems to be blooming between us. But I can't seem to silence the loud voice in my head that won't stop screaming WHAT THE HECK IS BLOOMING?!

What am I to Jake?

What is he to me?

We kissed once, a few days ago, but honestly, I've kissed my grandmama longer and with more gusto than the kiss that transpired between Jake and me. I feel like it doesn't count (and I really need a do over). But neither of us has mentioned it. I think about it all the time, but I don't dare bring it up because I'm a big stinkin' coward. I'm scared that if I mention it, he'll spook and run away. And I really don't want him to run away. I want this one to stay. To like me. Maybe even love me one day. Is that crazy?

"What's going through your head over there?" Jake's voice makes me jump.

"Huh? Oh. Nothing."

"Not nothing. You look like you're about to throw up all over my seats."

I laugh, and it sounds silly and put on like a theatrical dame on Broadway. *Ha ha! Oh, Jakey, Jakey, you're too funny!* But yes, I'm totally going to throw up. Nerves are overtaking me because I'm about to meet Jake's family. I almost chickened out this morning and said I was sick, but Jo texted me before I got the chance and basically forbade it.

JO: I better see photographic evidence of your cutie little bootie in a swimsuit poolside, or I will revoke your use of my washer and dryer.

Rude. She knows my weakness too well: clean underwear.

"I'm fine," I say, but of course my voice wobbles.

"You don't have to be nervous. My family's going to love you." *Really? Cause mine doesn't.*

A few minutes later, we are pulling into Jake's driveway, and there are already five other cars parked outside, and I'm mentally reminding myself how much I love having clean underwear, otherwise I would be hightailing my butt out of there. He gets out, and I stay put. I don't mean to stay put in his truck, but the super glue I poured on the seat before sitting down is really doing its job.

He laughs and comes around to my door and opens it. He's not being chivalrous; he knows I'm not getting out if he doesn't pry me out. "Come on, crazy. They aren't going to bite, I swear."

I hand him the brownies and slide out. My cover-up drags against the seat, and wayyyy too much leg is revealed in the process. Sure, I'm wearing a bathing suit under this cover-up, and it's going to come off soon, revealing even more of my legs. But in a driveway where Jake is still completely covered and there is not a drop of water in sight, it feels way too indecent.

Jake thinks so too because he's trying to hide his smile like a teenage buffoon. This is the distraction I needed, though. I slap his arm. "Can you at least try to be a gentleman?"

"I could, but I don't really want to."

Charlie jumps out behind me, and I think he finds this flirting between Jake and me annoying, because he grunts and then sits down right beside us, staring up with the most unamused expression I've ever seen.

"All right, Charlie, we're going." I wasn't the one to say that.

It was Jake. Which means Jake is now interpreting Charlie's facial expressions too, and *wow,* this thing is getting real.

Speaking of real, Jake takes my hand and guides me into the house. We're holding hands (we've never held hands before) and walking into a family event. This doesn't feel like friendship. This feels like dating. But are we? I've never felt more confused in my life. I also love Jake's hands. You would think from all the calluses that he's a contractor instead of an architect.

We walk through the front door, and Jake drops my hand to take the brownies from me and set them on the counter. He made fun of me for putting up a big fuss to take the brownies back to my place so I could bring them over again today—that way everyone could see that I was contributing something to the party. I'm disappointed that no one is here to witness my contribution. Now it just looks like the brownies were here all along!

"Wait. Let's go back and ring the doorbell so everyone can see me bring in the brownies."

Jake turns around with a grin. "You don't have to come bearing brownies for them to like you."

"But when has bringing brownies ever hurt anyone's chances of likability?"

In the next moment, the back sliding door is opening, and I'm out of time. I lunge for the brownies so I can hold them in front of me like a peace offering, but Jake is one step ahead and blocks the brownies. Now it looks like I'm lunging for him. Wonderful. He takes it in stride, though, and wraps his arm around my shoulder, holding me pinned to his side.

"Jake, you're back!" says a little blonde woman in a voice that is Southern and sweet as iced tea. I don't know why, but I did not picture Jake's mom sounding like Jo. Probably because Jake barely has an accent. But it's clear from her teased-up hair to her drawn out R's and A's that she's as country as bread pudding at a church potluck. And I love it. "Oh, and Evie, honey! You made it!" I don't think anyone has ever sounded so pleased to meet me in my entire life. "EVERYONE! EVIE IS HERE!" she bellows toward the back door.

I'm glad I'm only wearing a bathing suit under this cover-up, because there is definitely some back sweat starting to happen.

"Hi! It's so nice to mee—"

"Evie!" Sam busts through the door with Daisy at her side and throws her arms around my waist.

Jake doesn't let go of me either. So, I'm just standing here with one Broaden wrapped around my upper half and another Broaden wrapped around my lower half. And then, suddenly, ALL of the other Broadens are watching on, and I'm hyperaware of what a picture we must be painting.

"Who's here? Oh, Evie!" says a happy, middle-aged man who comes to stand next to Mrs. Broaden and looks a lot like Jake.

There are now four other women filing into the kitchen, followed by a trail of various-aged children and spouses to look on, too. They are all saying hi and smiling so brightly, and I feel like the room is spinning. Why do they all sound so happy to meet me? And how does my name sound so comfortable on the lips of people I've never met before?

But when Jake squeezes my shoulder, I feel like everything shifts into place. Like one glorious line of Tetris when you can get all the shapes to fit perfectly together. He likes me. Jacob Broaden likes *me*. He's told his family all about me. He's standing proudly beside me and not letting me go.

This is the beginning of something, and I think I'm going to let myself enjoy it this time.

The introductions are complete, and I have been given a moment to catch my breath by the pool. Jake and his dad are over by the grill, tossing hot dogs and hamburgers on, and Sam and a few of her cousins are all swimming in the pool.

Turns out, Jake has the sweetest family on the face of the earth, and I had nothing to worry about. Who knew that there were people out there with families who actually love each other without secret agendas?

I pull my towel out of my tote bag and drape it over a pool chair. I find myself smiling at all the sounds of splashing and laughter. Growing up as an only child with two very pompous and career-driven parents meant the only sounds that usually filled our house were that of Daddy typing on a laptop while Mama gossiped with her other elitist minions on the phone. Exciting stuff.

"Soooo," says Jake's sister June as she plops down, stomach first, onto the pool chair beside me. "You're the hottie with the body that my big brother keeps talking about." I feel my eyes widen to the size of oranges.

Jake appears out of nowhere, standing beside my chair and towering over me. "I never called her that!" he says to his sister before looking down at me. "I never called you that."

June huffs an offended sound. "So, you're saying she doesn't have a hot body? How rude, Jake."

He gives June a look, and now I'm stuck between two siblings in a game of monkey in the middle. "Cut it out, June."

"You're not helping your case here, big brother. Evie is going to leave today, completely dejected, thinking you hate her body."

I'm struggling so hard to keep a laugh from bursting out of me.

"She's not going to think that." I like the way Jake's face is turning the tiniest bit pink, and I wonder if I can push it over the top to red.

I give him a pouty look and decide Jake needs to be the one in the middle now. "I don't know. I might think that."

He's glaring at me but clearly trying not to grin. "Fine, I'll give. Evie…you…you've got a hot body." BINGO. Jacob Broaden is capable of turning bright red, folks!

I laugh, enjoying the feeling of victory far too much. Jake just rolls his eyes and goes back to the grill with his daddy.

"He's too easy to mess with," June says, shaking her head with a smile while watching her brother walk away. I like her. She's spunky and a little crazy in the best kind of way. And she has a really cute watercolor flower tattoo capping her shoulder that makes me wonder if I would look as cute as her with one? Probably not. And I really don't like needles, so I dismiss the thought instantly.

"So, are you guys dating?"

My eyes shoot to June, and I must look like a deer in the headlights, because she laughs. "You don't have to answer that."

"No. It's not that I don't want to answer. It's just…I don't know how to answer it." I fish around in my tote bag for my sunscreen to give my hands something to do. "I think Jake and I are just friends."

"Eh, I wouldn't be so sure. He's never talked about any of his friends like he's been talking about you lately." Wow. Okay. Not sure what to do with that statement other than try to hide the wings I just sprouted from that surge of joy.

"Oh. Well…" I laugh and shrug, letting the conversation dangle out on the line because I really don't think I should be having a DTR conversation with Jake's sister before I have one with him.

"What are we talking about, ladies?" Mrs. Broaden rounds our pool chairs in her sunflower-printed kimono, gives June a little pat on her bikini-clad rear end like affectionate mamas are known to do and then takes the third seat beside us.

"Just trying to figure out if Jake and Evie are dating or not."

"What!" says Mrs. Broaden so loudly I think the whole neighborhood heard her. All of Jake's sisters definitely did, because now they are swarming me like a gam of sharks.

"Honey, of course you're dating. He brought you around us, didn't he?" says Mrs. Broaden.

"Oh, well, I—"

Jake's oldest sister, Jennie, squats down beside my chair. "Isn't he taking you to a benefit or something in a few weeks? If you're making plans that far in advance, you're definitely dating."

I open my mouth, but it's useless because yet another sister, Julia (Mr. and Mrs. Broaden apparently have a thing for J's), leans over the back of my chair and says, "I don't know. Jake is pretty friendly in general. It doesn't necessarily mean anything that he asked her to the benefit. I can totally see him thinking this is nothing but a friendship thing."

Do I even need to be here for this?

June sits up and crosses her legs. "Have you guys made out yet? That would totally help us figure out his intentions." HA. What?!

I'm definitely sweating. I'm also wondering if it would be wrong to fake a seizure right now to get out of this conversation. *Psstt, Charlie! What are you thinking, lounging over there in the shade at a time like this?!*

"All right, all right. Everyone shoo," says Mrs. Broaden, riding in on her white horse. Forget Jake and Charlie; she is my new knight in shining armor. "Evie doesn't want all these questions, and our meddlin' is going to do nothing but scare the poor girl away. Go play with your children in the pool and let her catch her breath." She's waving them away, and they all disperse.

"So, Evie, you're the one I get to thank for bringing some happiness back into my son and granddaughter's life."

"I can't take that credit. That's all Daisy's doing."

"Oh really? And did Miss Daisy stay over last night and teach my Sammie how to make brownies? Did Daisy convince Jake to have a little more fun in his life and throw a pool party?"

I laugh. "Jake's quite the sharer, isn't he?"

"Actually, no. Jake's pretty private about his life. But Sam is an open book, and she and I talk every night on the phone. She's been keeping me apprised of all things Evie Jones." Her smile turns a little more serious. "She really likes you. And my Sammie is a good judge of character."

"I think Sam is pretty amazing, too."

We are both quiet for a moment, and I decide I need something to do, so I peel off my cover-up, revealing my bright-yellow, polka dot, high-waisted bikini and start applying sunblock to my arms and legs. Jo made fun of me when I picked this swimsuit out in the store, saying that she owns sexier swimsuits than this one, but I don't care. I like it. It's cute and sporty, and I don't have to worry about all my parts falling out during a game of water volleyball.

Yes, I know...I'm once again pretending that I have big enough parts to fall out of something, but just let me dream.

Mrs. Jones—or Bonnie as I've now been bid to call her—and I spend the next five minutes shooting the breeze and getting to know each other. No, not true...she only wants to talk about me. But I like her. I like her a lot, so I answer all of her questions. She's encouraging and cheerful, and I think she and Jo would hit it off right away if they ever get to meet one day.

When the conversation winds down, though, she throws me a curve ball. "Your mama must be so proud of you, Evie. You're quite a woman."

I have to look away as soon as she says those words, because I can feel tears pooling in my eyes, and this is SO not the place to start crying.

My emotions are sent on a rollercoaster, however, when I turn my head in just enough time to see a bare-chested man with a gorgeous six pack and tan, defined shoulders running up beside me. I only have time to blink at the vision of sexy masculinity rushing up to me before Jake's arms go under me and scoop me out of my chair.

I scream and kick like a little girl as he jogs us toward the pool. *Umm, hello! Have you never heard of the no-running rule at the pool?!* But I'm not concerned about my safety. I want him to slow down so I can savor the feel of his warm skin against mine.

"What are you doing?!" I yell.

"This is payback, Evie Jones," says Jake before he jumps off the side and plunges us both in the pool.

CHAPTER NINETEEN

JAKE

Evie is lounging beside the pool like a golden, suntanned goddess. The funny thing is, she doesn't even realize she's this beautiful, and she's definitely not trying to be sexy. I know it because most women angle themselves so that their abs are contracted and their legs look like they are barely putting any weight on them to look slimmer. Not Evie. In fact, she's put her oversized shirt back on and added a straw visor and big sunglasses. She is an ad for skin health at a dermatologist's office, and I swear I'll buy anything she's selling.

The best part of Evie: she's laughing. She's always laughing. Her smile lights up her whole face in a way that looks like she might explode from joy. She's talking to June right now about a date that June went on last week. I was hanging out nearby until my baby sister started talking about the guy kissing like a slimy wet fish and I decided it was time to go.

But the weird thing is, Evie fits here. My family gave her the ultimate hazing of no personal space and a rousing game of a hundred questions right out of the gate, and Evie accepted it all with that adorable dimpled smile of hers. I don't want to be that guy who's constantly comparing every woman he spends time with to his ex-wife, but I can't help it. The picture is a stark contrast.

Natalie never fit in with my family. She didn't like them. She thought June was childish and that everyone else was too involved in our life. I don't remember the last time we had a pool party like this, because honestly, Natalie wouldn't have wanted to spend the afternoon with my family. In the interest of making my marriage work, I went along with it. I had lunch with my parents by myself most Sundays, and for holidays, we got in and out of family functions as fast as possible.

I've missed them in my life, and I can't help but notice that I don't miss Natalie one bit.

"Well, I think this pool party was a success, Jakey," says my mom, using my shoulder to help her sit down beside me on the edge of the pool. My mom is cute. She's about five foot tall standing on her tiptoes, has the voice of Paula Dean, and her personality is like a shot of Fireball Whisky mixed with sunshine.

"You think? I'm glad. And I'm glad you guys could come."

Evie's voice carries across the pool and distracts me. "Sam! When's the last time you put on sunscreen, darlin'?"

Sam pauses her descent down the pool steps and looks over to Evie. "Oh. Not since this morning."

"Come over here and let me lather you back up before you turn into the world's cutest lobster."

I watch my daughter smile from ear to ear and then rush back up the steps to go perch in front of Evie on the lounge chair. Evie's sitting cross-legged now, smiling and talking away to my sister while thoroughly applying sunscreen to my daughter's back. I'm mesmerized by this scene. I couldn't look away if I tried.

I am the person who loves Sam the most in this world…and I

forgot to reapply sunscreen to her back. But Evie remembered. What does that mean? It feels significant.

My mom leans close to me, and from the corner of my eye, I can see her smile. "I think you found a good one."

I take in a deep breath. "Yeah. I've thought that before, though."

"True. But you were just a kid back then when you met Natalie. You didn't know the first thing to look for in a woman besides her bra size."

I grimace. "That was disturbing to hear. You're starting to sound like June."

She chuckles and rolls her eyes. "You kids think I'm so out of touch, but I'll have you know that I watch *The Bachelor* every week." She says it like that fact in itself should knock fifteen years off her age. "But that's not the point. The fact is, you're a grown man now who's lived a lot of life, and you know what kinda woman it's gonna take to hold your hand through the rest of it." She pats my back and then shimmies off the edge of the pool into the water to go swim by my dad who, at this moment, has approximately five grandkids leached onto him in the shallow end.

I turn my eyes back to Evie just in time to see her stand up, empty glass in hand, and head toward the house.

Next thing I know, I'm on my feet and striding after her. I suddenly feel like there is some unfinished business between us.

I step into the house, and the cool air hits my bare chest. I probably should have grabbed a shirt, but there was no time. Everyone else is outside, and Evie's alone in here, and I didn't want to waste this moment.

Turning the corner, I find Evie in the kitchen, pouring herself a new glass of lemonade and shoving a brownie into her mouth. She spots me and covers her mouth to keep her crumbs from spewing out with her laughter. "Caught red-handed," she says from behind her fist.

I round the island to get closer to her, and I notice her chewing slows and her body straightens a little. I stop just behind her, hoping she'll turn around to face me. "You're allowed to eat brownies, you know."

My plan works, because Evie turns around, and now she's trapped between me and the counter, and I'm loving how close we are. I can see the freckles dotting the bridge of her nose and the perfect bow of her full top lip.

"Yeah," she says with a final swallow, "but am I allowed to have *four* brownies?"

My eyebrows lift. "Did you really eat four brownies?"

"What?? Me? No. I was kidding. I'd never eat that many. That would be soooo unhealthy." That means she actually ate five.

I smile and lean in and set my hands on the countertop behind her—one on either side of her, pinning her in. Her eyes widen. I know this is bold. Other than that ridiculously tiny kiss we had the other night, our relationship has looked nothing like this. And speaking of that kiss, neither of us even acknowledged it after. I just kinda swept it under the rug because my body had gotten away from me and started something that I wasn't ready for yet.

I'm ready now.

I've been watching Evie all day, and there's not a chance that I'm letting this woman leave my house with us stuck in the friend zone. I get closer and breathe in the scent of Banana Boat suntan lotion mixed with the sweet brownie on her breath. Let me tell you, it's a ridiculously good combination.

"Jaaaaaake," says Evie in a slightly nervous, playful voice as she looks backward toward my hands. She takes a tiny step back toward the counter and puts her hands behind her to grip it. "What's going on right now?"

I smile because I like how frank she is. She doesn't try to

play games. She's straightforward. What you see is what you get —and *goodness,* I like what I see.

"What's going on is…I think our kiss was way too short the other night." *I can be frank too.*

She sucks in a breath and blinks before pursing her lips together. She looks over both of her shoulders before her green eyes hit mine again. "Do you think THIS is the place to discuss that?" She's cute when she's nervous.

"Yeah. I do."

"But what if Sam walks in here?"

"She'll probably be scarred for the rest of her life."

"Jake! I'm serious."

I smile and inch closer so our bodies are touching. "Me too."

Evie's eyes drop to my mouth and then lower to my chest. She swallows, and her cheeks pink, and I swear I've never felt more cocky than at this moment.

She looks back up at me. "You can't just switch gears on me like this in the middle of the day at your family pool party. I mean…all week, we've been friends. And now you're going to pin me against the counter and kiss me while you're half-naked? You're not allowed to do that. I think that's skipping a few steps."

I smile bigger and move my hand up to her neck, enjoying the way her skin is still hot from the day in the sun. "It's been a little while since I've brushed up on the rules, so you'll have to forgive me. Because, yeah, I'm going to skip some steps now."

She smiles, and I can't stand it any longer. I've gotta kiss her. I'm leaning down, and her hands move up to rest on my bare chest. The sudden skin-to-skin contact is electric, and it short-circuits my brain. I've been dead for the past year, and she just put two paddles to my chest. I'm alive now.

My lips touch hers, and then I'm having terrible déjà vu, because we get interrupted.

"Whoa!" says my dad from the doorway. Evie and I split

apart. "Sorry, you two. I didn't realize there was something going on in here." But his smile says he very well knew.

I lean my back against the opposite counter of Evie's and give my dad an unamused smile. "Impeccable timing, Dad."

He shrugs and struts right on over to the fridge to fill his glass with ice. "I've got four daughters, son. I've had loads of practice to perfect my timing." He looks at Evie and winks. WINKS!

One minute, I was a cocky son of a gun, and now I'm fifteen with a face on fire, and my dad is embarrassing me and my pretty girlfriend. How can I recover this?

Dad is taking his sweet time, adding one cube of ice to his glass at a time, filling it with water, taking a sip, and topping it off again. This goes on for two minutes, and I can see that Evie is trying so hard not to dissolve into laughter.

I give her a look that says, *Enjoying this, are you?* That forces her to cover her mouth with the back of her hand so a laugh doesn't spew out.

All right, enough.

I'm not fifteen, and this is my own freaking kitchen. "Okay, water boy, I think you're well hydrated. Why don't you take this outside now and stop doing whatever it is you're doing in here."

My dad laughs as I'm pushing him from the kitchen. "I'm going, I'm going…but you should know that we can all see you out there." He points toward the one sliver of an opening between the kitchen and the sliding door in the living room…and yep…it's a straight shot. Everyone is gathered and watching on like their cable got canceled months ago and they're starved for entertainment.

Once I forcibly remove my father from my house, I turn around and go back into the kitchen. I find Evie giving in to her laughter with both hands covering her face. I take one of her wrists and pull her out of the kitchen into the hallway—AWAY from the prying eyes of my creepy family.

"Are you going to sneak me away to make out in the hallway now?" she asks while laughing.

I stop and turn around when I know we are clear from the audience. "No. The moment's over."

"Boooooo," she says with a big smile.

I'm laughing now too, and I can't believe how bad I am at this dating thing. Turns out, it's something you *can* get rusty at.

"What are you doing Friday night?" I ask.

Her smile goes a tad serious. "Friday?"

"Mmhmm."

"Well…nothing that I know of."

"Come over Friday night then."

Her smile peeks again. "Come over?"

"Are you just going to keep repeating everything I say?"

"Only if you don't start explaining what you mean in full sentences. I mean, I know we just kinda kissed again in the kitchen, but I don't want to misconstrue anything." Gosh, I like this woman. I also really want to try to redeem our bad-kiss streak, but I refrain because I can't handle another interruption, and the potential for that happening is way too high.

"Sam has her slumber party that night, so I'm going to be off of dad duty. I was hoping you'd come over and let me cook you dinner…as a date."

"A date?"

"You're still repeating me."

She smiles wider and leans her back against the wall. The shadowy hallway we are encapsulated in only adds to the flirty look she's giving me. Evie is *not* rusty. "So…a *date*-date? Like…you *like* me-like me? Not just a friend thing?"

I chuckle and inch closer to her. "Yeah. Didn't you get my note I passed you in science? I like you. Check yes or no if you like me, too."

She scrunches her nose and dares to step closer to me. She reaches up and wraps her arms around my neck. "I check yes."

"So, does that mean you'll come?"

"You said you're cooking?"

I nod.

"Count me in."

She raises up on her tiptoes and kisses my cheek before breaking away and darting back out toward the pool.

CHAPTER TWENTY

EVIE

"Where do you want to go dress shopping this weekend?" Jo asks me around a bite of salad.

"Doesn't matter to me."

"Just prepare to get something skimpy to show off those legs for Jake."

I give Jo a flat look. "First of all, a man should like me for more than my body. And second, shouldn't you be the one telling me this? You're in your sixties. How am I the mature one here?"

Jo shrugs and steals a fry from my plate. "Now, why would I tell you something you already know? I'm pretty sure all you ever think about is how to be upstandin'. Think of me as your fairy godmother." She waves the fry like a wand over my head. "*Bibbidi-bobbidi, do yourself a favor and live a little.*"

I shake my head at my fairy godmother and take a bite of my burger.

My phone buzzes on the table with a new text, and I see the name *Jake* written across my screen. Jo sees it, too, and wags her eyebrows suggestively while reaching for my phone. I snatch it off the table and clutch it close to my chest before she gets a chance to swipe it open. "No one likes a Nosey Nelly."

"Even less people like a Boring Bessy." She steals another fry, and I smack her hand playfully.

I angle myself away from Jo, and I swipe open my phone.

JAKE: Only two more days until our date. It's been way too long since I've seen you.

I smile because it has felt like a long time. Jake and I haven't seen each other since the pool party last Saturday. It's Wednesday now, and I've never felt like a week has gone by slower. It's not that I haven't been busy. In fact, I've been crazy busy training a new group of volunteers who signed up to be puppy raisers. Our newest litter of pups will be ready to leave their mama and go into a volunteer's home to start learning their basic training techniques: potty training, don't chew the rug, sit, and lots and lots of socialization.

Our company literally wouldn't survive without these volunteers and the time they sacrifice in helping train our dogs. But these weeks of breaking everyone in and teaching them the rules is always exhausting for me.

Not only have I been teaching classes for the volunteers, but I've taken three dogs to the vet, had two match meetings with potential recipients, reviewed five new applications, and ignored three texts from my mama reminding me that I need to quit fooling around and do something useful with my life. Something like join the Powder Society of Revolutionary Ladies and drink martinis in the afternoon.

But, in the meantime, Jake and I have been texting every day and have even talked on the phone a few of those nights. Remember how I felt like he was out of my league? *Ha ha ha,* oh how wrong I was. Jake is out of my universe.

The more I get to know him, the more I like him. He's thoughtful, and funny, and tender, and truly and completely *rippe*d. You thought I was going to say something sentimental there, didn't you? Well, sorry, but thoughts of Jake's ridiculous body make my brain turn into mush, and all intelligent thoughts melt into steamy nonsense.

This morning I got lost in a fantasy of what a *real* kiss with him would be like, and I accidentally overflowed my coffee all over the counter. If this date on Friday goes well, I'm afraid my brain will be permanently fried.

EVIE: Oh. Is our date in two days? I totally forgot.

JAKE: You're not funny.

EVIE: *Screenshot of countdown timer, titled: Days until date with Jake.*

JAKE: Better. What time should I call you tonight?

EVIE: I'll be home by 7.

JAKE: I'll call you at 7:01. I mean…I'll call you at some vague time after that so you don't realize how much I like you.

"Oh, he's good," says Jo from over my shoulder.

"Hey!" I lock my phone screen again and give her the stink eye. "Mind your own beeswax."

"My beeswax is boring today. So, tell me, are things going good with you two?"

I can't hide my smile. "Really good. Too good, actually."

She rolls her eyes. "Only you would say that when a hot man is being attentive and flirting with you."

"I know! I don't want to feel this way, but…I have too much experience that's taught me it won't last long. Every guy I've ever dated has either moved on to easier and perkier pastures, or they see one of my episodes and it scares them right out of my life."

"Yes, and do you know what you outta say to those types of guys? *Don't let the door hit ya where the good Lord split ya!* Because if you don't know it already, honey, you've been known to date duds."

My mouth falls open. "What?"

"It's true. The few guys you've dated in the past have all

been a few eggs short of a dozen, and waayy below your level. It's like you're so desperate to not end up with anyone like your parents that you swing completely the opposite way. Jake is the first man you've ever been interested in that even comes close to being on the same tier as you."

"Ha! You think Jake and I are on the same level?"

"No." Her eyes slide to mine, and I see a twinkle. "I don't think anyone will ever measure up to you. But I get the feeling that Jake will actually try."

I don't know what to say. The fact that Jo thinks so highly of me makes me feel weepy. There's nothing else to do but lean over and wrap her up in a hug and then slide my phone onto the table in front of her.

"Just for that, you get unlimited access to my texts for the next five minutes."

She wastes no time in picking up my phone and scrolling through every text Jake and I have ever exchanged. While she continues giggling like a teenager, I decide to occupy myself by refilling my water.

I stand up, and Charlie does, too, but with a big yawn. Poor guy has been bored to death the past few days. Or maybe exhausted from all the running around and meetings we've been to. Either way, I need to devote some special time to take him to the park and throw the ball.

I'm filling up my water at the drink station and mentally planning on taking Charlie to the park on Friday morning so that he won't feel slighted during my date with Jake—*don't worry, Charlie, you'll always be my first love*—when I feel the presence of someone else beside me.

I cut my eyes to the side to get a look at whatever weirdo is entering my personal space, when I find an attractive man smirking down at me. He's not Jacob-Broaden attractive, but I'm still woman enough to admit he's good looking.

"Hi," he says.

"Hi," I reply back, and I'm a little embarrassed to say it sounded more like a mouse squeak.

Come on, water. Fill faster!

"I'm Garrett."

Okay. Nice. Cool. So, what's going on here? This never happens to me. I briefly glance down, worried that maybe Charlie ran away, because men NEVER approach me when Charlie is around. He's a giant man deterrent. *Do not come near the pretty girl. She's high maintenance.*

"Evie," I say with a polite smile and then turn to set my cup on the counter and put the lid back on. Annnnnd then Garrett is beside me again, doing the same with his lid.

"What's your dog's name?"

Huh. Okay, so he did see Charlie. And he's not scared off? I don't know how I feel about this. Actually, yes, I do. I'm not interested in this guy. Maybe a month ago, before I met Jake, I would have felt flattered. But right now, I just kinda want to extract myself from the conversation as quickly and politely as possible.

"This is Charlie."

"Sup, Charlie," he says, and I smile instead of telling him not to distract my dog while he's working. "Are you from around here?" Alrighty then. I guess we are going to do the *chit-chat* thing now.

This is so bizarre. Do men have some kind of scent tracker that helps them sniff out the women in town who are unavailable? Because, I swear, I never got hit on by cute, normal-looking guys before Jake asked me out.

"Yeah, I am. Are you?"

"Kind of. I just moved here a few months ago, so I'm still trying to get my bearings on the town."

"That's nice."

"I'm actually a physician's assistant over at Roper Hospital."

Cool, cool, cool. Didn't ask you, but that's all right.

"That's a great hospital."

"Yeah? You've been?" He's asking like we are talking about a hot new club that just opened or something. *No way, I love that place! Maybe we could go together sometime. I know people who can get you one of the good gowns without stains on it.* It's a strange topic of conversation, but I give him slack because I'm pretty sure he's just trying to find ways to keep me here talking and will likely want to punch himself later for asking that question.

I chuckle. "A few times, yeah." I glance down at Charlie, and Garrett follows my gaze to the patch that says *Seizure Assist Dog*. A look of dawning hits Garrett's face, and I expect him to start moonwalking away from me at any second.

He doesn't. "So, look, Evie, this is really forward of me and probably going to creep you out a little, but…I think you're really attractive, and I'd like to take you out sometime if you're free."

If I'm free? Does he mean if my schedule is free? Or if my relationship status is single and I'm free to date other people? Because honestly, I don't know. I mean, Jake and I talk every day, we flirt, we've sort of kissed a few times, and we have a date on Friday…but does that, technically, mean I'm in a relationship?

I cast a quick glance to Jo, hoping she'll give me a thumbs up or down for what I should do right now, but her eyes are still glued to my phone. *Useless.* I think she's even screenshotting text conversations to forward to Gary.

I look back to Garrett and do a quick assessment of him: nice, dark hair, well-trimmed beard, taller than me, a nice body, and an open smile. And overall, he's not setting off any alarms that make me feel like I should ask a security guard to walk me to my car when I leave here.

But the truth is, all I can think about is Jake. I like Jake. I want to date Jake, not this guy. "You seem nice, Garrett, which is why I feel like I should be honest and tell you that I'm sorta-kinda seeing someone."

Garrett gives me a nice-guy smile and nods. He then reaches into his laptop bag that's slung over his shoulder and pulls out a pen. After grabbing a clean napkin, he writes his number on it and hands it to me. "Well, since 'sorta-kinda' doesn't sound like you've set a wedding date yet, here's my number. Call me if you find yourself in need of a fun date."

"Hitting on my girl? Not cool, dude," says none other than Tyler Murray after somehow sneaking up behind me and dropping his arm over my shoulder like he owns me.

Tyler pulls the slip of paper with Garrett's number on it out of my hand and tears it in two. Because, yep, that's the kind of guy Tyler is.

Garrett gives me a look that says I'm an idiot for dating a jerk like Tyler. I flash an apologetic smile, but don't worry, I'm just waiting for Garrett to walk away before I throw my elbow into Tyler's southern regions.

He knows me too well, though, because the second that Garrett walks away, Tyler jumps back with a big grin. "You were going to hit me, weren't you?"

"Why are you saying it in the past tense? The threat is still real."

Tyler is still very much the same man who moved to New York five years ago. He's wearing a dark-gray suit that hugs his toned body. He's tall with chestnut-colored hair and dark-chocolate eyes. And he's still got the same smile as the devil. He openly scans my body and then raises and lowers his brows. "Well, shoot, Eves. You look even better than the last time I saw you."

I roll my eyes and turn around to return to my seat next to Jo. "Go away, Tyler."

He chuckles and tries to catch my arm, but I'm faster. "Wait.

Don't you want this phone number? I'd be willing to paste it back together for a kiss."

I would tell him he could kiss my butt, but he would likely just treat it like an innuendo and say something that grosses me out. "Nope. Don't need it. And now you've filled your douchebag quota for the day, so you can scurry on back to the vermin hole you climbed out of." Charlie and I are weaving in and out of tables, and unfortunately, Tyler is keeping pace with me.

"Why don't you need it? Have you finally decided to marry me after all?"

When I walk up, Jo hands me my phone and, before she realizes Tyler is right behind me, says, "Jake texted you something sappy again, and I asked him to send a picture of his backside." I know she's kidding, so I don't press it. At least…I hope she's kidding.

But I really wish that she hadn't just mentioned Jake's name in front of Tyler. It's not that I think Tyler is some crazy guy from the movies who will kidnap me and stuff me in his trunk until I agree to marry him, but I do know that he's enough like my parents to go to extreme manipulative measures to get what he wants. He's always been that way. It's why he's such a good attorney.

"Wait, who's Jake? Don't tell me my Evie Grace has a boyfriend," Tyler says, coming to stand far too close to me. He's like a pimple. I just want to pop him—or punch him, or step on his toes, or slap him—but I know that if I do, it'll just make things worse for my complexion. Best to ignore him and wait for the breakout to pass.

"I'm not yours, Tyler, and I never will be. Now leave me alone and find someone else to bug."

"Come on, Eves. You know we'd be good together."

"Do you seriously not think it's completely insane to marry

each other just because you own your daddy's portion of the business now?" I'm asking because I genuinely want to know.

"I think it makes sense. You know this life better than anyone else. You know what it takes to be a good wife to a man like me, and I know that you look ridiculously good in a cocktail dress. So, yeah…I'm willing to sign that contract."

"You mean marriage certificate?"

"Same difference."

"Yeah. Go away, Tyler."

He chuckles like he hasn't heard a word I've been saying. Like he thinks I'm cute for turning him down. I swear, if he pats my butt like he did last time he came to visit, I will tear his favorite limb right off his body.

"Tell you what. If you're so worried about it, let me take you out. I'll wine you and dine you, and if you're lucky, I might even—"

"If you finish that sentence, I promise you I will dump this drink all over that fancy suit of yours."

His eyes widen like I've just threatened to shoot him. He relaxes back into his sleazy grin and tugs on his suit lapels. "Your parents want this, Eves, and so do I. So, don't think that by me walking away right now, I'm giving up. I'll find a way to show you that us being together is the right choice." He tries to kiss my cheek as he passes by me, but I turn my head away. And *whoa,* someone should tell that man that a spritz is all it takes. He is a walking bottle of cologne.

"Oh, I hate him," says Joanna once Tyler is out of earshot.

"Me and you both," I say and then turn around just as Tyler makes it to the far end of the restaurant and is standing in line to order. I smile a big ol' blinding smile and call out to him so the whole restaurant turns and looks. "Oh, Tyler! I forgot to say that the ointment you had me pick up for you is on your desk at work! The pharmacist said it should clear your rash right up but that sex is not advised for the first three weeks!"

I have the privilege of watching the scumbag's mouth fall open, and the woman in line in front of him (who he had just been checking out relentlessly) turns her shoulder firmly away from him. Even from this far away, I can see his face turn beet red. And then, just as I had hoped, he steps out of line and leaves.

"That was too satisfying to watch," says Jo with a high five.

I should feel satisfied, too, but I don't. Because the only takeaway I have from this whole situation is that I have no idea what sort of relationship I have with Jake, and I really need to figure that out. Are we exclusive? Is *he* dating other people?

A minute ago, I was thrilled about my date with him. Now, I'm feeling nervous. I can feel a big fat DTR on the horizon, and if I know the male sex at all, Jake is not going to be excited about this conversation. But it needs to happen so I can know whether I should pocket the phone numbers from cute strangers in the future, or if I should put my blinders on and pretend that I no longer notice other males in the vicinity.

CHAPTER TWENTY-ONE

JAKE

It's Friday, aka a major day for me.

Not only is today the first time my daughter will spend the night away from home since being diagnosed with epilepsy, but tonight, I will have my first date with a woman other than Natalie in about eleven years.

As I'm searching through my closet for something to wear, I realize how out of touch I am. I think my mom got my birth certificate wrong, and I'm actually one hundred years old instead of thirty-three. Do I wear a T-shirt? Do I wear a tux? A tux is probably a little much.

Okay, breathe, Jake. You know you can't wear a freakin' tux.

My jeans are on, but I'm still naked from the hips up when I hear Sam scream from her bedroom. I drop the shirt I was contemplating wearing and run into her room, expecting to find her in a pool of blood on her floor.

Nope.

But I do find her in a pool of clothing. Her dark, wide eyes look up at me, and she says, "I have nothing to wear!" *What?! How can we be having the same dilemma?*

"What do you mean? I see lots of clothes."

"Daddy!" She rolls her eyes and sounds way too exasperated at me for stating a fact. "These are all day-clothes. I don't have any cute PJs! All of the girls are going to have the perfect slumber-party PJs, and I'm going to have to go in these old, stained, polka-dot pants that are way too small for me!"

This is catching me completely off guard. I had no idea that fashionable PJ attire was a must-have to attend an eleven-year-old's slumber party.

Although…now I feel like I should have known this. I've seen the cheesy teen movies.

I sigh and look at my watch. "Okay. We have an hour until I have to have you at Jenna's. Grab your stuff, and we'll swing by the store on the way and get you some new PJs."

"And a bra."

"What?!" I'm going to have a full-on panic attack now.

"Daddy, I'm almost a teenager!" *Hardly.* "All the other girls that will be there have already been wearing them. It'll be embarrassing if I'm not."

My gut instinct is to pull the emergency lever and shut this whole thing down here and now, because honestly, I'm having trouble breathing. My daughter is almost a teenager, and she's wanting to wear bras, and up next is the sex talk that I don't feel at all ready to give her. But after I give myself a mental slap, I remember that I've been training for this very moment. A man doesn't watch all seven seasons of Gilmore Girls for nothing. I know to stay calm. Don't panic. Stop, drop, and roll. Basically, do anything besides make my not-so-little girl feel uncomfortable about her changing body.

Channel your inner Lorelai Gilmore. I will not be that single dad that sucks.

"Got it," I say with a firm nod and start ticking things off on my fingers like it's no big deal. "New bra. New PJs. And probably a new toothbrush because I'm guessing you don't like that princess one I bought you last time?"

She smiles, and I feel like I can sigh with relief. And then she looks at my bare chest, and she scrunches her nose. "And a new shirt for your date."

"Perfect. Meet me downstairs in five minutes."

I go back to my closet, throw on a plain white tee that's good enough for shopping and dropping her off at her friend's house, and then hustle downstairs. Sam and Daisy are already waiting for me when I reach the bottom floor. It's then that I notice something in Sam's eyes that I saw in my own the last time I looked in the mirror.

We look at each other for a long minute, both of us heavy with emotion. We are moving on with our lives, not letting the obstacles of this year hold us back.

I pull her in for a hug, and she doesn't resist. "It's okay. I'm a little scared too, kiddo."

"You are?" she asks, sounding relieved.

"Yep. But we're both going to do great. The first steps into change are always the hardest."

She pulls out of my hug and picks up Daisy's leash. "I wish Evie could help me pick out my new bra. I don't really know what to get, and I'm guessing you don't either."

Should I be worried that she's wishing for Evie right now and not her own mom? I probably would be if I didn't completely get it. Natalie basically abandoned her. It's hard to want someone who doesn't seem to want you back. Evie, however, has been more invested in Sam's life over the past several weeks than Natalie has all year.

I would love to be able to call Evie right now and beg her to go with me and Sam to pick out a bra. I bet she would be perfect in that role. I've no doubts that she would make Sam feel special and grown-up without making it awkward like I probably will.

But Evie and I haven't even been on a real date yet. I can't call her.

I can feel myself trying to sprint. *Slow down. Turtle speed, remember?*

But maybe I can at least text her when we get there about tween bra sizes. Would she think that's weird?

EVIE: OMG. I loved my first bra. Get her a white one and a gray one so she has something to wear with both a light and dark outfit. Size: Small. No underwire and nothing with the words "push up" unless you want to have a heart attack. And whatever you do, get in and get out as quickly as possible without saying anything remotely close to "My baby girl is growing up so fast."

So…I guess she doesn't find it weird. And now I look like a major perv, standing in the girls' bra aisle, smiling like a lunatic.

I drop Sam off at Jenna's house with a backpack filled to the brim with turquoise-and-white PJs that have some kind of sequined koala face on the front of the shirt and the words "Don't wake me until noon" on the back. She talked me into not only a white and a gray training bra, but also a pink.

All in all, I think I've kinda crushed the single-dad thing today.

When we pull up in front of Jenna's house, Sam tells me I can stay put in the truck. I suggest dropping her off a block away so she can walk back—that way, no one will even need to know that she has a dad. And she just replies with a simple, "*Not this time,*" like it wasn't even a joke and she was really contemplating it.

She's in for a treat if she thinks, for one second, that I won't be sitting a row behind her at the movies on her first date.

Sam jumps out of my truck with Daisy in tow and her bag strapped on her back. She darts toward the house with one of her friends that has also just told her parents to keep the car running and drive off as soon as her feet hit the grass. But my kid—the good one—pauses and looks back at me. She comes sprinting back and jumps up onto the running boards of my truck to kiss my cheek through the open window. "Love you, Daddy."

"Love you too, Sam. Have fun. Call me if..." I let the statement dangle because, somehow, I'm afraid that if I say the words out loud, I'll be responsible for a seizure if she has one.

She smiles and nods. "I will."

And then my little girl goes into her friend's house for her first ever slumber party. My heart squeezes painfully, and I'm glad now more than ever that I had the forethought to plan a date to distract me tonight.

I put the truck in drive, and I'm headed home to get ready for my date with Evie when my phone buzzes with an incoming text. A text that makes my stomach plummet to the ground.

NATALIE: Headed back from Hawaii soon. Thinking of coming to visit when I get back. Hug Samantha for me. <3

CHAPTER TWENTY-TWO

EVIE

Jake asked if I wanted him to come pick me up for our date, but I thought that would be silly for him to come all the way over to my place and get me, only to drive right back to his house. We went three rounds until he gave up and let me call an Uber. But he was adamant that he was going to pay for it.

Now, I'm very aware that society would tell me to stand up for myself and own my female empowerment by showing him that I can take care of myself monetarily. But since I'm broke, I've decided that there's room enough for me to feel empowered and also let Jake feel like a hero. It's a give and take.

He's giving me his money, and I'm taking it.

I'll act more empowered next time.

The Uber pulls up in front of Jake's magazine-worthy farmhouse, and I'm still in disbelief that I get to even go inside this home, let alone date the man that owns it. (Don't get all judgy right now. I'm not after Jake for his money or his belongings—I'm after his abs.)

Charlie and I get out of the Uber, and I tug on my high-waisted jeans to put them back in their correct placement of hugging my butt and trimming my waist. I paired them with a cute pale-pink blouse, and I won't lie, I'm feeling pretty adorable right now. I even took the time to curl my hair in long, loose waves. I look like a walking ad for a beachy-waves hair product, and I wonder how I got so lucky to not wake up with a zit today.

Everything feels too good. I'm still waiting for that hammer to drop while also trying to be more optimistic like Jo suggested.

I ring the doorbell, and the feel of my heart thudding in my chest helps me count the seconds it takes for Jake to answer the door. *Ten.*

As he's opening the door, my nervousness overcomes me, and I wonder if it's too late to play ding-dong-ditch and hide in the bushes. Yeah, it's too late. He's seen me. And OH BOY, do I see him.

"Hi," he says in a sultry voice with a smirk that says, *Yeah, I know I look hot.* He puts Garrett's paltry little "hi" to shame. Jake is tall and muscular, and he's wearing a form-fitting, slate-blue shirt and day-old stubble on his jaw. His jeans are dark and trim, and I'm sure that he has them tailored to fit him like a glove. I like this look on him. No, I love it.

"Hi yourself," I say, and NOPE, sultry doesn't sound good on me. I sound delusional and like I have a throat bubble.

I'm just considering jumping into the bushes again when Jake steps out to where I'm standing and captures me around the waist. He leans down and brushes my cheek with a kiss from his deliciously scratchy jaw and whispers in my ear, "You look beautiful."

Well, okay then. I guess I'll stay.

I smile against his cheek, and then he releases me to pat Charlie on the head and take my hand, pulling me inside. The smell of herbs and spices fills my senses, and the sound of Leon Bridges plays softly from the speakers in the ceiling. It doesn't escape my notice that he's turned on the very album I was listening to the night he came over.

The lights are dimmer than normal, and my body is hyperaware that Sam is not home, and this is officially *Jake the Man's* house and not *Jake the Dad*. My nerves are humming, and buzzing, and ping-ponging with excitement, and suddenly, I don't know what to do with my hands. They don't make real pockets on women's jeans, so I'm forced to clasp them behind me like a kindergartener who's been told not to touch anything.

"Come on in; I'm just finishing up a few things." He goes into the kitchen, and I follow a few paces behind him, afraid to say anything.

Someone please tell me what to do right now! I've stood in this kitchen dozens of times. I've spent the last few weeks talking to Jake every single day. But this feels different. The air is different. It's rich with anticipation.

It's been a long time since I've gone on a date. Even longer since I've been on a date with a man I liked. Or a man that looked and acted like Jake. No one should look that sexy holding a ladle and stirring a pot. He's a safety hazard.

I decide to give in to my awkward and plaster myself in the farthest corner of his kitchen. The cold marble cuts through my shirt and stings at my lower back, but I don't care. I'm not moving. "How was Sam when you dropped her off?" I manage to squeak out.

Jake taps the wooden spoon against the side of the pot and sets it down. He takes note of me standing alllll the way across the room and smirks. "Great. She looked so happy running in with all her friends. I'm glad I let her go." He goes toward the fridge and pulls out a bottle of white wine. How did he know that was my favorite? "Want a glass?"

"Yes!" I say a little too eagerly.

He smiles and pours but stays put where he is. "Here you go."

He's smiling at me and holding the glass in front of him. I know what he's doing. He's bribing me away from my private island, and I have no choice but to comply if I want that wine. And I do want it.

I slowly move closer, and he chuckles. "Why are you so afraid of me tonight?"

"I'm not," I croak. But I am. I totally am.

My nerves are sizzling because I don't know what to expect from the night, or what he expects. We are two adults on a first real date, and let's face it, there's been a lot of tension building up between us lately, and I just don't know what he's thinking is going to happen tonight. What do I want to happen? What will I let happen?

When I come within arm's reach, he slips his hand around to my lower back and pulls me closer. *Ha ha, you fell for it, and now you're trapped.* I like being trapped. He smells incredible—like he used a body wash with descriptive words on the bottle, like *mountain* or *rain.* Somehow, the smell acts like a truth serum, because when he asks me to tell him what's going on in my head, I do.

"I'm nervous," I say, looking up and meeting his tender blue eyes.

He smiles, and a small chuckle runs through his chest. "Me too."

"Really?" Somehow, that surprises me because he seems so put together and sure of himself. He *always* seems that way. Like a sturdy tree that's been there for hundreds of years. You know that if a strong wind blows, it won't knock it over.

"I changed my outfit three times," he admits with a cute, guilty look.

I grin and relax a little more into him. "You didn't."

"I did." His voice is warm and rich.

Something changes between us, and I can feel the moment we both realize that we are completely alone in this house and no one will burst in and interrupt a kiss this time. Chill bumps fly across my skin as Jake brushes my hair away from my face and neck and then leans down. But he doesn't kiss my mouth. Nooo, that would be way too obvious a choice for him. Instead, Jake moves right on by my lips and goes to my neck, placing a light, lingering kiss right below my jaw. His lips are warm, and I can feel his day-old stubble tickling my neck where he's placing slow, heart-melting kisses.

I tip my head back to give him a better vantage point. He puts his hands on my hips and pulls me closer. His kisses are moving up toward my mouth, and as much as I'm loving this slow torture, I'm finding it hard not to tap my foot and tell him to move on to the main event.

He and I have kissed twice now, but both of those were nothing. I'm ready to find out what a real kiss is from Jacob Broaden.

Just as his mouth is rounding my jaw, I become aware of a bubbling sound on the stove. "I think something is boiling," I say.

"Mmhhmm," he murmurs against my cheek.

"Is that a bad thing?" I don't know why I'm suddenly so concerned with food prep. Actually, it probably has something to do with the way my nervous heart is about to explode from my chest.

"It's fine." He sounds like he's in a coma.

"Are you sure? Because—" I don't get to finish my thought.

Jake's lips take mine, and all thoughts of dinner are behind me. In fact, I don't think I ever need to eat again. I'll just stay here and keep kissing Jake for the rest of my life, and I'm pretty sure that will be enough to sustain me.

He pulls me flush with his body, and together, our kiss feels like a deep exhale. Like life has turned fuzzy around the edges and nothing else matters anymore. Except, he's too tall. I hook my arm around his neck to help pull him down to me, but Jake responds to my dilemma by picking me up and setting me on the counter in front of him.

My hands run over the tight ridges and valleys of Jake's shoulders, and I can't believe that I'm even allowed to touch this work of art. He should be boxed up and sent off to a museum where he can be adequately appreciated. I lace my fingers in the back of his hair and breathe in his clean scent. Jake's lips move, both soft and fierce like the tides of the ocean, and I fall into them and swim.

I can hear something on the stove bubbling into a frenzy, and I can't help thinking that whatever is cooking is perfectly mirroring Jake's and my kiss, because let me tell you, it's sizzling. I wind my arms tightly around his neck with a grip that says *you're not going anywhere.* He moves his hands up and down my back, pressing in and tugging me closer, and our lips part. And just like a three-Michelin-star chef, I'm able to taste the notes of everything he's been cooking.

As the minutes go by and Jake and I are lost in each other, I can't help but think of how surreal this feels. How perfect. I should have known. I should have prepared for how I would feel after a kiss like this with him, because Jake is an overachiever, and I feel a little in awe of him.

When I'm with Jake, I'm starting to have these feelings that scare me. They are possessive, and wanting, and wishing to claim Jake as mine.

And now I'm kissing him with the intent to brand him. I want everyone to be able to look at him and see my kiss planted across his lips and know that he's taken. I think Jake can read my thoughts (or my body language) because, suddenly, he's slowing things down. The weight of his hands splayed out against my back is lightening up, and I can tell he's putting on the brakes. He's not letting this go too far, and dang it if that doesn't make me like him even more.

He slowly breaks the seal of our kiss, and I can't open my

eyes. They are too heavy and kiss-induced to function properly yet. His hand moves to cup my jaw, and I feel his thumb tenderly caress my cheek as he says, “Let’s take it slow, Evie.” The way he says it, though—with a low, raspy voice—knots my breath and instantly makes me wish we were still kissing.

But with my eyes shut, I nod my head in agreement because *I am* in agreement. In fact, I’m pretty sure that’s what kind of girl I am: the go-slow kind. The old-fashioned kind. The ring-on-her-finger kind. I say *pretty sure* because I honestly forgot there, for a minute, but now I’m emerging from the most devastating, tender, passionate kiss of my life, and I think I can remember my full name again.

I open my eyes and find Jake giving me a lopsided grin that says he knows what effect he’s just had on me.

“Slow,” I repeat back to him like English is not my first language and I’m trying to commit this new foreign word to memory.

He smiles bigger and shakes his head a little, stepping back, and taking all of his fantastic body with him. With the new, cool air comes the feeling of embarrassment. I can feel that my lips are swollen and my cheeks are pink, and just a minute ago, Jake felt the need to remind me that we should take things slow… which means he was aware that I had my blinker on and was ready to change over to the HOV lane. *Move over, slowpokes.*

But I push that embarrassment right back down because I know that Jake wanted that kiss too. He wanted the HOV lane. And the fact that a man like him—wonderful and handsome and a champion kisser—could have used this opportunity of my kiss coma for his own gain, but instead chose to restrain…well, that’s filling me with all sorts of warm feelings. I don’t want to let him go. I don’t want to lay my head on my pillow tonight and wonder or leave any room for doubt.

“Jake,” I say, reaching out and grabbing his hand before he fully turns away. He turns back, and his eyes say, *Why yes, I would love to kiss you some more.* For a moment, I think that sounds like a great idea, but I hurry and speak up before he or I get a chance to act on that thought. “What are we?” There we go. It’s out now.

His brows pull together, and a thoughtful expression clouds his eyes. “What do you mean?”

“I know this is only our first date, but…I guess…I don’t know.” A-plus conversational skills are happening over here. Really top-notch stuff.

The problem is, I’m scared. I’m scared that making him *Define The Relationship* will scare him off. Because in history, this is the moment all of my dates bail. It’s like they see me approaching with a giant, man-sized net and think, *No way am I getting trapped in that one.*

“You want to know where this is going?” he asks, and I can’t tell if he sounds hesitant or not.

“Yeah. I guess I do.”

He bites his lips together and nods. He turns away, and I think that maybe I’ve annoyed him, but when he shuts off the burner and takes whatever has been furiously boiling off of it, I realize he’s just getting settled in. He turns around and takes both of my hands, pulling me back up to his warm body, and I wrap both of my arms around his waist. I like this. I like that I get to do this. It feels natural and new—but also like we’ve been doing this forever.

Jake looks down at me and fills his broad chest with air and then lets it out. “I think our title would be dating. I like you. You like me. We’re making out in the kitchen but not going too fast too soon.”

“Right. Good. Yeah.” But see…that’s not the answer that I needed. I want to tell myself to just simmer down and enjoy the ride, but honestly, it’s not safe to drive in a car at night with your headlights off. I need to see where I’m going. “It’s just that…a guy at a restaurant asked me out earlier today, and I honestly didn't know if I should accept or turn him down, because I wasn't sure what this thing between us is. I know we are dating, but are we exclusive? Are we casual? Are we seeing other people?"

Jake's brows pull together tightly. I can't tell if he looks upset or is just giving it a lot of thought. I think guarded is probably the best description. "You got asked out?"

I nod.

He nods slowly, too, and then his expression changes to something lighter. He shrugs, and suddenly, he's Mr. Yeah-Everything's-Cool guy. "I think we should be non-exclusive. Casual."

Oh.

That was so not where I was hoping this heart-to-heart was going.

"Casual."

"Yeah." He smiles softly. "Like I said, I want to take this slow with you. We should just have fun and keep things light. Date. Get to know each other. But by all means, feel free to go out with other people." He lets go of me and heads over to pull two plates down from the cupboard.

I'm staring at him numbly, trying to decide if I'm okay with this or not. I feel let down. As much as I don't want to admit it, I was hoping that Jake—the man that feels so out of my league—saw something in me that made him want me all to himself. But of course he wants to be casual. He's just come out of a long relationship, and he wants some time to explore his options.

I don't like casual. I don't like open relationships because they lead to nothing but heartache for me. But I do like Jake, and I think he's beyond wonderful. So, am I willing to sacrifice my wants for this? Play it cool and see where it goes?

I don't know because, right now, I feel so disappointed that I just need a minute to let my frown loose.

Jake is fluttering casually around the kitchen, looking just as cool and collected as he did at the beginning of the night, and I'm pretty sure my shoulders are sagging. "I…need to wash my hands before we eat." Surely, he can't argue with good hygiene.

I think my voice might have trembled, though, because he looks over his shoulder with an inquisitive look. I don't wait around for him to ask me if I'm okay. I turn on my heels and make a mad dash for the bathroom and shut the door behind me. I lean against it and give myself the freedom to pout for a minute. *Just one little indulgent pity party.*

My mind bounces from that devastating kiss, to his proposal of a casual relationship, back to the kiss. See, this is why I'm old-fashioned. This is why I'm not the kind of girl to sleep around with guys for the fun of it. My heart dives in deep, and if I added the physical layer to it, I'd be shattered when he decided he was ready to move on.

While I'm in here, I decide to stall by going to the bathroom. It's when I'm seated on the porcelain throne that I realize my obnoxious and never-appreciated friend, Aunt Flow, has arrived early for her visit. Wonderful! Just wonderful. Because guess what? I know for a fact that I don't have any tampons on me because I DIDN'T BRING MY PURSE.

I want to groan at the injustice of the last half hour. It's fine, though. I'm fine. This isn't my first rodeo. It's not glamorous, but I know what to do here. I wrap toilet paper around my hand a few times until I've made a nice, scratchy and uncomfortable pad for myself to tuck into my underwear until I can get home.

I don't know if I'm relieved or disappointed that this date has to end early. On one hand, I'm happy that I'll have more time to think over the *casual* proposition, but I'm also sad to leave Jake. I've missed him this week.

Oh well. I have to go because I don't really care to free bleed on Jake's couch. Now, I just have to make up an excuse that will get me out of here without having to sacrifice my dignity.

CHAPTER TWENTY-THREE

JAKE

I've been nervously pacing the kitchen, waiting for Evie to come out of the bathroom. I have a bad feeling in the pit of my stomach that the conversation we just had did not come out in my favor. It might have just been in my head, but she seemed spooked before she went to the bathroom.

When I hear the bathroom door open but Evie doesn't come right into the kitchen, I round the corner and find her in the living room. She has Charlie's leash in one hand and her cell phone in the other. She's looking down and typing on it, but when I enter the room, her wide green eyes shoot up to me, and she offers an awkward smile.

"Oh hey, yeah, so I'm really sorry, but it turns out I've got to cut our dinner date short." *What?!* "I had something come up, and…it's kinda important. Well, actually it's *super* important, and I have to take care of it right away. I'm really sorry."

Jake, you freaking idiot! I knew that I played it too cool back there in the kitchen.

When Evie told me she was asked out by some random dude,

I freaked out inside. That situation is exactly why I've been hesitant to date someone as young and gorgeous as Evie. But then, I thought about it and realized she had given me the perfect excuse to have my cake and eat it too. I could date her. I could enjoy time with her. I could kiss her. But as long as I never mentally plan to commit to this woman, I'll be okay. I can't lose someone I never really had.

But right now, seeing her frantically typing on her phone… I'm thinking that I made a mistake.

"Don't go," I say, reaching out to cover her phone with my hand. "Or…at least give me two minutes."

Her eyes hit mine, and there is a look of finality in them that makes my stomach twist. "Definitely not. I need to go."

Wow. I must have really butchered that conversation more than I realized.

I feel a little desperate. I tried to play it cool earlier, and clearly that didn't work, so now it's time to let it all hang out. "Evie, I know I made it seem like I couldn't care less about this relationship, but here's the truth: I really like you. I like you so much that it scares me. The last woman I cared for left me high and dry after nine years of marriage. I'm still a little banged up and scarred. I want to have a relationship with you because I think you're incredible, and gorgeous, and smart, and…" She looks so shocked right now that I'm scared I'm coming off a little stalkerish, but I keep going because I've opened the gates and the truth is all flooding out. "…way too good for me. But I have a lot of baggage, and honestly, I wouldn't blame you if you want to split right now. I've been playing it cool, but I'm scared of putting myself out there to have something real again. That's why I'm not ready for anything serious. I don't want to punish you by making you turn down other dates when I'm not ready for anything—"

"Jake!" Evie cuts off my long-winded monologue with a small chuckle. I don't really know what's funny about what I just said—laying my heart out on the line like that and all—but she chuckles, nonetheless. "You didn't have to say any of that." She shrugs and shakes her head. "I'm not leaving because I was mad or offended. I'm leaving because I just started my period early, and I don't have any tampons with me."

What? Her statement sinks in, and I feel my shoulders relax. "You started your period?"

She looks embarrassed as she nods, a tense smile on her mouth.

I stare, blinking at Evie and trying to wrap my mind around this new turn of events. Evie is not upset. She never was. I didn't have to pour my heart out to her. She was fine with casual.

She clears her throat and folds her arms. "So, can I call an Uber now? Since…ya know, I still don't have any tampons with me?"

"Oh." I snap back to life and take her phone out of her hands and toss it onto the couch. "No."

She sighs. "I don't think you fully understand my predicament."

I grab her hand, dragging her toward the guest bathroom. Once inside, I open the linen closet, revealing three shelves fully stocked with every kind of maxi pad and tampon known to man —or woman. I wave my hand over the selection like I'm Vanna White.

"Ta-da," I say and then feel really stupid. Is it weird to be proud of your selection of feminine hygiene products?

Her mouth falls open. "Why do you have a closet full of pads and tampons?"

"My sisters are never prepared, and I got sick of making tampon runs when they would come over to hang out or watch Sam. I decided to just stock my house. And it'll come in handy when Sam…well, you know."

She laughs and stares at the closet. "I've never been so jealous of anything in my life. I'm so cheap that I always buy the smallest boxes possible like I might not get a period next month." She pauses and looks at me hesitantly. "Was that TMI?"

I laugh. "Evie, I have four sisters, a mother, a ten-year-old daughter, and I was married for nine years. I'm very aware that you have a period, and I'm not at all embarrassed by it. You shouldn't be either."

She quirks a brow at me. "Are you about to give me a speech on feminism and how I should be proud of my womanly body and its functions?"

I let my gaze travel the length of her, and when my eyes meet hers again, I say, "You definitely should be proud of your body."

She shoves my chest with a guttural laugh. "If anyone but you said that to me, I would show him the new skills I've learned in my self-defense class."

"So, what you're saying is, I can deliver a line better than any other man in the world?"

"Okay, get out."

I agree, but not before leaning down to kiss her rosy cheek. "We're good?"

She smiles, brushes her wavy hair behind her ear, and I swear she's the most beautiful woman I've ever seen. "We're great. But we're going to have a whole different problem soon if you don't get out of here and let me steal one of these tampons."

I lean in a little closer and drop my voice to whisper seductively against her ear. "If you're lucky…I'll even let you take home a whole box."

She pretends to shiver. "I thought you didn't want to be my sugar daddy?"

"I'll be whatever you want me to be, Evie Jones." I said that in a serious tone because I am serious. In that moment where I thought she was going to walk out my door and out of my life, I was ready to throw all my fears out the window and tell her I'll do serious. I would have made a Facebook profile just so I could change my status to *In A Relationship* to make her happy.

Her dark-green eyes lock with mine, and she raises up on her tiptoes to lay the softest, most alluring kiss on my mouth. It's not nearly long enough. "And I'm happy to take things slow for you, Jake. I'm glad you were honest with me."

And this, people, is what a healthy relationship looks like. And yeah…I'm feeling hopeful about a woman for the first time in a year. The question is, how long will it last?

CHAPTER TWENTY-FOUR

EVIE

It's 9:30 PM and Jake and I have moved outside to swing on his back porch. The night is warm, and the stars are bright against the black backdrop of the sky. We leave the porch lights off and decide to swing with the moon as our only light. It's romantic and quiet and still.

When we sit down on the swing, Jake reaches over and pulls me closer, wrapping his arm around my shoulder. I've learned that he's an affectionate man, and I still can't believe I get to know that about him. I also like his deodorant. I briefly wonder if I could get away with using some before I leave without him noticing. That's creepy, right? Yeah, let's forget I considered it.

Jake picks up his phone again and checks the screen. He's had that thing glued to him all night, and if I didn't know the real reason he was checking it so much, I'd be worried he was waiting for a booty call from another woman. But I don't say anything about it because I know that he's just worried about Sam.

It strikes me how different this first date is from all of the others I've been on. Not only have we already made out in the kitchen and discussed my menstrual cycle, but usually on a first date, I would *maybe* be holding his hand with about twelve inches still neatly placed between the sides of our thighs (make room for the Holy Spirit as Grandmama used to say). But as it is, Jake has me tucked in so close to his side that I'm pretty much sitting on his lap. (Sorry, Grandmama.)

I feel like a little bunny rabbit, so I nestle in a little closer to his stupidly defined side and sigh with contentment inside my burrow.

"Sam's going to be just fine," I say when I catch him checking his phone again.

"I know."

"Do you?"

"No. I'm lying. If you weren't here to tether me to this porch swing, I'd probably already be in my truck, halfway to Jenna's house to get her back."

I reach across him and lace my fingers in his. His hands are calloused and warm. "Just say the word and I'll handcuff you to this swing."

He looks down at me with a big fat smirk. "Oh really? So now I know you're a butt girl AND a little kinky."

I poke him hard in the side, and he laughs. "Not like that, you weirdo."

How is it so easy with him? It's not supposed to feel like this. We're supposed to feel awkward and uncomfortable, and by now on a date, I'm usually texting Jo an "SOS" so she'll call and say my house is on fire and I need to come put it out.

Instead, I'm rubbing my thumb across the back of Jake's knuckles and wondering if he'd be scared if I asked to go ahead and move in? Truth is, I'm falling head over heels for this man, and it's scaring me to death. He wants to go slow. And I want to punch the gas. I feel safe with Jake, and the sensation is entirely new for me.

But I've watched enough movies and dated enough jerks to know that something is probably waiting around the corner to jump out and bite me. Maybe I don't have to take a turn at all, though. No corners. No dark hallways. And I definitely don't have to walk through any creepy doors that would have the audience yelling, *"Don't go in there, you idiot!!"*

I think Jake and I have this dating thing figured out. We're being adults, communicating through our issues, and honestly, I'm really proud of us.

I sit up a little and pull my knees up on the swing to be more eye level with Jake. He holds me tight, though, saying with his body, "*Uh-uh-uh. You're not going anywhere, you sexy lady."* I added the "sexy lady" bit to boost my own confidence. Don't judge.

"Let's play a game to distract you from worrying about Sam," I say, turning my torso to face him.

He smiles and picks up my legs and drapes them over his lap. So, *WHOA*. I guess he's feeling comfortable on this first date, too. I can hear my grandmama trying to remind me of the Holy Spirit, but I remind her—as every dutiful Southern child would —that the good Lord lives in my heart.

"What sort of game?" His blue eyes are sparking, and my whole body flushes. I can see his mind working, and honestly, it's not fair. These mixed signals are torture. We're playing tug of war between *fast* and *slow,* but I can't keep up with who's tugging for which end. What happens if we both give up?

Chills race across my arms, and I dust them off with my hands.

"It's called the honesty game."

"So, truth or dare?" Would he quit talking like that? In that deep, sexy, husky tone that's dripping with innuendos?

"Noooo," I say, tugging on the *slow* side of the rope. "Just the truth game. It goes like this: one of us asks a question, and the other answers truthfully."

He nods thoughtfully. "Yeah. So just basically talking, then? I don't think you can call it a game if one of us isn't daring the other to take off their clothes and jump in the pool if we don't want to answer the question."

I gasp and give him a big poke in the side again (because let's face it, I like feeling his obliques). "You wouldn't! I thought you were a gentleman."

He chuckles and grips my legs as he squirms away from my tickling pokes. "I would soooo dare you to skinny dip."

"I thought you were wanting to take this whole thing slow."

"Want? No. Will? Yes." Why am I let down by that? I want to smack myself with a ruler. *Behave, Evie.*

I'm supposed to be grateful for the good guys who want to respect me. I'm supposed to respect myself enough to make sure men do, too. Girl power. Feminism. And something else about milk and cows that I can't remember anymore because Jake is now massaging my feet. Like WHAT? What man does this on a first date? How is he so good at knowing what a woman really wants? I think I'm half in love with him already.

"Are you feeling okay? Need a heating pad or anything?"

Never mind. It's full-on love.

"I'm okay, thanks." What I really want is to get inside Jake's head and learn everything I can about him. I think the idea of the truth game freaked him out a little, and that's why he was side-stepping it with a joke. But guess what? I like to wave at the relationship *no-no* stop signs as I'm speeding by them. "Okay, first question: why did you get divorced?"

Jake's eyebrows raise, and he swivels his face to give me a disbelieving stare. "Wow. You didn't waste any time with that one."

"I like to live on the dangerous side."

Jake takes in a full breath and lets it out. "Can I just take off my clothes and jump in the pool instead?"

Not picturing that. Not picturing that. Not picturing that.

Shoot. I pictured it. And YEP. I'm debating letting him do it now. "No. You've gotta answer."

He winces and then settles back against the swing, busying himself while he talks by rubbing his hand up and down my leg. Not distracting at all. "All right, here it is. I didn't really date in high school. I was more focused on my grades and sports than girls. My mom likes to say it was because I was a really great kid —but actually, it was because we didn't have any hot girls in my grade."

I laugh and give him ten points for honesty.

"When I graduated and started college, I met this really forward girl. She was"—Jake takes on a distant look that kinda makes me feel jealous, but I decide to chill—"physically attractive and had a sort of larger-than-life attitude. She drew me in with her beauty and charm, and I fell for her fast and hard. I proposed after only a month of dating, and she said yes. We set the wedding date for six months after I proposed, and she was already two months pregnant with Sam on our wedding day."

"Whoa," I say with an awkward smile. I think I was secretly hoping for one of those divorce stories where he realized instantly that she wasn't the right woman for him, and he's been miserable for the last nine years. Yeah, I know, that was kind of gross of me to think. But I never claimed to be a saint.

"Yeah. It was intense. And honestly, those first few years were great. We were so wrapped up in each other and our newlywed bliss that it felt like nothing could stop us. I graduated from college, and Natalie, Sam, and I moved to Texas so I could work at a big-box architecture firm. Natalie decided to drop out of school right after she had Sam, so she never finished her teaching degree. After about five years of marriage, things started to get really rocky. I decided that I wanted to branch out and open my own firm—and also that I missed my family and wanted to be closer to them.

"We moved here to Charleston, and money was really tight

for the first two years of getting my firm off the ground. Natalie grew restless, so she started spending more and more time at the gym. She became a Pilates instructor, and then it was like, before I knew it, we were never seeing each other anymore. Natalie would still spend time with Sam, but not much. I felt guilty, thinking that maybe Natalie was so restless because she gave up her dreams to stay home with Sam while I went after mine, so I started taking over the brunt of the parenting responsibilities.

"Things just got worse, and she became more and more distant. She completely changed her appearance and lost like thirty pounds. It was like she was always chasing a happiness that I couldn't give her. Finally, last year, she told me that she met someone else who could give her the life I couldn't." He laughs a mirthless laugh. "He was a pilot." Jake finally looks at me. "Turns out, it's not just me who can't give her the life she wants. She's had three serious relationships in the past year."

"Wow. Jake. I'm so sorry. That sounds…terrible. You and Sam deserve better than that."

He shrugs. "Sam does, for sure."

I take his hand in mine. "You do, too."

"I wasn't perfect, Evie. No failed marriage is the result of one person."

I know he's right. But I also know Jake, and I'm sure that he's done nothing but beat himself up for his mistakes this past year and replayed a thousand different scenarios where he could have done better. I think right now he just needs someone on his side that can scoop him up off the ground, dust him off, and say *try again*.

But then again, maybe that's just me being selfish, because I really want Jake to try again…with me.

It breaks my heart to see how sad Jake looks right now, so I decide to lighten the mood. "Yeah. You're right. I think if you would have just sacrificed a little and gotten butt implants or something for her, it would have solved your problems."

Jake barks out a laugh and shakes his head at me. "You and butts."

I don't know how this has become my thing, but now I'm 100% certain that if Jake and I make this work, he's going to buy me a mug for Christmas that says *I like big butts and I cannot lie*. I'll worry about that bridge when I have to cross it.

"So," he says, giving me a vulnerable smile that melts me a little. "Now that you know all the baggage I'm carrying, do you still want to date me?"

I feign a look of contemplation for a second before my eyes shift to him, and I lean in slowly to place a soft kiss on his mouth. I hear him take in a breath through his nose, and his hand lands on my jaw. But then, before things get too interesting, he groans and breaks the seal of our lips. He's smiling and shaking his head. "Oh, no you don't. You're not going to distract me out of my turn."

"Shoot. I thought that was going to work." I lean my shoulder against the swing. "Fine. Do your worst."

"Tell me about your relationship with your parents." *Ouch.* So this is how it feels when someone goes right for the kill.

I scrunch my nose and try to decide where to start. Fifth-grade talent show, when my mama scolded me all the way home for missing the high note and coming in third? Nah. Instead, I tell Jake what it was like growing up in a house with parents who only care about money and status. I told him how the only time my mama ever showed me any affection was when we were in public and a woman that appeared to have better domestic skills was watching. "And now, they are trying to freeze me out. If I'm poor enough and hungry enough, they think I'll come to my senses and marry Tyler. But the joke is on them, because I know how to make a pack of Ramen noodles last a whole week."

"Which reminds me, I grilled an extra steak for you to take home." He just keeps getting better.

"Careful. I'm like a stray cat. If you feed me, I might keep coming back."

"That's what I'm hoping for." He smiles, and my stomach turns inside out.

"Anyways, I just decided that if I'm never going to be good enough for them, I might as well have them be disappointed in me for doing something I love rather than living a life that makes me feel like crap."

He reaches up and runs his hand through my hair. The look on his face says he's wanted to do that all night—maybe even since he met me. "Evie, let me say what your parents are too stupid to recognize: you're an incredible woman."

I'm not good with compliments. It's either because I'm not used to hearing them, or because I've heard so much criticism over the course of my life that I can't believe the good things people tell me, but either way, I want to throw my hands up and bat away those compliments like I'm Babe Ruth. "Eh. I'm messy, and forgetful, and I don't like greens."

Jake's eyes grow serious, and I'm sure he's about to try to convince me of my merits, so I stand up abruptly and smooth out my shirt. "It's getting late. I better call an Uber. Charlie's getting antsy."

Jake lifts his brows and glances around me. I follow his gaze to my traitorous dog who's curled up in a comfy little ball by the porch railing. "You're right. He looks super anxious."

"Yep. This is how he manifests anxiety. He looks chill, but believe me, inside, he's fit to be tied."

Now, run, Evie.

Jake grabs my hand and pulls me to a stop. "Why are you getting squirmy again?" He stands up and invades my space.

"I'm not," I lie. I'm squirming because Jake is the first man in a long time that I've wanted to look into my eyes and convince me that I'm worth something. I really can feel myself falling for him, and falling in love with someone on a first date is definitely not *slow* material.

"Stay with me tonight," he says quietly. *Well, that's definitely not going to help anything either.* "Not like that. I just mean, stay here tonight. We can stay up all night talking, or watching a movie, or whatever. I just…I won't get many chances like this to spend time with you without Sam, and I want to take advantage of every minute I get."

I should go home. I should NOT stay.

Ohhhhh, but I want to stay. Staying sounds like a dream. And Charlie does look awfully comfortable. What kind of a heartless terrorist would I be to wake my sleeping pup when he looks that comfy?

Jake squeezes my hand, willing me to say yes. I'm opening my mouth to say just that when our attention is distracted by the sudden buzzing of his phone.

He lets go of my hand and darts to his phone. Noticing the number, his eyes flash worry at mine. "It's Jenna's parents."

"Answer it!"

He puts the phone to his ear, and I can see the worry and dread filling his face. "Will. Is everything okay?" He listens for a minute, giving away no hints of what Will is saying. I wish I had asked him to put it on speaker. Is Sam okay? Did she have a seizure?

There is a silent panic I've never felt before welling up in my heart.

Jake mumbles a few mmhmm's and then says, "I'll be right over." He hangs up, and his shoulders relax. "She's fine. She didn't have a seizure, but she wants to come home."

I sigh, feeling deep relief. What is this feeling? I'm worried about how my heart seems to be tying itself to not only Jake, but his daughter. "Whew. That's good."

He gives me an apologetic smile, and I already know what

he's going to say, so I hold up my hand. "Don't apologize. I was going to decline your offer to stay, anyway."

He gives me a look that says he doesn't believe me one bit. "Yeah, okay."

"I was! Jacob Broaden, I am a Southern woman of great moral principle. If you think I can be easily seduced by your pretty blue eyes, you'll be sorely disappointed."

He laughs and wraps an arm around me, pulling me up close to him. "Come with me to get Sam. I can drop you off at your apartment after."

"You sure?"

He smiles and nods slowly before releasing me. He helps me gather all of my things, and Charlie, and the extra food bag that looks suspiciously less like "an extra steak" and a lot more like a full bag of groceries. I should turn him down, but…I don't want to. I think I even see the box of tampons I opened earlier on the top, and I smile to myself.

CHAPTER TWENTY-FIVE

JAKE

Evie and I pull up outside of Jenna's house, and the door immediately flies open. Out comes Sam and Daisy, waving to Jenna's parents who are decked out in stupid matching robes and slippers. They have their initials monogrammed on them (the robes and slippers), and they are giving Sam a pitying look as she barrels toward my truck.

I open the door and get out to help Sam and Daisy in and then wave back at Will and his wife, Beth.

Beth calls out, "So sorry you had to come all the way here in the middle of the night, Jake." Okay, well, it's ten o'clock, so not exactly the middle now is it, Mrs. Exaggeration? "We tried to get her to stay, but she wasn't having it." Beth's voice annoys me for some reason. I think it's because she's looking at Sam like she thought it was a bad idea to invite her in the first place. It's a pitying *I-told-you-so* look. As if my daughter is the first young girl in the history of girls to want to leave a sleepover early.

"No problem, Beth. I was glad to come get her."

"Oh," she says suddenly, tilting her head to get a better look through my window. "Sorry, I just noticed you have a friend with you." She's squinting hard, trying to get a good look at Evie, and I just wave and shut my truck door so the tinted windows will hide Evie's face.

Beth is queen of the rumor mill at Sam's school. She's on the board and is also the cheer coach. That woman doesn't like for anything to happen without her express knowledge and permission. I can see her chomping at the bit to catch a glimpse of my young, hot date so she can text everyone in her circle of moms that I now have hussies (that would be her word, not mine) sleeping over at my house, and no one should trust their daughters in my care anymore.

"Night! Thanks again," I say, opening the truck door and slipping in quickly before Beth gets a peek at my mysterious woman inside. I think I'd make a good bodyguard if this architect thing doesn't work out, because Beth isn't awarded even the tiniest glimpse of Evie.

The moment I turn the key and start the engine, Evie leans over to me and says quietly, "Stupid robes, right?"

I wish I could kiss her right now, but I don't know how Sam would feel about that. "You don't like the matchy-matchy couple style?"

She grimaces and shakes her head before turning her whole body around in her seat to face Sam like she always does. It's not safe in the least, but it's sweet, so I allow it. "How's it going, darlin'? Everything okay?"

I was literally opening my mouth to ask that very question. Why do I like it so much that she beat me to it? I shut my mouth and look in the rearview mirror to catch Sam's answer, but her downcast expression worries me.

"I'm sorry, Evie. I tried. I really thought it would be fun. But…I just couldn't stop feeling scared and wanting to go home."

"Oh, Sam. Why are you apologizing to me for that?"

She shrugs. "Because I know that that's why I have Daisy—to make me feel more comfortable and keep going on with my normal life like you do with Charlie. But even though I had her by me, and I knew she'd do her job, I just still kept feeling scared that I would have a seizure while I was sleeping. I just felt nervous and wanted to go home." She pauses and looks at me now. "I'm sorry I put up such a big fight to go, Daddy."

Her words pierce me. She thinks I'm going to be disappointed that she came home?

No way. I think she's brave as heck for even fighting to go in the first place. Once again, I'm about to say all of this when I notice Evie unclick her seatbelt and start climbing over the center console to get in the backseat with Sam. For a split second, her butt is in the air beside me, and I have to remember to concentrate on the road.

She settles in beside Sam and wraps an arm around her shoulders. The sight shakes me, and I feel speechless now.

"Listen to me, darlin', and remember this for the rest of your life: it's always okay to go home. Anytime you feel uncomfortable or scared, never worry about what anyone else is going to think if you call your daddy and have him come get you. Your house is a safe place, and you love being there, and that's something to be proud of, not embarrassed about."

A car honks at me, and I realize I've nearly just sat through a whole green light as I'm listening to Evie give my daughter the best speech I've ever heard. I kind of just want to roll down my window and wave the jerk behind me to go on by. Can't he see that I'm having a moment here?

"You're not disappointed in me?" Sam asks Evie, not me.

It also strikes me that Sam is not even questioning why Evie is in the car. It's like she knew she would be. Like she's a part of our life now. How do I feel about that?

Evie squeezes Sam. "Never. I'm so stinkin' proud of you for even giving it a try. Do you know that it took me a whole six months with Charlie before I felt brave enough to go anywhere without a friend with me? But there was nothing wrong with that either. We all find our bravery at different times, and that's perfectly fine."

Sam smiles and settles her head on Evie's shoulder. "Thanks, Evie."

"Anytime, sweetie." She kisses the top of Sam's head and brushes her hair away from her face.

The sight is tearing me up inside. In my little rectangular mirror, I see the most perfect picture of a woman that doesn't have to be here, caring for my little girl who adores her, and their service dogs on either side of them.

Evie connects with Sam in a way that I will never be able to. This should upset me, but for some reason, it relieves me. Maybe I won't have to do everything on my own after all. Maybe Sam will get to have a mother that cares for her like she deserves.

And dang it.

Those thoughts do not sound casual. They sound a lot like commitment.

CHAPTER TWENTY-SIX

EVIE

The morning after the best date of my life, I'm trying hard to focus while training a handful of our volunteers how to teach the newest batch of puppies to walk with loose leashes. But I can't keep my brain from wandering off back to last night and how it felt to sit on Jake's counter and kiss him.

"Evie, is this okay?" asks a volunteer.

"Yeah, it's fine," I reply, still in a daze until I realize that the pup is practically dragging the woman across the lawn to chase a butterfly. I snap into action, gaining both the puppy's and the volunteer's attention, and I quickly run back over the instructions on how to get the puppies to mind their manners on the leash.

We go on and on like this for a time, and I can't seem to keep myself from checking my phone every couple of minutes to see if Jake has texted me. Wow. I'm pathetic. I've gone from an independent woman to a needy girlfriend overnight. Actually, I'm not even his girlfriend. Just a needy girl with a Texas-sized crush on the guy she's seeing.

Finally, the workday is over, and I'm on my way home. I feel so let down from not hearing from Jake that I think my arms are actually dragging on the ground as I walk. There's sad music playing in my head, and I'm just about to break out in a melancholy ballad and let my hands drag across a field of wheat when I hear my phone ringing in my purse.

I pause on the sidewalk right outside of a bakery and grab my phone out of my purse. I don't even look at the caller ID because I'm certain that it's Jake. I think we have that special telekinesis that couples get when they've been together a long time. Technically, we've only been together for the span of one date (which was last night), but we connected on such a deep level that I don't think we need the same amount of time that other people do to develop couple superpowers.

"Hellllоооо." My flirtatious tone is dialed up to ten.

"Evelyn Grace, why do you sound like an inappropriate phone operator of some sort?" Ugh. Mama. Apparently, Jake and I do need a little more time for those superpowers to kick in.

"How would you even know what one of those ladies sounds like, Mama?"

She's quiet for a second, and I take that opportunity to give myself a tally in the book of Evie vs. Melony I started a few years ago. My therapist says it's not healthy, but what does she really know, anyways?

Mama apparently doesn't have a good rebuttal for that question, so she decides not to answer it. "I'm sure you're busy petting puppies, so I'll make this quick." I think she has a tally book too and is probably adding a tick to her column right now, but she would be wrong. That one didn't even hurt, because *ha ha,* the joke's on her, I already did my puppy petting this morning, and it was a lovely way to spend my time as well as an important part of socializing the new pups.

I decide to sit on the bench outside of the bakery to finish this chat instead of continuing my walk home, because I have a feeling that I'm going to need some carb therapy after I hang up. "Very kind of you to consider my time," I say and lean over to pet Charlie's head.

"I'll cut right to the chase. I want you to come to the house for dinner tomorrow night."

"Umm thanks, but no thanks."

"If you would have let me finish, you would have heard why I want you to come to dinner."

I wince and shut my eyes because I can smell a Melony Jones special coming down the line. A fancy dinner that costs more than my whole week's worth of groceries, dessert that melts in my mouth, and a big ol' helping of manipulation on the side.

"I would like for you to come to dinner because your daddy and I have decided to make a sizable donation to your little dog business." Yep. There it is.

"Actually, our dogs are pretty large," I say, but Mama doesn't snicker because I don't think she knows how to laugh at a joke. Jake would have laughed. I let out a long sigh and decide to be serious to get this over with faster. "A donation would be great. Feel free to make one at the benefit."

A family is walking by me, and I can see that they so badly want to stop and pet Charlie. Most people are pretty good about not storming up to pet him without permission. But occasionally, I get a few who don't understand that he is a working dog and will get right down on the ground and start loving on him without my consent. It's hard. Not only because it usually makes me have to stop whatever I'm doing, but because it distracts Charlie when I need him to be his most alert. But I try to give everyone as much grace as possible since I know it's difficult to ignore a dog as adorable and fluffy as Charlie.

But I'd be lying if I said I'm not relieved, though, when the family passes by me without stopping.

"Well, of course, we will make a donation at the benefit, but we would also like to make a special donation separate from the fundraiser." Oh, Mama. I wish so badly she would stop trying to pull these puppet strings all day. I'm tired of dancing for her.

I'm halfway tempted to turn down her offer, but I can't. We're desperate for the money. More money means more dogs we can give away to those who need them. I would feel terrible knowing that I had to turn someone away who couldn't afford the high-ticket price of our dogs because I was too insecure to have dinner with my parents. "And I'm guessing there is no way you would consider just mailing us a check?"

Mama makes a scoffing sound. "You know, Evelyn, you are starting to sound rather ungrateful for my offer. Maybe we won't give an additional donation since it sounds as if you're not in great need after all."

I sigh so loudly I'm sure it sounds like a windstorm on Mama's end. Looks like I'm going to be dancing tomorrow night. "All right, all right, I'll be there. What time?"

I can practically hear the wrinkles creasing around my mama's mouth as her lips form a smug smile. "Dinner is at 7:00. And please, for heaven's sake, be punctual. We will have a few other important guests at dinner who I'm sure would be more than happy to pull out their checkbooks if you make a good impression. So, come wearing that winning smile I taught you back in your pageant days and a dress with a hemline that hits below the knee." There is no doubt in my mind that this is all one big trap. I wish I knew what it was so I could be prepared before I get caught in it.

"I'll be sure and pick up my nun costume from the dry cleaner."

"Evelyn Grace, don't you da—"

I hang up, and my phone immediately starts ringing again.

"I wasn't serious. I don't even own a nun costume," I say, standing up and starting to walk home. I don't feel like eating my feelings anymore. My stomach is twisting uncomfortably now that I know I have to go to my parents' house for dinner.

"That's too bad. I bet you'd make a sexy nun."

It's Jake!

"Ha! We do have telekinesis."

"What?"

"Nothing. What's up?" I realize I'm practically skipping down the sidewalk now. That's what the sound of Jake's voice does to me: turns me into a skipper.

"I was just calling to see if you have plans tomorrow night. And before you say anything, I know I'm supposed to wait 48 hours before asking you out on a second date, but this is Sam's fault. She wants you to come over and watch a movie with us. It has nothing to do with me wanting to spend more time with you."

I stop skipping and groan because now I'm doubly upset that my mama has manipulated me into going to dinner. "I wish I could, but I have dinner plans tomorrow night."

"Oh. A hot date?" he asks in a playful tone, but I can tell he's only half joking. My heart swells a little that he's jealous of me going on a date with another man.

"Far from it. I'm being forced to go to a dinner party at my parents' house because they are evil overlords who have too much money."

"Gotcha. Okay, so do you want some company then? I can have June come stay with Sam." He's offering to go with me? I didn't even really give him a valid reason, and he's willing to go with me anyway?

"It's going to be torture."

"Will you be there?"

I laugh. "Yeah."

"Then it'll be worth it."

Yep. I'm a goner. I am no match for this man. He makes me feel wanted and valued in a way that I didn't even know existed.

As scary as it is, I'm starting to picture a future with Jake. One where, after forty years of marriage, he still pinches my butt in the kitchen.

Charlie looks up and sees my dreamy expression and shakes his head at me. I think he really is getting jealous now.

"All right then, yes. I'd love for you to come with me."

We continue to talk for my whole walk home, and before I know it, I'm lying on my couch and twirling my hair around my finger while Jake tells me about his day. Yes, he's made me a hair twirler too. Don't worry, I'm fully aware of how annoying I am to be around now.

Finally, he asks for details about what he should wear tomorrow night and what time we need to be leaving my house to get to my parents' place. I tell him 6:30, to which he replies, "Great. I'll be there at 6:15 so I can mess up your lipstick a little before we go."

I'm having so much fun in this flirty bubble with Jake that, at first, I don't even realize that Charlie has suddenly stood up and come to sit in front of me, staring. It's not a normal stare. It's a direct look that he only ever uses when he needs my attention most. My chuckle dies out, and dread takes its place. I know this look. I've seen it many times.

"Hang on, Jake," I say, and I think he can hear the worry in my voice, because he starts asking if everything is okay. I ignore him and focus on Charlie who is now whining, and I know it's not because he needs to go potty.

Annoyed that I'm not acting on his signals, Charlie takes his alerting to the next level. He takes the hem of my dress into his mouth and starts tugging me. I blow out a breath through my mouth, because now I'm certain that Charlie is alerting me of an oncoming seizure.

I know what he's telling me to do. "All right, buddy, I'm coming," I say to Charlie, and I follow our usual procedure and get down on a clear spot on the floor. I probably could lie on the couch or my bed, but I'm always worried that I'll convulse myself out of the bed and hit my head on the floor. Living on my own, I like to be more careful than necessary when it comes to my seizures. So, I lie on my back and take a deep breath. It doesn't matter how many times I've gone through this, though, it never gets less scary.

"Jake."

"What's wrong, Evie?"

"Charlie just alerted me. I'm going to have a seizure." My voice shakes even though I'm trying so hard to put on a brave face. I'm going to be okay. Charlie will watch out for me. Once I lose consciousness and begin convulsing, I know that Charlie will move me onto my side to keep me safe. He'll go push the button on the wall that calls Jo and then come back to stay with me and lick my face to bring me back into consciousness faster. Even now, he's going to the fridge and using the tug rope to pull it open and retrieve a water bottle for me for after the seizure.

When Jake speaks, he sounds as heavy as I feel. "How long do you think until it starts?"

"He always alerts me ten to thirty minutes before an episode."

"Okay." I hear him rustling papers around frantically. "I'm on my way from the office, so it won't take me long to get there."

"What?!" I start to sit up, but Charlie doesn't like it and tugs me back down. I comply. "Jake, you don't have to do that. I'll be all right. I'll call you later, once everything passes."

"Evie." His voice is deep and means business. If my heart rate wasn't already high from nervousness, it would be elevated for a whole different reason. "I want to. Please let me come over."

Honestly, I'm contemplating saying no. I'm nervous. What if he gets here in time to see the episode? I've never filmed myself, so I don't know what I look like during a seizure, but I've seen it reenacted by mean boys enough times to get a pretty good idea.

Jake has seen Sam's seizures, so it won't be totally foreign to him, but what if seeing me this way changes the way I look to him? I might be less attractive. Or he'll realize that I'll just be more of a burden in his life.

You might be thinking I'm overreacting here. I'm not. These fears have all evolved out of past experiences.

The truth is, Tyler Murray and I dated from freshman to junior year of high school. And remember those jocks that made fun of me for the way I convulsed during a seizure in class? Yeah, Tyler was one of them. Actually, first, he broke up with me, and then he made fun of me with his buddies.

I never told my parents about that day (and the weeks he spent reenacting my seizures in the hallway when I'd pass by) because I was too embarrassed—ashamed over something I couldn't control.

Later, when Tyler and I graduated, and before he moved away, he tried to get back together with me (most likely because his parents were beginning to convince him of the merit of marrying a Jones by that point), and when I turned him down because of how he treated me our junior year, he said the teasing was all good-natured fun and he didn't mean any harm by it.

It didn't feel good-natured to me. And to this day, he's never actually apologized for what he did.

Point is, it's stuck with me all this time, and I'm legitimately afraid that if Jake comes over and sees me like that, it will put an end to our relationship before it ever gets going. But then, I remember my own advice to Sam. *"If you think that these girls will be mean to you if you have a seizure, don't go—they're not worth your friendship."*

Jake is worth it.

I'm just about to tell him to come over when I hear Jake's keys jingle and he says, "Like it or not, I'm on my way."

I take a deep breath and shut my eyes. I guess that's that then. I put my arm over Charlie and wait.

I had a seizure; I know that much. Everything feels a little foggy, and my arms and legs are heavy. I'm coming out of the seizure, and everything feels like a dream where life is a blurry haze. I don't know how long ago I had it, but I know that I'm in the postictal phase and that I probably won't feel like myself again for a while. All I want to do is sleep.

Suddenly, I hear a voice. "Are we all clear, Charlie?" And I realize it's Jake. I peek open my eyelids, but they feel so heavy. The nausea is pretty intense too, so I shut them again. "That was a good boy," I hear Jake say, and I picture him petting Charlie's head.

The next thing I know, I feel a warmth over the side of my body, and Jake's voice is close. "You're okay, Evie. I'm here, and you're safe. I'm going to move you up onto your bed so you can rest, okay?"

I nod slowly because, really, that's all I feel like I can do yet. And then I feel Jake's hands slide under my body and he cradles me close to his chest. He's warm, and I wish I could stay in his arms forever. He's like a heating pad but even better because I don't have to plug him in to the wall.

Jake lays me down gently on my bed and pulls my comforter up over me. I feel the weight of the bed shift, and although my arms feel like they weigh a million pounds, I reach out and find his hand. "Stay with me," I say quietly.

I don't open my eyes because sleep is so alluring right now. But then I feel the bed sink beside me and Jake's glorious warmth engulf me. He smells like his cologne today. It's a clean, masculine fragrance that I hope never washes out of my linens. His big arm wraps around my torso and pulls me up close to him.

I feel tiny and safe in his arms. He brushes a stray hair out of my face and tucks it behind my ear before I feel him place a soft kiss on my temple.

I don't know how long he's been here. I don't know if he saw the seizure. But I do know that he's lying beside me right now and tenderly caring for me. He's not running for the hills.

CHAPTER TWENTY-SEVEN

JAKE

Evie is asleep in my arms, and I'm very aware of the feeling of never wanting to let her go. I got here on the tail end of her seizure and in enough time to see her body jolting with movement. My heart broke for her. Charlie did his job perfectly, but now that it's over, I'm stepping in and holding her as close as she'll let me for as long as she'll let me.

Yeah, I'm doing great with this whole taking-it-slow thing. Completely casual. No strings attached. Just call me *Casual Friday* because I am so chill about our relationship it's ridiculous. In no way am I stroking her long blonde hair away from her face and contemplating proposing here and now. She smells so good, too. Her soft feminine curves are curled up against me, and I can feel my heart splitting open. I have a feeling I'll be handing it to her on a silver platter before long.

When she told me she was about to have a seizure, it was like the world stopped spinning and all that mattered was getting to Evie as quick as possible. It's the same way I feel about Sam. Well, not the exact way. The same protectiveness. The same worry. But definitely not the same affection. I don't think I need to describe to you all the ways that it differs.

Evie makes a little groaning sound in her sleep, and I wonder if she has a migraine. Sam always gets a migraine after her seizures. But I see a water bottle with fresh condensation dripping down the side and a bottle of headache medicine on the bedside table. I know from talking to Evie and learning about all the ways she trained Charlie to aid her that he was the one to fetch her those necessities.

Has she taken the meds yet? I'll ask her when she's more coherent.

Charlie hears the groan and comes to stand beside the bed on Evie's side. He rests his head on the mattress and slices those big brown eyes up at me. I'm pretty sure he's telling me, "You're in my spot." I get it. I'd be possessive too if I got to share Evie's bed on a daily basis. It's way too small, though. My feet are hanging off the bottom. She needs a king-sized bed like mine. Or maybe just mine…

What if I just packed up all of her stuff and moved her into my house? *Good morning, darling. Did you sleep well? Yeah, I changed my mind on the whole no-serious-relationship thing, and we're married now, and you have to live with me forever.*

As gently as possible, I shift Evie and myself over to the far side of the bed. She's totally out because she doesn't even stir the slightest bit. I give Charlie a nod, and he gets it right away. He jumps up on the bed and snuggles up under Evie's arm and stomach. Suddenly, we are a family, and I wish Sam was here, too.

What is that? Why am I feeling this way? I'm out of my mind scared that I'm about to get my heart crushed by this woman. I can't hide away forever, though, right? Sooner or later, I've got to give in and risk heartbreak. Evie feels worth that risk. And she hasn't given me a reason to not trust her so far.

I spend the next hour like this, watching Evie sleep (it's only slightly creepy of me) and trying to work through some of the insecurities that Natalie left me with. Evie may be stuffing herself inside Tinkerbell's house, but she's not fooling anyone—me, especially. She's used to a different life. One of money and prospects and people who have a whole lot more to offer than me.

Natalie left me because she wanted more.

Evie's already had the kind of life that Natalie is chasing. She knows what she's missing out on. And although she says she doesn't want the kind of life that she grew up with, what's to say she won't want it back later on? Sam and I can't go through that again.

I'm saved from my own thoughts when I feel my phone buzzing. I hurry and silence it before it disturbs Evie. She hasn't moved, though. Her soft pink lips are slightly parted, and her dark lashes are fanned against her cheeks. Her blonde waves cascade around her, and I'm feeling so in awe of her that I'm glad I have to get up and talk to my sister on the phone. As carefully as possible, I extract myself from Evie's bed and quietly slip out the front door.

"Hey, June," I say, answering my phone.

"How is she?"

Sam was already with June while I was at the office this afternoon. When Evie called, saying she was about to have a seizure, I called June and told her I'd be later than I had originally planned because I needed to go be with Evie.

"She's okay. Resting now."

"I'm glad you're there with her," says June, and her concern makes me smile. She likes Evie a lot.

"Me too. And listen, what do you think about just letting Sam stay the night with you so I can stay here and take care of Evie tonight?"

There is a long pause and, at first, I think that maybe she disapproves. I should have known better, though, because I quickly realize that she's just taking a minute to stifle whatever celebration she's doing on the other end. "Eeeeekk, you love her! I knew it."

"Stop," I say, hoping to put an end to her pestering before she gets out of hand. "I just don't want to leave her like this."

"Mmhmm. Don't lie to me. You just want to be there when she's feeling better." She begins to sing, "*Jake and Evie, sitting in a—*"

"Is this going to go on for much longer? Because I need to go back in and help Evie."

She laughs. "Yeah, don't worry about Sam. I'll take good care of her." And do you know what? For the first time since Sam's diagnosis, I'm not worried. She's got Daisy now, and after today, seeing Charlie tend to Evie so diligently, I have more faith in service dogs than ever. Daisy will keep Sam safe until I get to her if something happens.

Later that night, I'm washing dishes in Evie's 6-inch wide sink when I hear her say, "You're still here."

I cut off the water and turn around to face her bed. She's sitting up, and her hair is all draped across one shoulder. Her eyes are heavy, and honestly, she looks more beautiful than ever. I lean back against the sink and cross my arms with a smile. "Did you think I wouldn't be?"

She looks down to pet Charlie and shrugs. "I didn't know."

Something about those words tears me up.

I uncross my arms and make my way back to Evie's bed. She watches me approach with shy eyes, and she pulls her covers up a little higher like she's naked under there, which she's not. She's still fully clothed in her yellow sundress just like I found her. But I realize as I get closer that she does feel naked. I've seen her seizure, and that's making her feel vulnerable.

I climb onto the bed beside her, and it's hilarious how unsteady this little thing is. It sags heavily under my weight, and Evie notices with a grin. I lean my back against the headboard and pull her to my chest. "I'm not going anywhere," I say into her hair, and then I kiss her forehead.

We stay like that for a minute, and I can feel her quickened breathing against my chest. It makes me smile to know that I have the same effect on her that she has on me. "How are you feeling?" I ask.

She tilts her chin up to me and wrinkles her nose. "I've been better." She then looks down to her hand resting on my chest, and she moves her index finger in a small circle. "I've also been worse." Oh, man. Can she feel my heart trying to pound out of my chest and leap into her hand? It's embarrassing.

Her smile grows, and her eyes peek back up at me, and yep, she can feel it and it's going right to her pretty little head. She then lays her head right on my chest where her ear is perfectly centered with my hammering heart. It's a pointed move. One where she's saying, *Yeah, I know how you feel about me, and I like it.*

We spend the entire rest of the day like this until I force myself to go pick us up some dinner. When her stomach settles and her migraine subsides a little, we eat on the couch and watch reruns of *Friends* with her legs draped over my lap and my arm around her shoulders. It feels so right. So natural. I don't think I've ever felt this content in my entire life. And I'll say one thing: it doesn't feel casual.

I think what we've shared together today has probably tied us together more than anything physical would have. Although, the night wasn't completely physical-less. We definitely spent an entire episode of *Friends* making out on her tiny couch. It was sweet and appropriate (at least that's going to be my answer when June asks me about it later), and we both cut it off before anything more serious happened. The self-control between us is outrageous. I wouldn't be surprised if we got asked to be the newest spokespeople for an abstinence program. But unless they pay me a billion dollars, there's no way I'm going to wear an "Abstinence is Cool!" T-shirt.

Sometime about midnight, Evie falls asleep on the couch beside me. I pick her up and carry her to bed and climb in behind her. Charlie is once again on one side of Evie, and I'm on the other. It's not the most comfortable thing to sleep in jeans and a shirt, and the bed is so small that my butt hangs off the edge. But honestly, I couldn't care less. Evie is here with me. I can smell the coconut scent lingering in her hair and hear her taking deep breaths as she sleeps. This feels right, and I don't know how long I'm going to be able to keep convincing myself that we're just two casual friends dating.

This feels a lot like falling in love.

CHAPTER TWENTY-EIGHT

EVIE

I can't stop smiling, and Jo notices. "Is it my imagination or are you glowing today?"

"I'm afraid I'm going to be glowing red if you aren't more careful with that curling wand," I tell her and try to inch myself away from the burning hot hair tool hovering beside my face.

Jake went home this morning but will be here soon to pick me up to go to my parents' house for dinner. I told Jo about the dinner, and she suggested she come over and help me get ready. But what I really think happened was she called me while I was still wrapped up in Jake's arms in my bed this morning.

My phone was going to buzz off my bedside table if I didn't answer it, so I did. That was mistake number one. Mistake number two was trying to whisper to Joanna so I didn't wake up the sleeping man beside me. But you guessed it, he woke up and leaned toward my ear (aka CLOSER to the phone) to huskily ask who I was talking to.

Want to take a wild guess what Joanna did before peppering me with 101 questions? She squealed. Squealed like a little teeny bopper at a Justin Bieber concert. "He's there with you, isn't he?! Oh my heavens, he's in your bed! It's only 7:00 in the morning, so I KNOW you aren't out of bed yet. Don't lie to me, missy!" She always calls me missy when she thinks her age will suddenly work as a rank card. Like she has the power to ground me or take away my phone.

"Oh, would you pipe down over there. I'll call you later," I said in a useless whisper because Jake was RIGHT there in my bed.

"*You better!*" she sing-songed back to me before I abruptly ended the call—pleased to finally get to end a call before she had the chance.

It was so strange waking up with Jake beside me. I thought I was waking up from the most wonderful dream where a strong, attractive man spent the entire day taking care of me and then snuggled me while we slept. And then when I opened my eyes, I realized a tan, muscular forearm was draped over my shoulder, and I nearly screamed.

I would say nothing happened, but that wouldn't be true. Oh, it would be true in the physical sense. We didn't do anything that Pastor Mike wouldn't have approved of…well, I mean a Southern Baptist mama might not have cared for the interlude during that one *Friends* re-run, but I'm getting away from myself. What I meant was, something happened in the form of my heart.

When I woke up with Jake's arms around me and felt his breath tickling my neck, I realized I wanted to wake up like that every morning for the rest of my life. Now, don't get me wrong. I realize that we are still so new that it would be insane to say something like that out loud. Those are the kinds of thoughts that you are allowed to have but must keep locked away in a secret compartment until somewhere around the six-month-relationship mark when you let them out in the form of a three-word phrase.

But I feel them. And I think Jake does too. He's just still too scared to admit it to himself.

He and Sam have been through hell and back this past year, which is why I'm perfectly fine waiting on him to adjust to the idea of another serious relationship. If he wants to go on pretending that this is something "casual", fine by me. But I know it's not…and I think that, deep down, he does too.

I don't know of a single man in the entire world that would drop everything, tend to an epileptic woman for a whole day, AND spend the night with her without having sex, and still have casual feelings. Not even a best guy-friend would do that. Well, he might share her bed if his best girl-friend's couch was as small as mine, but he wouldn't press soft kisses to her temple when she was sleeping. No. Jake is all romance, and it honestly takes my breath away.

Suddenly, the curling wand appears an inch from my face again, jolting me back into reality. "Tell me everything that happened." Wow. Jo has a real interrogation-officer thing going on right now, and I'm a little terrified of her.

"Nothing!" I say, craning my neck as far back as I can without falling off the stool.

Joanna lifts a brow. "You're not holding out on me, are you? I know he was in your bed this morning when I called. And no sense lying to me about it, because I already smelled your pillow, and it smells like Old Spice!"

"You smelled my pillow?!"

If someone was just tuning in, they might think that Joanna was about to scold me for having a man spend the night. Ha! I wish.

"Come on, Evie, didn't anyone ever teach you how to kiss and tell?"

I shake my head at her in mock reprimand. "Someone needs to teach you some manners."

She grins and picks up another section of my hair to wrap it around the iron. My hair is officially too long for me to curl myself, but I want it to be in pristine condition when I go to my parents' house later tonight. That way, Mama can't say anything about how I should really try putting an effort into my appearance before I go out.

"Fine. You don't have to go into detail. But just tell me this…are you happy?"

I meet my own eyes in the mirror and take a long look. And yep, right there, reflected in my green eyes, is a spark of happiness I haven't felt in a long time. I feel cherished by Jake, and I'm starting to trust that feeling. "I am happy. I feel like things are finally starting to come together in my life. Plans for the fundraiser are lining up nicely, and I really feel hopeful that we're going to make enough to achieve our goal for the year. I'm seeing an amazing guy that truly understands me and my lifestyle, and I get to spend time with his adorable daughter who makes me feel…"

"Whole?"

I meet Jo's eyes in the mirror and nod. "Yeah. How'd you know that?"

She smiles and then turns her attention back on my hair and gently wraps it around the iron. "Because that's what happened to me three years ago when I met you." My heart swells, and all of a sudden, tears are pricking my eyes. I sit very, *very* still because I despise crying in front of people.

Joanna unwraps a curl from the iron and sets it down, resting her hip against the counter and folding her arms in front of her. "Did I ever tell you that Gary and I couldn't have children?"

My heart tears in half. "No, you didn't."

"I don't like to dwell on it much. We found out back in the day before fertility treatments were as successful as they are now. The fact of the matter is, a family just wasn't in the cards for us. I always had this distinct feeling, though, that something or someone was missing in my life." She smiles softly. "All the way up until I met you, darlin'. I feel like you're the daughter I couldn't have…and…I probably don't say it enough, but I love you, missy."

I feel my smile stretch across my face and reach out to take her hand. "You tell me every single day, Jo."

Her eyes grow misty. "It's not enough."

Now my tears are falling too, and it's no use to stop them. "I don't know where I would be without you, Jo. I love you, too. And you've been a better mama to me than mine ever has been. So…thank you."

"You're welcome, honey. You know, I think the good Lord knew we'd need each other."

"I think you're right."

We stare at each other for a minute, and then, as if we truly are mother and daughter, we both scrunch our noses at the same time and let go of each other's hand. "Right. Well, no sense making your mascara run right before your evening at the palace. Wouldn't want to give the queen anything to remark on."

I laugh and turn my eyes to the mirror to finish up my makeup. I'm pulling out all the stops tonight. Mascara. Eyeliner. Blush. It's all happening. Sephora will be so proud of me. "Oh, I'm sure Her Highness will find something to her distaste."

"I wish you'd take me instead of Jake. I'd like to take that woman's hateful comments and shove them right up her snooty little—"

"Yeah, yeah, yeah, I know where you'd put them."

Jo gives me a mischievous grin and then leaves my bathroom. "I'll get your dress. Where is it?"

"On my bed," I call out to her, and then I hear her loud, overly dramatic gasp.

"Please tell me you're not going to wear this hideous thing."

I knew she'd hate it. It's a conservative little number I plucked from the sale rack of Ann Taylor Loft. It's a plain, navy pencil dress with a high neckline, and it hits me just below the knees. It looks like I should be walking into a courtroom with a briefcase at my side rather than a dinner party.

"But this looks nothing like you. Where's the color? Where are the flowers?" She sticks her head back into the bathroom, holding up the offending dress. "Oh gosh, don't tell me you got matching pumps to go with it."

"They're by the door."

"Why are you doing this?"

I sigh and stand up, taking the dress from her and walking out to lay it back down on my bed. "I know it's nothing like me. But I'm not trying to be me tonight. I'm just trying to get in, grab that check, and get out as fast as possible with as few mean comments stuck to my back as I can manage." It's probably a little wussy of me, but I don't care. I'm tired of fighting my mama at every turn. Might as well play the game and blend into their lifestyle until I can get back home and change into my sneakers and summer dress.

I peel off my clothes and slip into the dress, having Jo zip up the back. I spin around, and she gives me a begrudging smile. "Well…at least it hugs your curves. Jake will like that."

I laugh and shake my head at her. "I swear I will burn this dress as soon as I'm done with this dinner party. How about that?"

"Okay. As long as you let Jake unzip it for you." She winks with a devilish smirk, and I swat her arm.

I swear she pulled a Freaky Friday with someone back in the day, because there is no way this woman is actually in her sixties. And I'm also really jealous of her teal ribbon scrunchie wrapped around her top knot. I decide I'll steal it from her next time I'm at her house.

A knock sounds at the door, and Joanna and I both look at each other. She wags her brows and bolts to the door and, instinctively, I know what that crazy woman is after.

"Joanna, don't you dare ask him if we had sex last night!!" I say way too loudly just as she's flinging open the door.

I guess my door is paper-thin, because Jake smiles at Joanna and his dimples pop. "Sadly, we did not," he says, and my stomach flips over.

To say he looks amazing would be a gross understatement. He's wearing dark-blue slacks that cling to his muscular thighs and a white button-down tucked in with a brown belt. A light-gray suit jacket hugs his big shoulders, and his jaw is clean shaven. I also think he must have called some kind of hair-and-makeup artist to come style his hair, because it's molded into a soft, tousled look that only a movie star should be able to achieve.

My mouth is hanging open at the sight of him, which gives Joanna immense pleasure. She chuckles and grabs her purse. "I think I'll just be on my way, then. Have fun tonight, darlin'!" She squeezes Jake's arm on her way out and then flashes a wide-eyed look back at me after she realizes he's all muscle.

Jake steps inside with a chuckle and shuts the door behind him.

His eyes take me in, and they hitch on the curves of my waist before he shakes his head with a smile. He walks up to me and lightly sets his hands on those curves to tug me closer. "I think we might have to have a talk later about the whole *casual* thing we discussed."

"Oh yeah?" I ask with a smile and a lifted brow, looking as cool as a cucumber and not at all like my stomach is exploding with butterflies.

"Yeah." He bends down and kisses me…and yep, I'm going to have to reapply my lipstick before we leave, just like he promised.

It's a good start to the evening, and I think dinner is going to be more bearable with Jake at my side. But really, I can't wait until it's all over and I get to have that conversation with him. I can feel everything falling into place, and it feels good.

CHAPTER TWENTY-NINE

JAKE

"So. This is where you grew up?" I ask, staring up at the white, three-story Charleston mansion that has a wraparound porch on every level. The house is obscenely big for this part of town. I now know it's possible for a home to look smug.

It's tucked off the main road, and we had to punch in a number for the large iron gates to give us access to the driveway. I can see a well-manicured tea garden off the right side of the home, and the landscaping is so well manicured I wouldn't be surprised to see a staff of twenty on their hands and knees, cutting each blade of grass with golden shears.

I design homes for a living—some a lot like this one—but for some reason, knowing that this house is a part of Evie's history is leaving me a little dumbfounded. It's what this house represents. Wealth. Status. Power. Truth is, I'm feeling a little insecure right now. It's dumb, but I really thought she was impressed with me and my life. Now, I know that she was just humoring me.

She grabs my arm and tugs me out of my trance. "Don't look

it in the eyes. That's how it traps you." Evie lifts up on her tiptoes and kisses my cheek and then drags me and Charlie up to the front door. I think he wants to be here just about as much as I do. "There are two rules tonight: stay close and keep that pretty mouth of yours shut," she says while nervously running her hands over her dress that shows off all of her gorgeous curves.

I think she was trying to go for a modest look, but really, she just looks like a hot businesswoman. I'm not going to let myself get distracted, though, because I'm pretty sure I should be offended right about now.

"Did you say keep my mouth shut?" Surely, I didn't hear that right.

"Yep. Seal it up."

Huh. Well, yeah. Now, I'm a little annoyed. Does she not think I'm good enough for her family?

She's still fidgeting with her clothes and fluffing her long blonde waves (gosh, it's hard to focus when she's doing all that), and I've never seen her look so insecure before. She finally looks up at me, and her furrowed brows soften. "What's wrong?" she asks.

"You just told me to not speak during this dinner."

"Oh!" She steps closer. I want to be annoyed, but her nearness does strange things to me.

I can see two future paths forming in my mind. One, we go inside and have a tense dinner with her parents. Two, I toss her over my shoulder, haul her off to my truck, and we peel out of here before anyone knows we were ever on the premises, and then we spend the whole night together. She makes me feel greedy. I want Evie all to myself.

"Jake, I'm telling you to not talk for your own good. It doesn't matter how wonderful you are, or how successful you are. If your last name is not Murray, they will eat you alive. They want me to marry Tyler, and so trust me, anything you say tonight will be twisted around in some way to bite you in the butt."

"They are really that serious about this Tyler guy?"

She nods, looking remorseful…like it's her fault somehow. "We are only here to get that check and run. The less we both say, the better. Are you ready?"

I feel like we are about to step into battle. Suddenly, I feel naked. Where's my sword? Where's my armor? All I've got is this stupid button-down shirt and slacks.

I nod. "I'll cover you. And if you get in over your head, squeeze my hand three times, and I'll execute an extraction."

Her green eyes glow bright. "What if we get separated?"

I step a little closer and put my hands on her hips. "Don't worry. I won't let you out of my sight."

Evie's eyes darken, and they fall to my mouth.

I'm bending down to kiss her when the front door suddenly flies open. Evie jumps, and I let go of her. We both look to the woman watching us with, somehow, both a bored and angry expression. It's hard to explain, but you'd know it if you saw it. Kind of like she hates you but also knows she can crush you at any moment.

"Wonderful," Melony says with mock enthusiasm. "You brought your friend."

It's in this moment that I wish Evie and I had already had the talk that's been rolling around in my mind all day. Because, yeah, that's all I am to her, technically. A freaking friend. *Not for long, Melony.*

"Hi, Mama, you look nice," says Evie, being really generous to her mom.

Melony's hawk eyes scan down Evie, and she sighs. "At least you're wearing something on your bottom half tonight."

You. Have. Got. To. Be. Kidding. Evie looks perfect. I can see her shoulders slumping with dejection, and all I want to do is sit Melony down and force her to order a spring wardrobe from a Walmart catalog until she apologizes.

Evie flashes a tense smile up at me and wraps her arm around mine. “Alrighty then. Let’s get this party started.”

EVIE

I hate being in this house. It’s wrapped in memories that I despise.

“Do you feel that?” I whisper to Jake as we follow Mama from the foyer into the parlor where, supposedly, the rest of the guests have been waiting on us for the past fifteen minutes. I call bull. We were right on time! If they were waiting, it’s because those snooty booties got here early.

“Feel what?”

“That plunge in temperature. My mama’s heart is so cold it keeps the house at a chilling 63 degrees.”

Jake laughs, which draws Mama’s attention. She looks over the shoulder of her powder-pink linen dress and scowls. “I know you’ve been out of society for a while now, but do try to remember your manners, Evelyn Grace. None of your jokes at the dinner table if you want to leave here with a check in your pocket.”

“No, all you said was that I had to attend tonight to get the check. You can’t change the rules now, Mama.”

“As long as I am holding the pen, I can change the rules whenever I like,” Mama says with a lazy smirk as she pauses outside of the parlor threshold.

Everything looks exactly as it did the day I left home. Dark-chestnut hardwoods, cream walls, and the same color wood as the floor lines the molding of the windows and doors. Plush rugs with various shades of slate-blue, cream, and burgundy dot the floors, and in the center of the foyer, there is the same round antique table that would make Joanna Gaines salivate.

Mama's house has been featured in *Southern Living* as one of the most beautifully designed houses in Charleston, but it's not my style. Everything feels overdone. Over-decorated. It's not warm and inviting like Jake's house. And instead of smelling of vanilla and teakwood, I think the candles they burn here have wicks made from hundred-dollar bills, giving it the overall aroma of wealth.

Mama gestures with her hand for us to enter before her. She casts a disgusted look at Charlie, and I know she's annoyed that I brought him. I feel a familiar prickle of dread roll over me, and just as I'm considering kicking off my heels and running for the door, I feel Jake's hand land on my lower back. I glance up at him, and he winks at me with a smile that makes my heart grow.

That's when I realize this night isn't going to be anything like all of the rest. Jake is by my side. I have a sidekick. Someone to shoulder some of the weight and help me deflect the fiery scowls my mama will throw at me.

I'm feeling lighter and hopeful as we step into the room together. And then, as plain as day, I can spot the trap, and I want to turn around and bolt again. In fact, I do. I spin out of Jake's hand and make a beeline for the door, but Mama catches my arm before I can escape, and I realize it's too late. We're toast. Done for. All good feelings are gone.

Mr. And Mrs. Murray are seated on a loveseat, and Tyler is standing by the beverage cart with something amber-colored already floating in the glass in his hand. I hate when he drinks. It makes him cockier. And handsier.

I'm now realizing that this is what my parents were hoping would be a *family* dinner. Because that's what they want all of us to be: one weird, competitively dysfunctional family. I wouldn't be surprised if I looked in the corner and found a preacher gagged and tied until they were ready to force him into officiating a ceremony.

"I thought you said we would be having a dinner party with important guests," I hiss at my mother. She's no longer Mama to me. It's Mother from here on out. I knew she was underhanded, but this feels like too much. Forcing me to eat and be merry with people whom I have clearly been avoiding.

She's got her fake pageant smile on and that disgustingly sweet voice that gives me PTSD. "Of course I did. Because these are the *most* important guests, dear. It's been much too long since you've seen Tom and Amy." She's spinning me around, and old habits really must die hard, because I'm pasting my fake smile on too, even though I really want to stomp on my mother's foot and yell "NEVER!" before running out of the room.

I just keep reminding myself, though, to not rock the boat tonight. Get in. Grab the check. Get out.

"Evie, how nice to see you again!" says Amy Murray. She's as feline as I've ever seen. The only woman who could ever give my mama a run for her money. Keep your friends close and your enemies closer, right? Mama and Amy act like friends; they keep everything Southern sweet, but there is the unspoken code between them that says *if you double-cross me, I will destroy you.* "Tyler, dear, come see Evie! How long has it been since you two have seen each other?"

My eyes meet Tyler's, and he's smirking like the devil as he looks between me and Jake. I feel a chill settle over me, and I'm worried that Tyler is in on this trap. I fall in line beside Jake, and suddenly, I feel his hand wrapping around my shoulder. "*Mine,*" says his arm, and I like it. Maybe if I Sharpie his name across my forehead for the rest of the night, everyone would get the picture that I'm never going to be Tyler's, and whatever they are planning won't work.

"Actually, Tyler and I already ran into each other a few days ago. By the way, how's that rash treating you these days, Tyler? I hope it's all cleared up."

"Evie Grace, always such a jokester," says Tyler, rounding the loveseat to come stand in front of Jake and me. He's wearing a suit that I'm sure costs upwards of five thousand dollars and sticks his hand out toward Jake, giving him his most winning (vicious) courtroom smile. "I don't think we've met. I'm Tyler Murray. Longtime friend of Evie."

Looking on, you might think this is polite. No way. This is a strategic power move, because now, Jake is forced to let go of me to shake Tyler's hand.

"Jacob Broaden. Guy who's lucky enough to be dating Evie," says Jake, and I cringe because he's broken my second rule. *Keep your mouth shut.*

Everyone in the room chuckles like they've already somehow rehearsed this little skit before we arrived and know their cues.

Daddy swoops in out of nowhere. "You'll have to be more specific than that, Jake. Any number of men could boast that same title." Umm, that is so not true. Not even a little. Well, actually, it's just a tiny bit true. But it's not my fault that guys don't want anything serious with me. If they take me out, it's only for one night, and when I don't sleep with them at the end of it, they don't call again.

My smile tightens, and I look at Jake, afraid that he's going to be mad by what he's heard, given his past relationship with his wife. I know he's skittish. But when I look up, he gives me a reassuring smile and puts his hand on my lower back again. "I'm just grateful to have made the cut, then."

We all continue on with small talk for a few minutes about the law firm and how much Tom misses being in the thick of the action. After that, they spend a solid ten minutes gloating over Tyler and all of his achievements and cases he's won since taking over at the firm. I want to gag. Tom and Daddy then volley back and forth about whose golf swing is better between the two of them while my mother and Amy gossip about Cathey's new nose. All in all, everything is mind-numbingly boring—just the way I like it. No boat rocking tonight, and Jake and I get to sit quietly and observe.

It's when we sit down to dinner that I realize we have exactly enough place settings for everyone. That's odd. I never told Mama that Jake was coming with me. I look up and notice that Tyler is staring at me from across the table. Staring like a serial killer finalizing his plans. He raises his glass to his mouth, smirking at me and never breaking eye contact. My heart rate picks up speed, and I can feel that he has something up his sleeve. Something that I'm not prepared for, but he is. Something everyone at this table is prepared for, because there is an extra place setting here. Oh, crap. *This* is the trap. They knew I'd bring Jake. Planned on it.

Suddenly, Tyler's gaze cuts to Jake, and he sets down his glass. "You own your own architectural firm, do you not?" Now, how did he know that? I know that I didn't tell anyone in my family, so how in the world would Tyler know that? *Shoot.* My parents must have had Jake investigated.

I look around the table and notice how it looks like everyone is running their lines in their head, waiting for their cues again.

"I do, yes," Jake says with a kind smile, completely oblivious to the knife they are about to launch to his chest.

"Ah, yes," my daddy says from the far end of the table. "Evelyn told us all about it. She went on and on about how proud she is of you for owning such a successful company." I did not! I look at Jake and hope he will feel my thoughts meld with his. *This is a trap!! Something is afoot!* "I've got to say, I'm impressed by you, Jake. To own Goddard Smith is something to be proud of."

WHAT?!

Jake's brows twitch together, and his smile dims. "Oh…uh—

I don't own Goddard Smith, sir. My company is Broaden Homes."

My father looks at me with a put-on frown that could win him an Oscar. "Why did you tell me he owned Goddard Smith, then?" Oh, he's good. They're all good. Sitting here, acting like this wasn't a battle strategy to put a wedge between Jake and me while also making him feel belittled.

My eyes widen. "I didn't!" I flash my eyes to Jake next. "I really didn't. I never told him you owned that company. In fact, I haven't told them about you at all!" Oh. But that just made things worse, didn't it?

Jake's smile is oh so tight now, and I can see that he's trying his best to not let this situation eat at him. I touch his arm, and he whispers, "It's fine."

It's not fine. I can feel that it's not.

"Evelyn Grace, tell Amy all about your wonderful little service dog company." *Now it's a wonderful company, is it?*

"Oh yes!" says Amy, eyes twinkling in rehearsed anticipation. "You know, a few girls from the club and I were just saying that we needed a new little project to keep us busy. And from what your mama says, it sounds like your company could use a few patrons." She pauses. "Or…" Blink. Blink. Blink. She turns her doe eyes to Tyler. "Actually, Tyler might be just the person for the job."

"Tyler?" I ask, not bothering to keep the disgust from my voice.

"Well, yes! Who better than him? I'm sure that he could drum up all kinds of high-profile sponsors for you with all of his connections from New York. You two could get together and brainstorm through a game plan. You would be happy to work with Evie to further her company, wouldn't you, son?" GAG ME. Do they really think I don't see through this charade?

"I'd love to help you with your company, Evie," he says in a way that sounds like he's undressing me with his words.

I give him a tight-lipped smile. "Thanks, but I've got it all handled. Our benefit is tomorrow night, and I already have lots of big companies signed up to donate services and items for everyone to bid on. So, yep. Don't need your help."

"A benefit?" says Tom, stepping into his part now. "We didn't hear anything about a benefit. Is it open to the general public?" *Oh, shoot.*

"Well…no. It's by invitation only."

"Surely, we are invited, though, and our invitation just got lost in the mail."

"That's exactly what happened, isn't it, Evelyn?" says my mother. "Because you specifically called me and asked for their address a few weeks ago. And are you and Tyler still going together like you two talked about?" Okay, so first, Mama is manipulating me into inviting Tom and Amy to the benefit, and now she is flat-out lying about me and Tyler. Where to start?

One quick look at Jake, though, answers that question for me. "I—no. I'm going to the fundraiser with Jake. He's my date. He and I are going together." How many more ways can I say this? *Jake es mi cita*. Jake + Evie = Together.

My mother pouts and turns a broken-hearted smile to Tyler. "Oh. I'm terribly sorry, Tyler. I hope you'll be able to find a date on such short notice." Unbelievable.

"I'm sure he'll be just fine calling one of the many girls from his little black book and asking them to leave their Barbie dream houses for the night." Wait. What? He isn't even invited to the fundraiser! Did I just get tricked into inviting him, too?

"Don't be jealous, Evie. You know you're my number one choice. Just say the word, and I'll go with you."

My mouth falls open, and I look at Jake. He's looking at me, and his expression is so hard to read it could be an instruction manual from Ikea. "Like I said, I don't need you to go with me, Tyler, because I'm going with Jake. The man sitting right here beside me."

"Right. Sorry, man. I didn't mean to make you feel weird."

"You didn't," Jake says, but his voice is so hard that it's clear he's annoyed.

"Oh, Jacob, you'll have to excuse all of us," says Mama. "We tend to go on and on about Tyler and Evie because...well, there's no other way to say it, but we've all been waiting for the day they finally get back together and tie the knot."

Honestly, I'm shocked. I shouldn't be, but I am. I knew my family was capable of some manipulative stuff, but this is so out of bounds. "*Mother,*" I say, using that title as a warning. I'm about to lay into her at this table in front of everyone when my daddy pipes up, blotting his mouth and setting his napkin down.

"Come on, Evelyn. Enough's enough. It's time you stop this hippie lifestyle of yours and get back to real life. Tyler is your future. No offense to Jacob, because I'm sure he's working very hard in his business, but he can't give you the life you're accustomed to by owning a small-scale *residential* architectural firm. But Tyler can give you the life you deserve right now, and he's willing to do it. I'm sure he would even bankroll your little dog business, too, if it means that much to you."

"Don't you remember how good together you two were in high school?" asks Amy, jumping in with a smile that I want to smack off of her plastic face.

"It's true, Eves. We were great together, and I'd like for us to be a *we* again. What do you say?"

Is this really happening? Please tell me this is just a nightmare, and any minute now, I'm going to look down and realize that I'm not wearing pants. I'll wake up in a cold sweat and then immediately call Jake, and he will make me feel better by laughing and saying it was just a dream, because in real life, we would never be so stupid as to set foot willingly in my parents' house. I feel so stupid for believing her that this was ever about her giving me a check for the company.

I don't want to look at Jake. I'm so humiliated by the way

my parents are treating him, especially when his parents were so kind and welcoming to me. But I do, and the look on his face breaks my heart further. His brows are pulled tightly together, and he looks deep in thought. I can feel him slipping from me. I want to cry right here at the table. This night had started out so well for us, promised so many things for us, and now, here we are, sitting at this table, and a wall is physically being constructed between us for all to witness, just like they planned.

And now, I'm pissed. I shoot up out of my seat and make the legs scrape painfully loud against the floor. Good! I hope they leave a big ol' scratch! "That's it. We're leaving. Come on, Jake."

He stands up beside me, but his movements aren't as full of fire as mine are. I grab his hand and Charlie's leash, and we start walking from the room, hearing everyone's protests behind us. I then whirl around and level each of them with a searing glare. "For the last time, I'm not going to marry Tyler. And all of you should be ashamed of yourselves and the way you treated me and Jake tonight. Consider yourselves uninvited to the benefit."

"Evelyn Grace," my mother says, fire blazing in her eyes. "Are you forgetting about something?" She's referring to the check she's trying to dangle in front of my face.

"Keep it. I don't want your manipulative blood money supporting my company, anyway."

I grip Jake's hand tighter and race us through the house and out the front door like we just robbed a bank. The second we have put enough feet between us and the enemy, I drop Jake's hand and turn around to face him. "Jake, I am so sorry! I had no idea they were going to gang up on us like that. It was a trap, and I should have seen it coming!" He's not meeting my eye. He's looking over my head into the distance, and I can feel that wall between us grow taller. "Jake, look at me." He does, but the look in his eyes says things have changed. My heart squeezes painfully.

I feel desperate to get him to understand that I do not share my family's opinions, so I put both of my hands on his face to hold his attention on me. "Everything they said was a lie. They are master manipulators, and you can't trust anything they say. Please believe me. And I swear I didn't tell them you own Goddard Smith…because I don't even care what company you own. I just want you."

Jake doesn't say he wants me too. He doesn't say everything is okay and that he trusts me. His eyes are meeting mine, but I don't think he's really even seeing me anymore.

"I don't know…." is what he says before pulling away and walking toward the truck.

My arms fall back to my sides. "Where are you going?"

"To get in the truck and take you home."

"So that's it, then? We're just done talking because you decide we are?"

He pauses and turns to look at me—but he looks so hollow I want to cry. "Believe me, Evie. You don't want me to keep talking right now because I will say lots of things that I'll regret. I just endured an hour of belittling that has my blood boiling, and I have a lot to think about."

"Jake!" I say, taking a desperate step toward him. "None of what they said was true. Are you worried because of Tyler?"

He grimaces at the sound of Tyler's name and shakes his head. "No. That guy's a tool, and I know you'd never go for him."

"Then, what is it? And why are you looking at me like that?"

"Like what, Evie?"

"Like you've already said goodbye to me!"

Jake holds my gaze for a minute, and every breath I take sounds excruciatingly loud in my ears. His jaw flexes, and he breaks eye contact to look down. "Maybe I have. I heard them in there; they don't think I'm good enough for you. And…I'm not entirely sure that I don't agree with them."

"No," I say as an expelled breath. "That's not true! You're so much better than those people, and I don't want the life they have!"

"Maybe not now," he says, raising his eyes to meet mine with a new look of fire and determination. "But what about in two years? What about when you start missing your old life? When I don't make as much money as you need? Or have the connections you need? What then, Evie?" I hate the way Jake just said my name. It was like a jab to my stomach. "*This* is the opposite of what I need right now. Sam and I need support and stability. We need someone we can trust. And…"

I shut my eyes. "Don't say it."

He holds my gaze for the span of three breaths and then quietly says, "And I don't know that that person is you."

He turns around and gets in his truck and starts it. I stand there motionless, feeling like I've just been hit with a stun gun. I feel angry and hurt and betrayed. But it's odd because I know that's exactly how Jake feels too. The selfish people in that house accomplished exactly what they set out to do, and now my heart feels shattered.

I look back up at my parents' house and spot Tyler watching us from the window. He sees me looking at him and raises his glass in a mock toast. I wish I had a brick I could throw through that window.

I'm not quite sure that I'm welcome in Jake's truck right now, but I also know that there's no way in Hades I'm going back in my parents' house and asking for a ride.

I look down at Charlie, and his big chocolate eyes promise me that I get to order in a dozen cookies and eat them all when I get home. At least Charlie is always there for me.

CHAPTER THIRTY

JAKE

I dropped Evie off at her apartment after a completely silent drive home where I played the part of the brooding jerk perfectly. It wasn't a part I wanted to play, but I felt like I wasn't in control of myself anymore. This night couldn't have gone any worse, and as I'm driving home in the dark, I still can't quite pinpoint the moment it all went south.

One minute, Evie and I were united, and I was happy to be her shoulder to lean on during a difficult night, and the next thing I knew, I needed a crutch of my own to lean on as I dragged myself off the battlefield of the war I just lost.

I pull up out front of my house and cut the engine but don't get out of the truck. I need a minute to myself to think over everything that just happened. I run my hands over my face and hair and then groan as a sinking feeling fills my stomach.

Evie and I both just got played. Me more than anyone.

Now, away from the haughty smirk of Tyler, I can see it all clearly. They said exactly what they needed to push my buttons and hit me in all my sore spots. How they knew what my sore spots are is a little frightening, but I guess that people with as much money as them can accomplish just about anything they want to. Tonight being evidence of that.

Why did I listen to them? Deep down, I know that Evie doesn't want their life. She doesn't fit in in that manipulative social-elitist world any more than I would fit into one of Sam's training bras. And yet…I let them get into my head.

I'm still raw from Natalie. I'm still scared. And hearing them confirm my biggest fears that I'm not good enough for Evie and she'll leave me and Sam just like Natalie did, well, it undid me. I wanted to run away with my heart clutched in my hand to keep it safe.

But I was wrong. I overreacted.

My only hope now is that Evie will forgive me and forget all the accusations I tossed at her. I let out another groan because the more I think about it, the worse I feel. I remember the hurt I saw filling her eyes, the betrayal she felt. I sided with those people over her, and now I'm fearful she won't forgive me. I wouldn't blame her, either.

I pull out my phone, ready to call her and grovel at her feet for forgiveness, when movement on my porch catches my eye. I forgot to turn on the porch lights before I left the house, so I can't see who it is. For a split second, hope soars in my chest, and I think that it's Evie. But then I realize she can't drive, and there is no way she could have called an Uber and beat me here.

Maybe I should be worried that it's a robber. But I haven't heard of many criminals who like to leisurely swing on porches before breaking and entering, so I think I'm safe in that regard. Curiosity has me slipping my phone back into my pocket, and I get out of the truck.

It's when I approach the porch that I remember the old saying "curiosity killed the cat."

"What are you doing here?"

"Not exactly the welcome home I was hoping for, but hello

to you, too." Natalie, my ex-wife, is smiling and swinging on my porch like she never left me a year ago. Like she has spent every day of the past year caring for our daughter as she should have been. Like she belongs here.

She doesn't.

"You want me to throw you a party? Sorry, not going to happen."

"Too bad. I love parties."

"Cut the cuteness, Natalie. We're not friends, and we're not going to banter tonight. Now, tell me what you're doing here."

Her smile fades, and she stands up to walk closer to me. I take a step back for two reasons:

1. She's not my wife anymore, and it's not appropriate for her and I to be in close proximity when I'm seeing someone else (and I AM seeing someone else, because I fully intend to make amends with Evie as soon as I get rid of Natalie).
2. I just had a really crappy night, and my anger is at a boiling point, making every cell in my body completely aware of how much this woman has wronged me and my daughter.

In short, I don't want her anywhere near me.

"I thought it was obvious. I'm here to see you and Sam." She looks over my shoulder like maybe I carry Sam in a backpack or something. "Where is she, by the way?"

I so badly want to say something snarky like *maybe you'd know if you had cared enough to stick around and be a part of our life.* But I don't because I've already been a jerk once tonight, and I don't feel like being one again.

"She's spending the weekend with June."

Natalie makes a disgusted face. "With June? I hope you're not letting your sister rub off on Sam."

I bite the side of my cheek so hard that I taste blood. In an attempt to not lose my cool with Natalie, I turn around and start unlocking my front door. "You lost the right to make parenting decisions when you left last year. And if you have any hope of talking to me about whatever it is you're doing here, you'll want to talk nicer about my sister who has sacrificed an enormous amount of her life to help me raise my daughter."

I go in the house and think it would feel really good to slam the door in Natalie's face, but she's following me too closely. I'd end up slamming the door *onto* her face, and Natalie having a good reason to fight for custody of Sam is the last thing I need right now.

"You're right; I'm sorry. I shouldn't have said that."

Natalie comes in the house and looks around, wide-eyed, as I turn on the lights. *Oh, right.* This is the first time she's been in here. I was in the process of building this house when she left, so she never got a chance to enjoy it. It's a good thing, too. It gave me and Sam a clean start. A place where we could move on and not have to be plagued with memories of what our life was like before in that old house. The one that was much smaller. And older. And probably part of the reason Natalie left me.

She always had an eye for new and shiny things, and when Dr. I-Don't-Care-to-Remember-His-Name offered her a new life, she took it.

"Wow, Jake. This house is gorgeous." She smiles at me, and I try to squint to see the woman I used to love. But nope. She's not there anymore. This raven-haired woman with overly full lips and a whole new bra size is not the woman I loved. She looks plastic now. Even her smile looks too tight to be real.

"So, I'm guessing you're here to see Sam?"

She frowns and lets her too-skinny shoulders slump. "You don't have to be so gruff with me. I know I messed up, okay?"

I cross my arms, not giving in to her wounded-bird act.

"Natalie, are you trying to tell me that you're ready to be a part of Sam's life again?"

She tips a shoulder and gives a light grin that I realize is supposed to be flirtatious. She starts advancing toward me. "And yours."

HA! When hell freezes over, maybe.

I shake my head and give Natalie a look that conveys my dislike of her nearness. "First of all, you can't just do this, Natalie. You can't leave us with barely any contact for a whole year, then surprise me on my front porch late at night, hoping to play house whenever you want to. You needed to call, give us some notice, and I would have arranged a time for you and Sam to spend together. I've never kept you from her; you're the one who abandoned her, and honestly, I don't know if *she* will even want to see you. Second, you and I are done for good, so let's just get that out of the way now."

"Arrange a time for me and *my daughter* to spend together? You've got to be kidding me, Jake. Sam is just as much my daughter as she is yours, and I have a right to come and see her whenever I want to."

"Really? Because it seems to me that if she was just as much your daughter as she is mine, you would have been here when she had the flu…or when she won first place in her school talent show…or when she was diagnosed with epilepsy. I don't remember seeing you sleeping beside me on the floor in her room every night for the past six months." I'm fighting hard to keep my voice from raising, but I don't know how much longer I can stand in front of Natalie and keep it even.

Natalie doesn't seem to sense that every muscle in my body is flexed with anger, because she steps closer and tries to press herself up against me. I keep perfectly still because I'm afraid that any movement I make will end up being rough and hurting her.

"Jake, I know that I haven't been the mom that I should be

for Sam. I'm so sorry. I'm sorry I left you to deal with this all alone. But I'm here now, and I've changed. I'm ready to be a family again."

I laugh, but it doesn't sound cheery. "Just when did this change take place? On your flight back from Hawaii? And what did your latest boyfriend have to say about you wanting to become a family woman again?"

She casts her long, fake eyelashes down to my chest. "He and I broke up."

"Mmhmm. I see. So, are you out of money now?"

Her eyes shoot back up to me. "Jake! What a mean thing to say. I'm not here for your money." Yes, she is. "I want to be with our daughter again. With you again!" Maybe for a minute she does. But it won't last. I can't trust her, and I know it.

I take a deep breath and force my muscles to relax before I slowly extract myself from her grasp and the new fake boobs that she's trying to press on me. "Tell you what, Natalie. You rent a hotel and stick around here for one whole week, and I want you to call and talk to Sam every single one of those days. If you can do that, I'll think about letting you spend more time with Sam. But what I won't do is let you jump in and out of her life whenever you want and crush her little heart more than you already have."

"But Jake! It's late. You really want me to go get a hotel right now?" She's pressing up against me again. "Surely I can stay here with you. I mean…we were married, for goodness' sake." Yeah, I know what she's implying.

And guess what? Not gonna happen.

I abruptly step away from Natalie and head toward my room to pack a bag. "You can stay here tonight since Sam is with June," I yell while quickly tossing a few pieces of clothing in a duffel bag.

When I reemerge in the living room, I see that Natalie is already lounging on my couch with a glass of MY wine in her hand, and she's also already changed into a tiny tank top that flaunts her newest accessories. She sees my bag and frowns. "Wait. You're leaving?"

I nod and start heading toward the door because I'm not falling for any more traps tonight. "Yep. Surely, you didn't think I was going to stay here with you. I told you, Natalie, we're over."

She shoots up to her feet, looking angry, and crosses her arms. "Who is she?"

I sigh and pause only long enough to turn the thermostat down to 55. If she's going to be here, I want her to be so cold she has to wear a parka. "*She* is none of your business."

"So, there is someone?"

"Sure is." I'm not about to tell Natalie that I'm really going to my parents' house to sleep tonight. "Oh, and Natalie, check out time is at 10 AM. If you're not out by then, I'll send June over."

"You're going to sic your sister on me?"

I smile. "Definitely." Maybe I'm being a little bit petty now, but I'm so over this day that I don't even care anymore. I'll deal with Natalie more like an adult tomorrow, when the sun is up and she's wearing real clothes…or maybe even just over the phone. Yes, I decide the phone is a better choice because I feel physically sick having to look at this woman who I don't even recognize anymore.

She shakes her head and starts to spit an ugly comment at me, but I don't even hear it because I shut the door and walk toward my truck.

Once I'm down the road a little way, I let out a full breath. I feel like I just dodged a semi that had every intention of running me over. Not today. Not tomorrow. If anything, this little encounter with Natalie has only solidified the conclusion I came to on my way home from dropping Evie off earlier.

Evie Jones is a woman who can be trusted. A woman whose

word is as solid as gold and whose heart is as soft and warm as her skin. She's nothing like my ex-wife, and I'm ready to stop letting my hurt get in the way of what I know will be a very good thing between us.

Suddenly, her face flashes in my mind, and I remember how badly I left things with her. When I pulled up out front of her house and put the truck in park, I couldn't even bring myself to meet her eye. I kept my hurt little ego perched on my sleeve and my eyes cast forward on the road. I could see from the corner of my eye that Evie had opened her mouth to say something before deciding against it and going into her apartment. I wish so badly I knew what she was going to say. I hope it's not too late.

I want to call her, but I feel like this apology is something that needs to happen face to face. But not tonight, because this day has taken too much out of me. I'll go to her place tomorrow. I'll bring all of the muffins that the bakery has to offer. I'll tell her how sorry I am. How wrong I was.

It will all be okay tomorrow.

CHAPTER THIRTY-ONE

EVIE

I didn't sleep a wink last night. Not one teeny-tiny microscopic minute. I went back and forth between wishing Jake would call me and trying to print out a picture of his face so I could draw devil horns and a mustache on it. Actually, yeah, I would have done that, but I remembered that I don't own a printer.

I probably made 200 laps around my apartment, cleaned out all three of my cupboards, vacuumed under the cushions of my couch, and folded all my panties into neat little triangles and matched my socks.

Finally, the sun came up, and I decided I was tired of waiting around for Jake to come apologize to me—and he DOES owe me an apology. If he thinks that I'm just going to let him get away with mistreating me and ending our relationship, he's got another thing coming.

I'm fighting for you, Jake...because...I freaking love you.

Yeah, you heard me right. I love that big jerk. Because normally, he's not a big jerk. I'm giving him a little slack because I know, firsthand, what it's like to be on the other end of a Harold and Melony Jones Special. They whisper words in your ear that sound so true and real. And poor Jake got hit where he's most hurt: in the I'm-not-good-enough pants.

Well, guess what, buddy, you're good enough for me!

I know, I need to simmer down. I'm fired up because I drank a whole pot of coffee between the hours of 3 AM and 6 AM. So, now I'm on a caffeine high and *also* deliriously tired. Not a great combo. Or perhaps…the best combo! I laugh maniacally to myself, and Charlie shoots me a look that says he's going to tie me to my bed and force me to sleep if I don't chill the freak out.

So, I do.

I take a shower. I blow-dry my hair. I put on my favorite sundress that shows off too much of my legs, because—*why yes*—I do plan on pulling out all the stops to get Jake to listen to me. And then I call an Uber, and Charlie and I climb in the backseat and set out for Jake's house. My knee bounces the whole way, and I *know* that my Uber driver notices, because she keeps giving me looks that say she's afraid I'm going to pee in her backseat.

Honestly, I'm so nervous and caffeinated that I just might.

It's when we are pulling up out front of his house that I start to wonder if this was a bad idea. What if he turns me down? What if he's still angry? What if he's still asleep and I wake him up, making him even angrier?!

I give myself a mental slap and get out of the car. I have a man to get back.

Charlie and I walk with determined strides all the way up to Jake's door. I ring it, and as I wait for him to answer, I have deja vu of the first time I rang this doorbell. Not unlike that day, I kinda want to throw up in the bushes.

I have my speech all rehearsed:

Jake. Hear me out. I know that you think I will miss my old life, but that couldn't be further from the truth. I hate everything about my parents' society, and I left it for a reason. I want you…

all of you. I don't want to share you with anyone else or pretend that we don't have strong feelings for each other. Because honestly, Jake, I love—

The door opens, and a woman stands on the other side. A woman with shiny dark hair, swollen lips, a tight (pretty much see-through) tank top painted over her very large and obscenely perky breasts. She's not wearing a bra. And…she's not wearing pants. She looks as if I just woke her up, and…that's because I did.

No, no, no.

Now, I really think I'm going to be sick in the bushes.

"Can I help you?" she asks, looking mildly annoyed.

She's annoyed?! I'm annoyed!! Who is this woman? Did Jake seriously call a random girl to come hook up with him last night because he was so angry with me?

The thought sours in my mouth. *He did.* That's exactly what he did.

"I—" I have no idea what to say to this woman. I'm so hurt. I'm afraid I'm going to melt right here on his porch, and then that will be the end of me, and someone is going to have to come mop me up. "I was just…"

"Looking for Jake?" she asks with a taunting smirk. "He's not awake yet."

Of course he's not. Clearly, he had a late night.

"Okay." I wish I had something better to say or do than just stand here like an idiot. But I'm shocked. I never thought Jake would be that kind of guy. I thought he… I thought he loved me too.

"Do you want me to go wake him up for you?"

"No!" I'm backing away from the door now, fisting Charlie's leash and wishing it was transmitting superpowers into my palm that would help me blast this skank out of Jake's house. "I mean…don't worry about it. I'll just..."

I don't finish my sentence. Instead, I sprint back to the Uber, and luckily, I'm able to catch the girl before she drives off. I practically dive into the seat and then yell, "Drive!" like I'm in the movie *Baby Driver*. I expect her to squeal the tires as she puts the pedal to the metal, but OF COURSE she doesn't, because nothing in my life is going my way anymore.

"Are you okay, lady?"

"No. I'm not. Please just drive."

"Where to?"

"Anywhere!" Tears are now running down my cheeks. "Mexico! Let's go to Mexico."

"I can't drive you to Mexico." Seriously?! Where is this girl's sense of sisterhood? Girl power? I would even just settle for a smidge of empathy.

I let out a big puff of air and then just tell her the address of Joanna's house.

Because right now…I need a mama.

———

JAKE

I went by Evie's apartment, but either she wasn't home, or she just didn't want to talk to me, because my knock went unanswered. So did my phone call. And all fifteen of my texts. I even tried to bribe her out of hiding by texting her a picture of the muffins I brought sitting outside her door. That didn't work either.

Clearly, I'm in deeper with her than I thought.

I'm not giving up yet, though. Tonight is the benefit, and since I know she'll be there, I intend on going and sweeping her off of her feet. *That's all right, Evie. You can hide for now. But I'm going to find you very soon.* Wow, that sounded creepy.

This morning, I called June and filled her in on my chat with

Natalie. My sister begged me to let her go over there and rip every last extension out of Natalie's head, but I couldn't bring myself to give her the green light. Instead, I told her to keep Sam away from the house until I could drive back by and make sure that Natalie was gone.

She was, and when I went inside, I was immediately assaulted by the smell of her perfume. I'm pretty sure the crazy lady sprayed it all over my house like a dog trying to mark its territory. Ridiculous.

I used disinfectant spray on every piece of upholstery, and now my house smells like a hospital. But that's worlds better than the way it smelled before.

Finally, Sam came home, and I told her, very delicately, that her mom was back in town, and I asked Sam if she would even be interested in seeing her. I knew that answer before I even asked the question, and I was right: no.

It's sad when a ten year old knows that her mom can't be trusted. But she did agree to talking on the phone if Natalie did, indeed, call. I hate that I have to even give Sam a glimmer of hope that her mom will call when I'm not even certain that Natalie stayed in town. For all I know, her boyfriend left her high and dry, and she was only coming back to milk me for some spending money.

Sam and I spent the rest of the afternoon together, watching movies and playing in the pool (while I continued to sneak glances at my phone to see if Evie texted me back, even though I had the ringer on loud and knew for a fact she hadn't), and then FINALLY it was time to put on my suit and go to the benefit.

"Are you sure you're not upset about spending another evening without me?" I ask Sam before walking out the door.

She just laughs at me. "I spent all day with you, Daddy. I think we've had plenty of togetherness time." Oh, great. My kid is already over me. "Besides, Grandma said she and I are going to do some online shopping for new school clothes after you leave."

I raise my eyebrow at my mom who's come over to watch Sam for me. "Oh, she did, did she?"

"Yes, she did," my mom says proudly with her dainty little nose stuck up in the air. "Now, get on out of here, and go make that woman of yours swoon."

I can only hope.

it in the eyes. That's how it traps you." Evie lifts up on her tiptoes and kisses my cheek and then drags me and Charlie up to the front door. I think he wants to be here just about as much as I do. "There are two rules tonight: stay close and keep that pretty mouth of yours shut," she says while nervously running her hands over her dress that shows off all of her gorgeous curves.

I think she was trying to go for a modest look, but really, she just looks like a hot businesswoman. I'm not going to let myself get distracted, though, because I'm pretty sure I should be offended right about now.

"Did you say keep my mouth shut?" Surely, I didn't hear that right.

"Yep. Seal it up."

Huh. Well, yeah. Now, I'm a little annoyed. Does she not think I'm good enough for her family?

She's still fidgeting with her clothes and fluffing her long blonde waves (gosh, it's hard to focus when she's doing all that), and I've never seen her look so insecure before. She finally looks up at me, and her furrowed brows soften. "What's wrong?" she asks.

"You just told me to not speak during this dinner."

"Oh!" She steps closer. I want to be annoyed, but her nearness does strange things to me.

I can see two future paths forming in my mind. One, we go inside and have a tense dinner with her parents. Two, I toss her over my shoulder, haul her off to my truck, and we peel out of here before anyone knows we were ever on the premises, and then we spend the whole night together. She makes me feel greedy. I want Evie all to myself.

"Jake, I'm telling you to not talk for your own good. It doesn't matter how wonderful you are, or how successful you are. If your last name is not Murray, they will eat you alive. They want me to marry Tyler, and so trust me, anything you say

CHAPTER TWENTY-NINE

JAKE

"So. This is where you grew up?" I ask, staring up at the white, three-story Charleston mansion that has a wraparound porch on every level. The house is obscenely big for this part of town. I now know it's possible for a home to look smug.

It's tucked off the main road, and we had to punch in a number for the large iron gates to give us access to the driveway. I can see a well-manicured tea garden off the right side of the home, and the landscaping is so well manicured I wouldn't be surprised to see a staff of twenty on their hands and knees, cutting each blade of grass with golden shears.

I design homes for a living—some a lot like this one—but for some reason, knowing that this house is a part of Evie's history is leaving me a little dumbfounded. It's what this house represents. Wealth. Status. Power. Truth is, I'm feeling a little insecure right now. It's dumb, but I really thought she was impressed with me and my life. Now, I know that she was just humoring me.

She grabs my arm and tugs me out of my trance. "Don't look

CHAPTER THIRTY-TWO

EVIE

I stand outside of the venue where the benefit is being held and try to not cry. I've been crying all day, so I'm pretty sure that without the help of all the concealer I slapped on I would look like I've been punched in both eyes. You know how they say time heals all wounds? Apparently, they meant a lot of time, because with every hour that has passed today, my wounds have only grown deeper. My heart hurts, and I wonder if it's possible for an organ to physically split down the middle just from emotional pain.

It's silly, but…I really thought Jake would end up being *the one*.

Too bad he just ended up being *the one* to sleep with some skank when I made him mad.

Even still, it doesn't make sense to me. The woman that opened that door this morning doesn't line up with anything Jake has been telling me over the past month and a half. But maybe he was just lying. Maybe he really is into sleeping around…he just didn't want to sleep around with me.

Great, more tears.

"Nope. Uh-uh. No more tears from those pretty green eyes," says Jo, rushing up beside me to hand me a tissue. "You look too pretty to waste your night thinking about that frog leg for one more second!"

I spent the whole day today at Joanna's house, lamenting everything that happened over the last 24 hours. Her advice was that we try out a new Pinterest recipe she found, where you boil lemon and various items that belong to an ex-boyfriend and then pour the "juice" into a spray bottle and go spritz that person's house to bring them bad luck. Or maybe it was to keep the flu away… I can't remember because I was too busy ugly-crying into a pillow while she explained it.

"I know, I'm trying to stop crying, but I can't. This is the worst night to have to host a fundraiser."

"Or it is the best night to host a fundraiser. Because now you get to look hot and keep yourself busy all night. And who knows, maybe you'll find someone new here tonight too."

"I don't want anyone new."

"You're right. Too soon. But I'm just saying…I think I saw a Calvin Klein model walk in earlier, and if Gary didn't make such good chili, I think he might be in trouble."

Gary chooses that moment to walk by us. He gives Jo a little pat on her rear and then winks at me. "Chili is just an innuendo."

I cringe. "Yeah. I figured."

"I'm going on in. Y'all coming in soon?"

"Right behind you, honey," says Jo with adorably pink cheeks. I thought I had finally found a man who would make my cheeks rosy like Jo's even after years and years of marriage. Nope. And now the waterworks are happening again.

"Okay, okay, let's get you inside so everyone can see your handsome date."

Charlie does look ridiculously cute in his bow tie. I bet Jake would have looked horrible in a bow tie. But when I walk into the venue and look around the warm, glitzing room, I spot Jake standing by a cocktail table, one hand in the pocket of his black suit and the other holding a glass of something bubbly—and man, am I disappointed to see that he looks freaking amazing in a bow tie.

"What is he doing here?" I ask Jo, who follows my gaze to Jake.

Her eyes widen, and she looks back at me. "I don't know, but you can't tear him apart here. There are lots of people watching us right now, and if we both go all crazy ex-girlfriend on him, there's no way we will get any sponsors."

I sigh, knowing she's right. "Fine. I'll deal with him and then get him to leave."

"Are you sure you don't want me to do it?"

"No. I can handle him."

I think Joanna notices the way my eyes are trailing down his body in that fine-looking suit, and maybe a smidge of appreciation shows on my face, because now she's stifling a grin and humming a *mmhmm*. "You just go deal with him, then. Make sure you lock the bathroom door before you do, though."

I turn my saucer eyes at her. "Joanna!"

She just laughs and walks away to go mingle with the many guests already gathered.

I steel myself and then turn to look at Jake again. He's on the opposite side of the crowded room, but then he sets down his glass and starts crossing the center of the venue toward me. My heart starts racing, and I have to remind myself that I now hate him. I do. I hate him. I don't want a man that's not going to cherish me—who's going to sleep around with other women to make himself feel good when we've had a fight. No, sir, I do not like this man anymore.

I don't like his dimples when he smiles.

I don't like his tousled hair.

I don't like the way his muscles fill out that suit.

Okay, I like all of those things, but those are just physical attributes. And if you've ever visited a nursing home, you know that beauty fades, my friends.

I decide that Jake is not going to have all of the upper hand here, so I lift the front hem of my floor-length evening gown and start walking to meet him in the middle. His eyes scan over me as we approach each other, and I can see that he likes the way my black satin gown is clinging to my curves. He hasn't even seen the plunging back yet.

Eat your heart out, Jakey.

We stop right in front of each other in the center of the room, but Jake doesn't make a move to touch me. Smart. He can probably read the murderous scowl on my face and knows I'll bite if he does.

"You look…"—his eyes rush over me again—"gorgeous."

Right. His flattery is not going to work on me. I cut right to the chase. "Why are you here?"

"I'm your date."

"You most certainly are not my date. Not anymore. Not after…last night." Those last two words come out in a whisper because I know my voice will shake if I try to say it at my normal volume.

Jake's shoulders sink a little. "Evie. I've been trying to call you all day. I'm so sorry. Can we go somewhere and talk?"

I shake my head. I don't want to hear anything he has to say. *You slept with another woman last night. I saw her with my own eyes.* That told me everything I needed to know. "I'm busy tonight, and I need to focus on the event."

His lips press together, and he nods slowly. "Of course. I understand. Maybe after?"

I look away from him toward the tables where vendors are set up. A few couples are starting to slow dance near us, and everyone else is beginning to mill around the room and place their bids on various vendors' items and services. We have a live string quartet playing in the corner, a cocktail bar of which all proceeds go directly to Southern Service Paws, and later in the night, there will be a sit-down dinner. All in all, everything is going well, and I'm hopeful that it will be a success.

"I won't have time," I say, giving Jake my best cold shoulder. "If you'll excuse me, I see a few people I need to speak to."

Jake catches my arm before I walk away, and I wish so badly that my whole body didn't hum from his touch. When I turn my head, I find him so close to me that I have to tip my chin *up*, *up*, *up* to look into his eyes.

He smiles, and one of those dang dimples surfaces. "I'm not giving up on us, Evie. And I plan on trying to prove to you every single day from here on out just how sorry I am."

I want to lean into him. I want to lift up on my toes and press warm kisses up his neck all the way to his mouth. But I don't… because *I'm sorry* isn't going to fix what he did last night.

I rip my arm from his grasp and turn away from Jake and go to the far end of the room to get myself a drink. I'm going to need it if I have to get through a whole night with Jake's gaze following me around like it is now.

For the next hour, I try to pretend that Jake doesn't exist. I laugh too loudly with guests, I check in on all the vendors and am pleased to see that every clipboard is nearly full with bids, and I field about a thousand questions about our company and Charlie who has been dutifully standing at my side all night.

I feel exhausted from keeping up this fake smile, and I just need a minute to myself to let my mask fall off. I look down at Charlie, and I can tell that he is exhausted, too, so I do something that I very rarely do, and I go hand off his leash to Joanna who is sitting at a table with Gary and a few other guests. I'm going to let him have a five-minute break to lay at Joanna's feet while I go get some air, and then he and I will face the rest of the night together.

I open the main doors and let the fresh air wrap around me

and fill my lungs. I wish it were cooler, but it's the middle of July, and even with the sun down, it's still a balmy 80 degrees out here. I move toward the side of the building and cross my arms, staring at nothing in particular.

My thoughts wander to Jake, and I hate that I have to tell him later that I don't want to see him anymore. I don't think I'll ever be able to trust him again. And yes, I know that, technically, we were both keeping it casual and seeing other people, but what Jake did was sleazy. What he did wasn't dating other people. It was nothing more than booty-calling some random woman after my parents bruised his ego.

I'm pulled from my thoughts when a warm hand suddenly lands on my lower back. I turn, thinking I'll meet Jake's eyes, when instead, I'm assaulted by Tyler's devilish smirk.

"Ugh," I say, pulling away from him. "Not you again! I thought I made myself clear that you were not invited tonight."

"Don't be that way, Eves." He starts advancing toward me until he has me backed up against the wall of the building. His hands move to rest on my hips, and I try to push him away, but he doesn't budge.

"Get off of me, Tyler!" I say, feeling more annoyed than frightened. Although he's being a prick right now, I know he's not going to force anything more than a kiss.

"Just give me one chance to show you what you're missing." He's dipping his head down while I'm still trying to squirm out of his grasp and away from his lethal-potency cologne.

"Gross. No. Get off of me or—"

Suddenly, Tyler takes two falling steps backwards, and I realize that he's been grabbed from behind and physically peeled off of me. Jake is holding Tyler by the back of his suit, and the look on his face says everything: *I'm going to knock you out.* And he does. Jake punches Tyler square in the jaw so hard that Tyler falls back onto the ground.

Jake hovers over him like a victor from a *Rocky* film. "Don't ever touch her without her consent again. Do you understand me?" Tyler just stares up at Jake, stunned and holding his face. "This is the last time you will ever try to pursue Evie. She's made it perfectly clear that she doesn't want you anywhere near her, and from now on, you will respect her wishes."

Huh. I had no idea that I had a thing for hot guys going all bodyguard on me…but yeah, it's a thing, apparently.

Usually, this is where Tyler would say something sarcastic in reply, but he rubs his jaw and looks up at Jake instead and nods. It makes me think I should have punched Tyler myself a long time ago.

"Not good enough. Let me hear you say it along with an apology," says Jake in such a stern voice that it sends a chill down my spine.

Tyler's eyes meet mine, and I can see that he'd rather die than apologize to me, but he does it anyway. "I'm sorry, Evie. It won't happen again."

"Thank you." My voice sounds puny. Why can't I have a Rocky voice like Jake?

Tyler stands up and dusts himself off before walking toward the doors of the venue again. Jake makes a sharp *eh* sound like I use when training my dogs, and Tyler freezes.

"Wrong way," Jake says, and I swear that Tyler wants to hit him back but knows he would never be a match for Jake.

So, to my great delight, Tyler turns around and walks away from the fundraiser, back toward his fancy BMW, with his tail between his legs and then speeds off. When he pulls away, I sigh with relief. Not because I ever felt like I was in real danger, but because I'm so sick of seeing Tyler's face, and now I'm pretty sure I won't have to anymore.

Jake turns his head and pierces me with his gaze. "Are you okay?" His voice is so tender it nearly melts me right here on the sidewalk.

I shake my head no, and in an instant, he's walking up close to me and putting his hands on my arms, rubbing them up and down. "Did he hurt you?"

I shake my head no again and let my tears roll down my cheeks. "No. But you did."

Jake's hands still, and he meets my eyes. He looks like I physically stabbed him. "What can I say to make this better, Evie? I'm so sorry for making you think I don't trust you. Because I do. I trust you more than anyone. I let your family get in my head, and I reacted poorly. But I won't make that mistake again—"

I cut Jake off and shove away from him. "This isn't about what happened at my parents' house, Jake."

His head kicks back, and his brows dip together. "Then, what's it about?"

My mouth falls open, and I let out a sad mock laugh. "Did she not tell you I came by?"

Jake blinks a few times. "Evie, I have no idea what you're talking about. Came by where?"

"Your house, Jake!" I shove his chest because, apparently, I'm *that* kind of girl when I'm angry. He lets himself rock back on his feet to make me feel stronger. "I saw her. The perky little brunette with the big boobs, standing in your doorway in her underwear! I saw her, Jake! How could you turn around and sleep with someone right after dropping me off at my house? I thought we had something special, but—"

Jake shakes himself from the trance he's been in since I started my monologue and rushes up to me, grabbing my shoulders again. "No, Evie. You have it all wrong. I didn't sleep with her. In fact, I slept at my parents' house last night."

...What?

What in the freaking *what* did he just say?

"You...didn't sleep with that woman?"

Jake's face cracks into a tentative smile, and he shakes his head slowly. He opens his mouth to explain but is cut off by the sound of his phone ringing in his pocket.

"I've got to answer this; it's my mom. But I'll explain everything in a minute. Don't go anywhere, okay?"

I nod and wrap my arms around myself because the past 24 hours have felt like a roller coaster, and I'm not sure I'm off the ride yet.

"Mom? Everything okay?" He pauses, and I watch as a heavy expression settles over his face. He stays perfectly frozen.

Something in me knows. "Is it Sam? Is she okay?"

He nods, and I didn't realize that I had walked up to him and wrapped my arms around his middle, but apparently, I did, because his hand is wrapping around my shoulder, and he mumbles a few replies to his mom before he says he's on his way and hangs up.

"Sam had a seizure," he says, gripping my shoulder like he needs me to help hold him up. "But she's okay. Apparently, she went upstairs to get her PJs on, and then Daisy rushed back downstairs and started alerting my mom. Sam did fall, but it was on the carpet, and Daisy rolled her on her side just like she and Sam practiced. She stayed with Sam and hasn't left her side since the seizure ended." I see Jake's eyes welling with tears, and I squeeze him tighter. "Daisy made sure she was safe."

I smile. "Good. That's so good, Jake."

He nods and squeezes my shoulder again. "I need to get home to Sam, though."

"Right, of course." I let go of him and look back toward the venue. "Let me just go get Charlie, and we can go."

"We? You're going to come with me?"

I freeze, hoping that wasn't presumptuous of me to invite myself along. "Oh, I'm sorry, you probably just want it to be a family—"

"No," he quickly cuts me off and grabs my hand. He raises it to his mouth and lays a soft slow kiss just under my palm. "I want you to come with me. But I know you have the fundraiser going on here and probably don't need to leave."

I smile. "You and Sam are most important to me. Joanna can handle the fundraiser just fine without me." I fully intend to find out who that woman was at Jake's house later, but for now, I'm not going to let anything else get in the way of my happiness with this man. I trust him again. And he trusts me. We'll figure out the rest later.

A slow smile spreads across Jake's mouth, and then, before I have time to breathe, he tugs me up closer to him and captures my mouth with his. His hands are on my jaw, and then they slide down my bare back to press me up closer to him. His lips shift gears back and forth from tender to firm to demanding, and I'm just trying to keep up. The kiss doesn't last long enough, but it certainly did enough damage that I touch my fingers to my swollen lips when we part. I blink, feeling drugged, and then start walking. Jake turns me around so I'm actually headed in the right direction.

"Right. This way. Okay, so I'll just be right back."

CHAPTER THIRTY-THREE

JAKE

Evie and I got home about twenty minutes ago. We both raced up the stairs together to get to Sam's room. She was still on the floor when I got there with her head resting on Daisy. My mom is still a little nervous about Sam's seizures, and this was the first one she had ever been present for, so she wasn't sure whether it was safe to move Sam to her bed or not.

Sam is in her postictal period of her seizure, and I know that, like Evie's seizure the other day, she won't feel or respond like herself for a while yet. Her episode progressed normally and didn't last too long (Mom was able to time it, thanks to Daisy coming to get her at the start of it), so I felt good about letting her just rest here at home and not taking her into the hospital. I drop down to my knees, though, and brush her hair away from her face to plant a kiss on her forehead. She smiles and mumbles a "Hi, Daddy" that feels like an instant balm to my heart.

"Hi, kiddo. We're here now, and you're safe."

She hears me say *we,* and Sam's eyes peek open and instantly find Evie. Her little hand reaches up, and Evie takes it, coming to kneel down on Sam's other side. In short, Sam is surrounded, head to toe, by people who love her.

Evie adjusts so that her legs are curled up beside her, her fancy evening gown draped around her, and she leans in closer to Sam to continually brush her fingers in such a motherly way across my daughter's hairline. It's a sight that will likely stick with me until the day I die.

"Do you want some water, darlin'?" Evie asks, and Sam nods yes.

I go downstairs, trying to catch my breath while I fill up a glass of water for my daughter. It's been a heck of a day, and the minimal amount of sleep I got last night is catching up to me. Once the water glass is filled, I set it on the counter and unbutton my cuffs to roll up my sleeves.

My mom walks into the kitchen and comes around the island with a look that tells me to brace for a good, old-fashioned, Southern-mama-bear hug. That's exactly what she gives me. I squeeze her small frame back, kiss the top of her head, and thank her for taking care of Sam tonight.

Finally, she pulls away and smiles up at me, patting my cheek like she's a hundred-year-old senior citizen in a nursing home rather than the spunky 57-year-old mother that she is. "I'm gonna get going."

"Are you sure? I can make you some tea or something..." I'm not even sure if my mom drinks hot tea (or if I have any in my pantry), but it seems like a comforting thing to offer after the evening she's just gone through with Sam.

She looks at me with that same smile that I'm just now realizing is heavy with hidden meaning behind it and shakes her head. "I'll make some tea at home with your dad. I love you, Jakey. Go be with your family."

Ah. My family. So that's what was with the secret smile.

"You know we haven't even had the *let's-be-a-couple* talk yet, right?"

She shrugs, slings her leather purse over her shoulder, and heads for the door. "Doesn't matter. I've got eyes, and I know what I see. And what I saw up there was a family." With those parting words, she leaves the house.

I can just picture the self-satisfied smirk she'll be wearing during her whole drive home. She loves leaving a house on a monumental final thought.

I should be rushing back upstairs to get to Sam, but the truth is, I just need a minute to myself to breathe and soak up everything that's happened today, and I know that she's safe with Evie. For the first time this year, I don't feel alone in this parenting job. Someone who I can trust is upstairs right now, taking beautiful care of my daughter. And apparently, thanks to Natalie, I almost lost Evie.

After allowing myself five full breaths and a moment to run my hands through my hair, I head up the stairs with Sam's water. I crack open her door and pause in the doorframe, letting the picture before me steal the last bits of my heart. Evie has moved Sam up onto her bed and tucked her in. Daisy is on one side of Sam, and lying on Sam's other side, is Evie. Her black silk gown is a sharp contrast to Sam's unicorn bedding.

She looks like a movie star, home from receiving an Oscar and skipping the after-party in favor of coming home to tuck her daughter into bed. She's singing a quiet, sweet version of "Somewhere Over the Rainbow," and I have to try very hard not to drop down onto one knee here and now.

My mom is right. This feels like a family.

That thought would have scared me last week, but now it fills me with hope.

Evie must feel me watching her, because suddenly, she looks over her shoulder and finds me. A slow smile blooms on her face. I cross the room and set Sam's water glass on her bedside table. It looks like Evie has already put Sam to sleep, so I nod toward the door. Evie carefully extracts her arm out from under

Sam, looking like she's been doing it every day for the past ten years of my daughter's life, and tiptoes with me out of the room.

I leave Sam's door open so I can hear her if she calls for me and take Evie's hand to silently pull her back down the stairs to the couch.

EVIE

Jake's house at night is my favorite place in the world. He has the kind of lighting that can be dimmed in every room of the house, and so, right now, the house is blanketed in a soft warm glow. A candle is lit on his coffee table, letting my favorite vanilla scent fill the air, and everything feels peaceful and still.

Jake tugs me toward his couch and then, without dropping my hand, dives onto the couch, landing on his back and pulling me down on top of him. We both laugh as we settle into a comfortable position on the couch where our feet are intertwined and I'm lying half on the couch, half on Jake. He has one hand cradling mine and is kissing every single one of my fingers, and his other hand is lightly brushing circles on my back.

It's so romantic it makes my chest ache.

"Jake," I say somewhere between breathlessness and a reprimand. "We need to talk…" I say, trying not to smile as he pulls me up a little closer so that I'm level with his mouth. He tucks his hand into my hair, and his gaze lands on my mouth. He gives me a half smirk and mumbles against my lips, "I don't want to talk."

I know that look. He looks half drugged, and I know that if I have any hope of figuring out what's happening in our relationship, I need to drop a tray of ice cubes down his shirt. Or maybe a different article of clothing…

He leans up just enough to take my bottom lip between his. *Okay, so I guess I need some ice cubes too.* "Jake!" I say, giving the worst protest anyone has ever heard, and half-heartedly pull away. He tugs me back, and his grin nearly undoes me.

"All right, let's talk," he says as he's kissing the spot right under my ear. "What do you want to talk about?" He's lacing kisses down my jaw, and...*huh,* turns out I don't have anything I want to talk about anymore. I give in and press my hand to his chest to give me better leverage.

I make eye contact with Jake long enough to say, *Fine, you want to kiss, then let's kiss.* Fire lights his eyes, and I dip my head down and slant my mouth over his. Our mouths dance, and fire crackles somewhere in the distance even though there's not even a fire lit in the grate. I feel tiny pressed up next to Jake and his muscular body, and I love every second of it. Images of him defending me outside of the venue flash in my mind, and it shifts the kiss into something deeper. Buckle up, folks, because this train is leaving the station—or at least I thought it was.

But in the next moment, Jake breaks the kiss and sits up abruptly and slides all the way to the opposite end of his couch. He doesn't look at me for a solid minute...just stares wide-eyed at the black TV. And then slowly, he blinks, and his face turns to me.

I grin, and he grins.

"Maybe we should talk," he says, and I can't help but laugh.

"Can I sit by you?" I ask, because seriously, we are six feet apart right now, and I don't want to have to have a serious conversation over walkie-talkies.

"Are you going to behave, Miss Jones?"

My mouth falls open, and I bet my eyes are sparkling. "Me?! You were the one trying to put the moves on me."

"I'm completely innocent. I thought we would just kiss a little. But you..." He breaks off and puffs out a big breath.

"I, what?" I say with flirty, narrowed eyes.

He smiles and lifts a brow. "You had other ideas." I feel my cheeks flame because, *yep,* he's totally right. "Don't get me wrong… I have other ideas too. But, yeah, we need to talk because…" His demeanor softens, and he scoots back over near me. "Because you're important to me, and I want to make sure we are on the same page." He reaches up and brushes his fingers over my ear.

My heart starts racing again, and I shoot him a look of warning. "Okay, well, if we're going to talk, you need to stop doing things like that!"

He laughs and pulls his hand away to cross his arms. I do the same. We look ridiculous. Like two teenagers that can't be trusted to keep their hands to themselves. "Who was the woman I found at your door this morning?" I ask because I've decided we're just going to cannonball right on in.

He nods firmly. Down to business. "Right. That was Natalie."

My arms drop. "Natalie! As in, Sam's mama and your ex-wife, Natalie?!" Images of that woman's perfect body assault my memory, and without really thinking, my gaze drops to my own tiny boobs.

Jake notices. "Stop that. I know what you're thinking, and you need to stop it. You're perfect, Evie."

"But…she's so—"

"That woman you saw this morning is not at all a reflection of my personal taste. And she wasn't even the woman I married. The Natalie you saw this morning was the woman who left me, not the woman I stood next to at the altar."

I still feel a little self-conscious, but I say, "Go on."

"Over the last year of our marriage, she majorly changed. She became obsessed with seeking ways to try to improve her physical self. And yesterday, I was just as shocked as you when I saw her."

"Shocked in a good way?" I ask, not wanting to ask this question but knowing that if we are going to be a constant part of each other's lives, I'm going to need him to answer it so when I have to see Natalie again, I won't be a crazy jealous girlfriend.

Jake smiles and shakes his head. "Not in a good way." He squints one eye and suddenly looks a little shy. "Evie…I—" His gaze falls to scan my body for a millisecond before it bounces back up to my face. "You're perfect. You don't ever need to doubt that."

I smile and resist throwing a blanket over my head for the remainder of the conversation. But I'm an adult. I can do this. "Okay. So Natalie came back?" I'm putting the conversation back on the rails.

"Yeah. When I got home last night, she was on my porch. I didn't know she was coming or else I would have told you. But we talked for a few minutes, and she said she wanted to be a family again. She tried to get me to sleep with her, so I went to my parents' place for the night. The end."

His eyes meet mine, and I can feel my mouth hanging open. I'm speechless. I have no words.

Jake laughs and scoots closer to put his arms around me, completely wrapping me up. "Evie, Natalie and I are over. I don't have any affection for her anymore. I would like for her to step up and be a mom for Sam, but I don't have high hopes of that happening. In fact, I told her that before she could see Sam again, she had to stay in town for one week and call Sam every day. This evening, she texted, saying she was sorry, but she heard back about a job in LA and would be flying out tonight. What that really meant was she was in between boyfriends, hoped I would fill the position for a minute, but when I turned her down, she went seeking someone else."

"I'm sorry, Jake. For Sam's sake, that really does break my heart."

"I know. Me too." He kisses my head. "Hopefully, one day Natalie will get her act together, but until then, I'm not going to let her hurt Sam any more than she already has."

I touch his cheek and feel his five o'clock shadow beneath my palm. "You're such a good daddy."

He looks down at me, and his gaze pins me in place. "Evie. Let me be perfectly clear with you. I don't want something casual anymore." He adjusts himself to face me, and his big hand raises to cradle my face, making my hand drop to his shoulder. "I want Jake and Evie. Stupid kissing profile pictures. Cute ringtones for the other person. I want *serious*. Exclusive. Us. I don't want anything less than planning months out for a vacation and obnoxious Christmas cards that have you, me, Sam, and the dogs on the front. Can you handle that?"

My skin is tingling, and my heart is racing. It's trying to leap out of my chest and jump into Jake's lap. In fact, yeah, it turns out it wasn't my heart doing that—it was my body. I scoot up onto Jake's lap (again, sorry, Grandmama) and wrap my arms around his neck, smiling down into his face.

I hover an inch from his mouth and then narrow my eyes. "Do we have to wear matching robes?"

A rumbling laugh breaks from his chest, and his head tilts back, squeezing me a little tighter. He doesn't answer my question, because with his head tilted back like that, it gives me a perfect shot of his neck. His skin is warm against my lips as I place kiss after kiss up his neck.

I make it up to his mouth, and his gaze is sultry, and passionate, and full of… "I love you, Evie Jones." *Love. His gaze is full of love.*

"I love you too, Jake." I dip my head, and his lips caress mine for a luxurious, top-of-the-line, special-edition kiss.

Just as it's heating up again, we both hear a soft little voice on the stairs. "Ew. Are you guys kissing?"

Jake and I break apart and both wipe at our mouths. "No… we were just…just…" He looks at me, but what in the heck is he thinking I'm going to do to help this? He's been a parent for ten years, and I've been in this role for all of five minutes.

"Just looking for something in my eye!" I say.

"Through your mouth?" *Busted.*

I can see Jake trying so hard to contain his laughter. He rubs his hand firmly across his face and mouth and looks back up at Sam. "We'll stop kissing. Are you feeling better, kiddo?"

I scoot off his lap, and Jake stands and walks to Sam.

"A little," she says, coming down the stairs with the help of Jake. Daisy is right behind her.

Jake brings her over to the couch, and without hesitating even a second, Sam sits down beside me and curls her little body up next to mine. I wrap my arms around her and hug her close. I don't know who is benefiting from this connection the most in this moment. I feel like my heart is physically expanding. It's making room to accommodate all of the new love I have.

Jake disappears into the kitchen for a minute and then comes back out with a bowl of popcorn. He sits beside me, sets the bowl in my lap, and drapes his arm behind me to rest over my shoulders and let his fingers dangle over Sam's, effectively snuggling both of us at the same time. Charlie and Daisy both come over to hunker down at the foot of the couch, draping over our feet. Jake turns on a movie, and we spend the rest of the night just like that. Snuggling, laughing, stealing kisses when Sam isn't watching, and eating popcorn.

I hope with all of my heart that this is what every day for the rest of my life will look like.

EPILOGUE

1 Year Later

I wake up to the feel of Jake's mouth against mine. Turns out, I love being kissed first thing in the morning. This is the way Jake has woken me up every morning since we married nine months ago. "Rise and shine, Sleeping Beauty," he murmurs in my ear.

I peek one eye open and take one long look at his muscled, tan chest beside me and then to the clock on my phone. I groan because I know that I have no time to spend in bed with Jake this morning. "You let me oversleep."

"Mmhmm. You need all the sleep you can get." His hand lands on my swollen stomach as he kisses my cheek.

"I also need to get to the venue to unlock it in time for the vendors to get set up." Last year's fundraiser was such a success that we've decided to make it an annual thing. Thanks to all of the vendors who donated their services and items last year, we exceeded our fundraising goal.

Jake's voice turns husky, and he starts nibbling at my earlobe. "Let Joanna do it." Joanna technically retired a few months ago, but the poor thing was bored to death and driving

Gary crazy. Unsurprisingly, one week after she retired, she signed up as a volunteer for Southern Service Paws. I think she's putting in more hours now than she was before, but since I'll be going on maternity leave in two months when our baby boy is born, I don't mind. In fact, I'm downright grateful.

"I know, but I want to be there. I *like* my job, remember?"

"I know something else you like," he says, undeterred.

But *I* won't be deterred today. So, I roll my eyes and push him away. He laughs and reaches out to drag my body up close to him again, and I lay my head on his chest. Jake and I both feel our baby boy kick him in the side, and I laugh.

Jake looks down at my round stomach and shakes his head. "You're not even in the world yet, and you're already taking your mama's side? I thought I would have at least one of my kids on my team."

In that exact moment, Sam busts into the room, and I'm OH SO GLAD that I had put a stop to Jake's advances.

"Morning!" she says with a cheery smile and a bouquet the size of her head in her hand. She approaches the bed and sets them on the bedside table. "These are for you, Mama."

Yep, you heard her right. Sam calls me Mama, and it still melts my heart every time. This girl and I have bonded like we were always meant to be mother and daughter. Her biological mom still hasn't been in the picture much, and I know it hurts Sam more than she lets on, but I've been trying my best to always make sure that Sam knows she has a mama that loves her more than life. And also, I'm going to have to have a talk with her about opening the door to flower-delivery strangers first thing in the morning.

But for now, I smile and sit up, sending a questioning glance to Jake. He sits up too, and the sheets fall off his chest, and WHEN am I going to be immune to this man's incredible body? I'm betting never. "Don't look at me," he says. "I was saving my flowers to give to you after the benefit tonight."

I frown and pluck the little white card from the bouquet and tear into it.

Evelyn Grace,
We're proud of you. See you tonight.
- Mama and Daddy

"What stupid man am I going to have to go murder for sending my wife flowers?" asks Jake, leaning over to grab the card.

Sam jumps on the end of the bed to pet Charlie. Charlie adores Sam. But turns out, his love is pretty cheap. She devotes five minutes a day to throw a tennis ball with him in the yard, and he is putty in her little hands. I'm not mad about it.

"Wow. What's it feel like to read those words from your parents?" asks Jake after his eyes scan the card.

"I don't know yet. It's still hard to trust that they mean it. But I'm trying to let it sink in." About three months ago, Daddy had a massive heart attack that almost killed him. Since then, his and Mama's whole life has changed.

He gave up his position at the law firm, and he and Mama have started checking things off of their bucket list with all of their free time. Something happened to my parents after that heart attack. It was a wake-up call for them, and ever since, they have been trying their hardest to mend their relationship with me. I won't lie; I wish that it hadn't taken a heart attack to make them see my importance, but I know that beggars can't be choosers. I've been cautious in letting them into my life, but so far, they've proven that their motives are pure.

They've even been trying to get to know Sam and make sure that she and Jake know we are all a part of their family. Mama is still snooty, but she's getting better with every passing day. My hope is that, soon, we will have a real relationship and that they will be better with my child than they were with me.

Oh yeah, and this pregnancy has been a miracle in and of itself. I've had to grow accustomed to closer monitoring and *lots* of doctor visits (especially after seizures), but so far, everything has gone smoothly. We are all hopeful that I will carry to term and have a healthy birth. The doctor has assured me that epilepsy patients have safe deliveries all the time.

Jake kisses my temple. "Well, I love you, and I'm proud of you. And you can trust that."

I smile and meet his gaze. "*That* I do know."

"Me too!" says Sam, squeezing my feet. She inches up in the bed to lie down on my pillow beside me and rubs my belly. "How's my baby brother doing today?"

Jake puts his hand on my belly, too. These days, my stomach seems to be a public attraction. Even a random old lady in the grocery store rubbed it yesterday. Maybe everyone knows something that I don't, and they are all being granted three wishes. "He kept his mama up all night last night, dancing circles in there, the little booger," I say.

Sam starts whispering to my belly something about joining forces to annoy me and Jake, but I tune out when I feel Jake's eyes on my face. I turn to look at him, and he and I stare at each other, lost in the same thought: I can't believe this is our life.

"I love you," he mouths.

"I love you more."

TWO MONTHS LATER

Jonathan Timothy Broaden came into the world this morning around 2 AM. He and I are both perfectly healthy, but pray for Jake because I think he might be losing his mind. The poor man has cried more in the past 24 hours than I thought possible. I allow it, though, because I know he has so much love pumping through his heart that he can't keep it contained. I love him. I love my daughter. And I love our son. And of course, I love our dogs.

I don't think this life of mine can get any better.

Except it does when I spot Jake walking into the hospital room with a chocolate-chip muffin.

THE END

To stay connected with me, sign up for my newsletter, or follow me on Instagram and Facebook. I love getting to know my readers!

A NOTE FROM SARAH:

Hello, darling readers! I am so grateful to you for taking a chance on my book, and I hope that it made you laugh and filled your heart with warm fuzzies! This story is especially close to my heart because my mother-in-law, Lesley Adams, runs a nonprofit called Retrieving Independence that breeds, trains, and places service dogs with people who are living with physical, mental, or emotional disabilities.

The amount of time, energy, and love that Lesley and her volunteers put into these dogs and the recipients they go to is inspiring and life-changing for those living with disabilities. If you are interested in learning more about Retrieving Independence, check them out at: WWW.RetrievingIndependence.org.

ALSO BY SARAH ADAMS

It Happened in Charleston Series:

The Match: A Romantic Comedy (book 1)

The Enemy: A romantic Comedy (book 2)

It Happened in Nashville Series:

The Off Limits Rule (book 1)

ACKNOWLEDGMENTS

First, thank YOU, wonderful reader, for making it this far :) Without you, my stories would just be collecting dust in my imagination. Thank you for helping me bring them to life!

Thank you to my sweet beta readers: Ashely, Lesley, Kadi, Kari, Kasey, and Carina. You guys are my heroes for helping me find all the places my story needed to get stronger!

Thank you to my wonderful parents (Mark and Karen) for being absolutely nothing like Evie's terrible parents and everything like Jake's sweet southern parents. I'm proud to share your accents and love of sweet tea, and I'm thankful for how much you love me and my girls :) I would never have made it this far without you!

Thank you to Lesley Adams for letting me ask you a million questions about training service dogs and never once telling me to stop bugging you :) Thanks for encouraging me to write this story and helping me make it accurate! Also, thank you (this includes you, Dave) for being amazing in-laws and loving us all so well! I'm so blessed to be a part of your family.

Thank you to my true inspiration, my husband's six-pack abs

:) Oh, also a huge thanks to Chris as well for being the best husband and daddy in the world. I love you!!

Last, but definitely not least, Jenn Lockwood my brilliant editor!! Thank you, thank you, thank you! You are nothing short of fabulous and I'm so impressed by you.

ABOUT THE AUTHOR

Born and raised in Nashville TN, Sarah Adams loves her family, warm days, and making people smile.

Sarah has dreamed of being a writer since she was a girl, but finally wrote her first novel when her daughters were napping and she no longer had any excuses to put it off.

Sarah is a coffee addict, a British history nerd, a mom of two daughters, married to her best friend, and an indecisive introvert. Her hope is to always write stories that make you laugh, maybe even cry; but always leave you happier than when you started reading.